PLEASURES AND FOLLIES

PLEASURES AND FOLLIES

ANONYMOUS

Carroll & Graf Publishers, Inc.
New York

First Carroll & Graf edition 1989

Carroll & Graf Publishers, Inc.
260 Fifth Avenue
New York, NY 10001

ISBN: 0-88184-490-X

Manufactured in the United States of America

TABLE OF CONTENTS

PLEASURES AND FOLLIES

CHAPTER I

The stiff-pricked youngster.

I was born in a village which lies near Rheims and I was familiarly known as Cupidonnet. From earliest childhood I had a decided fondness for pretty girls; I had a particular weakness, above all, for prettily turned feet and cunning little shoes, in which predilections I bore a resemblance to the Grand Dauphin, son of Louis XIV, and to Thevenard, the actor at the Opera.

The first girl to get my youthful stem up was an engaging peasant who used to take me to vespers. With one hand posed on my unclothed bum, she was wont to tickle my wee ballocks and, feeling me rise, would kiss me upon the mouth with an entirely virginal impetuousness, for, although well-behaved, she was also hotblooded.

The first girl upon whom I in turn laid my hands, in consequence of my enthusiasm for pretty footwear, was the youngest of my sisters, Genovefette. In all, I had eight sisters, five older than myself and by a former marriage, and three who were younger. The second-born of the earlier crop was as pretty as can be: I'll have a great deal to say about her; the hair upholstering the trick of the fourth was so silken and fine 'twas all by itself a delight; the rest were ugly; each of my three younger sisters was more of a provocative little minx than the others.

Now Genovefette, the most voluptuously attractive, held the first place in my mother's preference, and, returning from a trip to Paris, she brought back an exquisite pair of slippers for her. I watched Genovefette try them on, and the sight caused me to get violently erect. The following day—it was a Sunday —she donned some new sheer white cotton stockings, a corset which drew in her waist, and with that luscious ass of hers, although she was still of tender age, she must have made my father's prick stand up, for he bade my mother send her from the room. (I had hidden myself under the bed so as the better to see my engaging sister's shoe and lower leg.) Directly Genovefette was gone, my father had at her (my mother) and there, upon the bed below which I lay concealed, set the clapper to ringing the bell, the while saying: "Oh, I tell you, keep an eye on your beloved daughter, she's going to have a devilish temperament, I warn you... but she'll have to compete fiercely, for I fuck like a steer, and look at the rewards I have for my trouble, cunt-juice, you're squirting it out like a princess..." I noticed that, behind the half-opened door, Genovefette was watching and listening to what was happening. My father was right: that pretty rascal was handselled by her confessor, thereafter fucked by virtually everyone, but today she's all the wiser for it.

After dinner Genovefette came into the garden, where I chanced to be by myself; I stared admiringly at her, and lo! up soared my device! Having stepped close to her, without saying a word I squeezed her waist, touched her foot, her thigh, fondled as pretty a cuntlet, as superb a cuntlet as ever there was. Genovefette was silent too; I had her get down on all fours, on, that is to say, her hands and knees, and in imitation of the manner of dogs, I wanted to plumb her thus, whining and snapping and jerking with all my strength the way a dog does; powerfully clutching her groin with both hands, I made her arch her flanks so that two holes were equally well at my disposal; therewith I closed in and poked the end of my stem between her lips, beseeching her to raise her ass: "Get it up so that I can get in," I repeated several times. But, and the truth of it was, only too plain, so youthful a crack was not readily able to accommodate a prick whose foreskin had not yet reached the back-slipping stage (what I needed was a well-beaten path, and I obtained one shortly afterwards.) I could do no better than pry open her cunt's shutters, there ensued no discharge, for I was still a little fellow and very new at the sport. Unable to encunt her, following the example of the creatures I had chosen to emulate, I set to licking that strait but infinitely delectable gap. Genovefette experienced a no doubt agreeable titillation, for she showed no sign of tiring of the game, and when at last I got back to my feet she kissed me a hundred times over. She was called back to the house and ran off.

As her breasts had not yet begun to develop, she promptly—the next day—outfitted herself with false bubs, probably because she had overheard praise spoken of my mother's or some friend's. I perceived these latest accoutrements, had her put on her new shoes and having placed her upon her bed in a suitable posture, we fenced away for a good two hours. I believe she did indeed ejaculate for my cunt-lickery induced her to writhe and thrash like a small demon. Two days later she was packed off to Paris to begin an apprenticeship. There, in the capital, she lived up handsomely to my father's predictions.

CHAPTER II

The silken-haired cunt.

Of the younger sisters left to me, one was properly behaved and kept me at bay (since those days I have fucked both her daughters in Paris), and the other sister was still too young. The first, with whom nothing availed, was a superb creature of eighteen; I had to fall back upon the child when it became evident that Cuthos, Genovefette's twin, was unapproachable. Ever since having had one within reach, I absolutely could not do without a cunt near at hand. I put Babiche through her preliminary paces; at last one Sunday, when she was dressed in her best and after my mother had given her a bath, we had a sucking spree.

'Twas during that enjoyable operation I was surprised by the ardent Madeleine of the silken-haired cunt; she spent a long time quietly observing us before interrupting our antics, and remarking that the little one was in the throes of pleasure, she was herself tempted to go under the tongue ; she broke her silence and we two who were at grips separated in keeping with decency. Madeleine said almost nothing at all, only asked Babiche to leave, then hazarded a conversation with me. Our gossiping lead to teasing; it was not long before she had thrust me into the hay (I had led Babiche into the barn's loft) and, as I lay sprawled on my back, she tickled me, covering me with her body, straddling me, one leg to this side, one leg to that. By pure accident I reached my hand beneath her skirts and found there that admirable silken-haired cunt. That divine fur sealed my passion for her, I straightaway went mad over Madeleine's cunt; I besought her permission to kiss it. "Why then, little rascal," said she, "wait a moment." She went out to the well, drew a bucket of water, fetched it back up to the hayloft and squatted down above it; that done, she returned to me and we prattled some more. Inflamed, beside myself, in my youthful erotic fury I exclaimed to her: "I've got to lick that little hole!" She lay down on her back, her legs spread wide; I licked; the lovely Madeleine elevated her ass: "Drive your tongue inside, dear little friend," said she, and I inserted it and she raised her fur; I burrowed furiously in!... She all but screamed from pleasure's onslaught. My member was as stiff as a Carmelite friar's, and as I had not the capacity to discharge, none of my ardor deserted me; 'twas surely on that account she adored me. Obliged to leave me, Madeleine gave me some cakes as a present, and I ate them in Babiche's company.

"Cupidonnet," said my downy-cunted sister one evening, "that dear little prick of yours is always hard when you lick me. It seems to me that were we to get together into the same bed, you'd be able to insert it into that little muff of mine which you so like to suck and whose fur is so soft. I'm certain that would give me all sorts of pleasure, and you too; come visit me tonight."

When everyone in the house had retired, I slid into my elder sister's bed. "Once, " said she, "I saw Father, just after he'd done caressing our sister Marie,"—Marie was the lovely one who had left for Paris—"run straight to Mother, his stick as long and tough as a rake-handle, and pop it straight into her fur—I'll show you how he went about it, you'll do the same thing he did." "I also saw him do it." "Did you really? So much the better." She arranged herself, situated me atop her, told me to thrust and then to retire and thrust again, but she was a maid, and although I was in strong martial form, I was unable to introduce the weapon, and succeeded only in hurting myself. As for Madeleine Linguet, I dare say she discharged, for she began to pant and came near to swooning away.

Oh, how I regret that pretty silken-haired cunt I licked and prodded for six fine months! My father, Claude Linguet, to whom I bore no resemblance in this matter, sent his daughters away as soon as their vicinity aroused him significantly... It was even claimed that Madeleine had attempted to get herself stuffed by him. However all that may be, she departed for Paris three days after the charge was leveled, and in Paris our dear ecclesiastical brother found her a governess' place in the household of a rue de Saint-Honoré canon. That beggar wasted no time determining what her talents were. There was a hidden door—about whose existence only he knew —which opened into the apartment occupied by his governess, whom he used to pass the night exercising. But never had he set eyes upon a cunt to match Mademoiselle Linguet's silky-haired article; he went repeatedly to stare at it. Its beauty enthralled him, and he knew he would have neither rest nor peace until he had fucked it. One night as she lay sleeping very soundly—or rather as she appeared to be sleeping soundly and was making a great effort to maintain that appearance—he applied his mounth to that singular cunt, and to her assailant 'twas plain she discharged; he immediately mounts and encunts her; she hugs him in her arms, the while stirring her ass rhythmically. "Ah, my precious," says he, "you do dance wonderfully well!... But it's not hurting you, is it? You mustn't overdo it... else I'll be obliged to think you somewhat a whore..." But her bloodied nightdown, and the bloodied sheets also, proved to him he had a novice under his belly; he adored her. She fucked blissfully, sacredly with this saintly personage and their liaison lasted two years at the end of which she buried him; however, his testament left her an inheritance, and thus endowed she married the son of her mother's first husband.

CHAPTER III

My mother is fucked.

More mature by the time Madeleine had acquired a husband and returned to Rheims, I had a very imperious desire to get into her. For a space of more than two years I had been reduced to sucking and frolicking with Babiche and several of my first cousins, but either my prick was thickening or all those still beardless cunts were shrinking. I solicited a nocturnal rendez-vous with the recently wedded Madeleine, and Madame Bourgelat granted me an interview for that same night. We were at our parents' farm: her husband had just been called away to Rheims on business. By I know not what coincidence or for what cause, my father was not feeling well that night and, after having treated whatever ailed him, my mother, in order to avoid disturbing his sleep, left his bed and went to share the one her daughter was occupying. The latter, observing that our mother had dozed off, rose quietly, and came to lie with me; I however had in the meantime got up and gone in search of her: unluckily, our paths did not cross. I stretched out beside the woman I discovered in Madeleine's bed; she was on her back; asleep though she was, I climbed into the saddle and made my entry; I was surprised to make such an easy way in; she folded me in her arms, squeezed, and, still half-conscious, bounced her ass about for a few moments. "Never, oh never have you given me such pleasure," she sighed through her drowsiness. I also discharged and promptly collapsed from too much delight, my face lying upon her breasts which, while she was not young, were still firm, for she had not raised her children and those charms had never been much handled. Madame Bourgelat returned from her fruitless quest at about the same instant I released my seed; she was greatly bewildered by the words her mother and substitute had just uttered; then she grasped that I had been fucking her, and led me away to my bed where she deposited me, still in a swoon... And thus it was in the maternal womb I began effectively to sow my wild oats... I returned to my senses; Madeleine went back to my mother's bed. Wide awake by now, Mother asked what my sister had been up to and then added in a whisper: You surely have odd ways..." "My husband," replied Madame Bourgelat, "often has me get on top; I was dreaming, that's how it all happened and when I woke up I must have jumped out of bed." The which my mother apparently believed.

However, the shot had been fired good and true. Madame Linguet's belly began to swell, she secretly gave birth to a son, and a splendid son to boot, whom she very cleverly substituted for her grown son's child, this latter infant having been stillborn; this son I bore my own mother and who was known as Petit Coq, my nephew, will return to figure later on in my narrative.

A week went by; at its end, completely recovered from the state into which that first discharge had hurled me, I sallied forth from my bed once again, and to another rendez-vous; now, reader, bear admiring witness to my misfortune: our activities had been remarked by a strapping big-bosomed wench, a country girl who worked in our fields as a harvester and who had her lodgings in the barn. As Madame Bourgelat was upon one occasion readying to join me in my bed, Mammelasse (as our full-blown girl was called), who was in love with me, for she frequently frigged herself in my honor, but who was not however a bad sort, took it into her head to advise my brother-in-law to lock his bedroom door at night and to keep an eye on his lady. He did as she recommended... and judge for yourself what was my astonishment when, instead of a soft-haired cunt and round delicate bubs, I found myself fisting two well inflated balloons and tumbling through widesprung gates into a veritable mineshaft. I pushed valiantly on into the unknown notwithstanding and had myself a pleasant time—but dizziness all but claimed me again and I came near to having to retake to my bed.

Finally, I did have the opportunity to stuff Madeleine and that was in the hayloft. I was performing like a madman, I encunted her prodigiously, but at her third reply to my thumpings, I exploded... and properly fainted.

CHAPTER IV

Another brother-in-law cuckolded.

Madeleine avoided according me favors whose effects upon me terrified her. Deprived, I suffered. But not for long. A week after this last scene I took leave of the farm and journeyed to Paris whither I went in the pursuit of learning; but it is not by relating my life as a student that I propose to entertain the reader. I went at once to see the lovely Marie, the second of my elder sisters; she offered me her hospitality and a room.

I had begun my career by making a cuckold of my father; I had cornified my brother-in-law, fucking and causing his wife to discharge and impregnating her into the bargain, for Madame Bourgelat, who was never to have but this one child, brought my bastard into the world nine months after our scuffle in the hayloft; but much remained to be accomplished with those seven other sisters of whom six, or at least five, were supremely encuntable.

But let us return to Marie, the most beautiful of the lot. She was one day dressed and adorned with that certain taste pretty women usually have. A superb bouquet shadowed her fair breasts. The sight of her caused my prick to rise approvingly up. I was fourteen years of age, and had already fucked and fattened three women, for Mammelasse had a daughter of whom, according to her boasting, I was

the sire and who looked so much like Genovefette
Linguet you would have supposed them two peas in a
pod. I was not a lad susceptible of vague or name-
less desires; I inclined directly towards my amiable
elder sister's cunt. Dinner over, she retired for the
night; the conjugal couch was situated in a dimly-lit
alcove; she had perceived a bulge in her husband's
fly, for his white breeches fitted him snugly; she was
eager to give him the pleasure of a full-dress fuck.
I concealed myself in a place whence I could see everything that transpired. But, after having toyed with
my sister's teats and her cunt, after having increased
the light in the alcove and subjected her cunt to an
admiring appraisal, my brother-in-law elected moder-
ation, decided to postpone his pleasures till the
morrow, and to my surprise, went out on tiptoe. I saw
him take his cane, his hat; then he was gone.
I entered the room: the husband had left his wife's
skirt around her neck and the door unlocked. I bolted
it and, untrousered, with the Devil's own erection,
I made a bee-line to her. I stoppered that yawning
cunt, now sucking her bared bubs, now her slightly
parted lips. She mistook me for her husband; the tip
of her tongue thrilled in my mouth. My prick went
in wearing its hat: at that period I had not yet had
the foreskin snipped and, stunting my device, it made
it seem stouter, as bulky as the departed husband's...
I drove sturdily ahead, my beloved quivered and
squirmed, and my inspired weapon touched bottom...
whereupon my sister, half out of her mind, convulsed
in a spasm... I discharged and... fainted.

'Twas for that reason I was found out. Marie
savoured the final oscillations of my militant prick,
but as soon as she had experienced the charming sensation of a copious discharge, she ridded her cunt of
its visitor by pushing me aside; she drew apart the
alcove's curtains and regarded me. "What! Ye gods!

it's... it's Cupidonnet... he's pumped himself empty... poor boy, he's fainted!" I waked from my swoon, she scolded me, demanding to know who'd taught me to behave that way. "Your beauty," I replied, calling her my adorable sister. "But you're so young!" With that I recounted my entire history to her, told her how I'd fondled and licked Genovefette's cuntlet, how I'd mouthed and subsequently fucked Madeleine's silken-haired cunt, next fucked Madame Linguet thinking all the while she was Madame Bourgelat, I told her how Mammelasse had got herself stuffed by me, how, unable to do without cunts, I'd explored Babiche's diminutive one with my tongue, and how I had got with child the three women I had properly fucked... "Good heavens! you are certainly indiscreet!" "With you, yes, because you are my elder sister, and because I've fucked you as well."

The tale I'd just brought spilling out, Marie's dazzling bubs, the shoes she'd donned, everything conspired to stiffen me afresh. "Divine Marie," quoth I, "'tis not yet over, methinks I'm going to fuck you again." "But my husband?" "The door's bolted." She pressed my head against her magnificent breasts, the while murmuring: "Are you also going to give me a baby, little scamp?" I re-encunted her and shot off joyously, but without fainting this second time.

Not until then had the glorious Marie been pregnant. The months flew by. I became the father of Mademoiselle Beauconin, the only child of my brother-in-law of that name.

I shall pass in silence over all the common fuckeries in which I had a principal rôle: 'tis only by dint of the singular voluptuousness in libidinous scenery such as it will appear in the tasty pleasure-takings which I plan to describe in the sequel, that one may touch the heart and mind of blasé libertines and advantageously combat the atrocious penchants quickened by the abominable literature of the infamous and cruel Sade; and so I reserve all my energy for representing almost ineffable, almost indescribable love-makings, couplings which outdo everything the racked imagination of *Justine's* author was able to invent.

CHAPTER V

The complacent and very Spartan husband.

Before moving on to the tableaux I have just promised, I must nevertheless devote a few lines to relating an extraordinary adventure I had during my stay in the rue Saint-Honoré, at the age of twenty and while engaged in my studies of the law.

Directly opposite the house lived an old watchmaker who had a youthful and charming wife; she was his third; the first had rendered him very happy indeed for a dozen years—life with her had been uninterrupted drunkenness, delight; the second had also done mightily well, but for only eighteen months and with the aid of a younger sister by whom she would have herself replaced in his bed whenever she felt in the slightest way indisposed—because she did not want to have her husband fuck under unfavorable, and possibly disgusting, circumstances. This excellent and thoughtful wife having left this life, the watchmaker, then sixty, married the pretty and gracious Fidelette, putative offspring of an architect, in reality the natural child of a marquis.

What for mellowness and poignancy, this third wife's beauty had no equal. Her husband idolized her, but he was no longer young; however, being wealthy, he lavished upon her everything her heart could desire. But his gifts and kindness failed somehow of the mark, and with every passing day Fidelette grew more despondent. "My angel," her good husband said, "I worship you, and you know it; all the same, you are sad, unhappy, and I fear for your days; do what I can, there is nothing I would not do for you, none of it avails, and so speak to me... 'tis a loving friend who begs you to speak, tell me what it is you desire... anything... no matter what, provided it is in my power to secure your happiness, I shall do as you bid me..." "Anything? no matter what?" asked the young woman. "Anything, yes, anything... were it to be... but say, is there something wanting to your heart, or to your divine little cunt?" "You fill my heart to overflowing, my dear, but elsewhere... I have a spirited temper and warm blood, and though my hair is ash-blond, my trick itches terribly..." "Does it make any difference to you who undertakes to appease your dear little hungers? or have you some special taste, some particular caprice?" "I love no one but you." "Is there not anyone who attracts your regard? only speak and I shall this instant go and bring him hither." "Ah well... there is that neighbour of ours who lives across the way, the young man who looks at me and of whom I've already complained." "I understand, 'tis enough, my sweet. You must have thought me thick-skinned indeed. Go take your bath, my beloved one, I'll return in a trice."

He dashed off to find me. "Neighbour," said he upon entering my room, "'tis rumored you are in love with Madame Folin, the watchmaker's wife. Is it true?" "Upon my soul," said I, "it is indeed, I am wild about her." "Then come with me and we'll see what's to be done, come at once." He seized me by the hand and led me to his house. "Remove your

24

clothes, go into this bathroom my wife has just left; there you see some of my undergarments, put them on, go regale her, play the new husband or settle the thing for some other night... for twenty other nights, suit yourself so long as you also suit her. I worship my Fidelette, I would do anything for her and am content simply to see her happy, satisfied... After you've done fucking her, after she has had her fill of discharges and discharging, I'll encunt her in my turn... and thus bestow my own modest little present."

He had me climb into the bed his wife had been occupying since finishing her bath; he started to take himself off. "Oh dear friend," exclaimed that timid dove, "you leave me alone with a stranger? Will you not stay and witness the pleasures I owe to none but you?" and she kissed us both. The bed was wide and capacious; the considerate Folin got into it with us; I climbed upon his wife's belly. The fires were already burning brighty, my own torch glowed red; there, before the husband's eyes, I buried my prick in the wife's cunt... She replied to my attack, and furiously. "Courage, dearie," cried that excellent watchmaker, fingering my nuggets, "let fly, my duckie, raise your ass, get your tongue into his mouth!... this brave young fucker's ready to flood you... You, my buck, dig in, dig in... head for bottom, ring the bell!..."

We discharged like a pair of angels; I fucked her six times before the night was over; husband and wife were equally pleased with my performance.

I revelled in this remarkable situation and repeatedly tasted these celestial, more-than-human delights until Fidelette perished out of this world while in the act of bringing the fruit of our fuckery into it.

CHAPTER VI

The husband who took to bumtupping.

I shall omit giving the full details of my amorous exploits with the person who was my clandestine wife, since I have never publicly acknowledged that marriage with Conquette. Although her looks had been marred by smallpox, she was a robust, splendidly-made creature, with a cunt so insatiable that I was obliged to let her take the bit in her teeth and wander abroad to fuck whomever came her way. She was the daughter of an innkeeper in the rue Saint-Jacques and the sister of a bookseller; she died, syphilis-ridden, long after she'd borne me two girls. Ah, but that one knew her job to perfection! Never did woman encunted treat her rider to a finer outing. Conquette was the first woman I ever embuggered; but that came about in reply to her invitation and at a moment when she was in doubtful health. Afterwards she foisted off her younger sister's ass on me, telling me 'twas her own: we were in the dark and I believed her, but the target the young lady presented me was not her ass but her cunt: I detected the fraud... but have no real grievance to express: it was delicious howbeit everyday fuckery.

When my sister-in-law married and ceased to be at our disposal, my wife seduced her hairdresser whom she heartily urged to submit to an anal penetration, alleging, as argument, that I was habituated to navi-

gating the narrower strait; but this girl, having dis-
cussed the problem with me during the day, got her
cunt plumbed that night without Conquette noticing
into which aperture I inserted my device. In this way
I had six all very pretty hairdressers in the course of
twelve years; my wife paid them, thinking by this
means to conceal from me the fact she had the pox.
And 'twas thus I enjoyed a feast of those delightful
cuntlets for which Nature had given me such a powerful appetite.

It was after the sixth hairdresser that Conquette,
gravely ill, noticing that one of my schoolfellows was
paying court to Mademoiselle Beauconin, my niece-
daughter, that obstacles to his success were being
created, and that she loved him, suggested to Mariette
that she allow her lover to have his way with her; but
fearing lest the lad be unable to depucelate her, she
told me that the last of the hairdressers was sending
one of her pupils who stood in dire need of a good
encunting, but, she added, I was not to say a word
while doing the task, reminding me that my niece
was sleeping in the adjoining chamber. She gave
me further instructions to which I hardly listened,
as I was eager to be off. A hairdresser's pupil? Provided I fucked a fresh young cunt, I cared damned
little to whom it belonged. Naked, I approached
the bed, stepped in; I found newly burgeoning breasts
at hand, and a cunt which lay quivering... I entered,
I demolished the maidenhead... I had repeated the
exercise three times when I was summoned from the
bed; at first I fancied this to be some convention of
which hitherto I had been in ignorance, but having
listened more closely, I was most surprised to hear
the spur being applied to my mount and my wife,
while proffering encouragements, giving directions to
her niece and my comrade. I went back to my own
bed, pondering these curious events; the following

day, I asked Conquette for an explanation. "Why," she said, "'tis all very simple. You handselled your niece before your schoolmate stuffed her, for I doubted whether all alone he would be able to manage the deflowering." I was enchanted: I had made mine the first fruits of the daughter emplanted one remote holiday in Marie Linguet's cunt, but I dissimulated my joy: this augured well for the pleasures I had for ages held hopes of enjoying and whose hour of realization was arriving: I was nearing my objective.

CHAPTER VII

Concerning yet another downy cunt.

The reader will recall that I spoke of two daughters: I said they were mine, or at least thay they were my clandestine wife's, for she used to declare that her veritable daughters had died while being suckled and that... and that... she would speak of the king... mention some princess... but she always lied a blue streak, one simply dared not believe a word she said.

Conquette Ingénue, my elder daughter, had no sooner reached her tenth year than she started to incite desires in me. While her mother, whose syphilis was not yet apparent, was off sleeping and fucking with some gallant or other, she would send little Conquette to keep me company in bed... she had the world's prettiest crack; I made a regular practice of kissing it every night, after having spread her thighs. She would fall into a light sleep, I would insert my tongue, but would refrain from licking; then I too would go quietly to sleep, having eased her onto her side, her buttocks against my thighs and my prick squeezed between her legs.

During the daytime I encunted either the mistress of a certain Monsieur Rivière—a barrister—or a pretty hunchback, who always wore delightful shoes and who lived in the same building, or a woman who limped in both legs but who had a delicious face and was about to marry. She had let her intended deflower her and since that initiation had given her pretty blond cunt an absolute minimum of rest. When not at work on one or the other of these three projects, I would poke my prick between Conquette Ingénue's tightly squeezed thighs and she, feeling that uncomfortable presence, would seize it, sound asleep as she was, and cause me a spectacular discharge. She was eleven years old by now; she caught the drift of things and started to chatter about them: we sent her away to learn a trade. She learned to draw when she was thirteen or fourteen. At the end of a two years' absence she returned to the house—I was now left alone in it by my wife's death. Conquette Ingénue slept in a small room adjacent to mine; she was a tall, handsomely formed girl; she had perfect feet; I had the cleverest artisan in the quarter make her shoes modeled after her mother's last which was also that of the Marquise de Marigny; then I fell head over heels in love with the creature. But never was anyone more chastely virtuous than that heavenly girl, although her mothers, real or supposed, had been a pair of sluts and had both succumbed to the pox. Conquette Ingénue would not tolerate insolent behavior, there was no possible way of taking liberties with her... Fate doubtless willed it that her austerity would only make her the more voluptuous and the more desirable.

And so I found myself reduced to virtual buggardom: there was nothing for it, and I continued to tongue her during her sleep which, happily, was invariably profound. Directly she began to slumber I would fly to my post, lift her night gown, gaze worshipfully at her delicious cunt which a faint growth of down was beginning to cover, and apply my mouth with caution. Not before the tenth night after her return home did I sense her respond to these attentions; I redoubled my tongue's activity and was rewarded by an emission. The light was out when Ingénue awoke sighing and moaning happily: "Ah," she murmured, "ah... that tickles so nicely..." She imagined she had been dreaming; however, she nudged her young sister (who slept in the same bed beside her) with her elbow as though she had thought the child had been responsible for what she had felt. I regained my bed, enchanted by the fact my daughter had discharged; her emission encouraged me to hope that, her spirits now set in commotion and become aware of her temperament, she would soon be susceptible of encuntment, become my mistress, and make me the happiest of mortals... But how far astray my calculations led me! And what a great number of pricks were to attempt to martyrise that glorious cunt. Alas, it was to be the cause of a myriad of disappointments.

Nevertheless, such were my wholehearted, my unswerving, my voluptuous inclinations—that was the adorable girl whose only rival for my affections was her sister. No, I can say it with all the conviction of a man who has had the experience, no, there is no pleasure to be compared with that of plunging one's straining prick into the last depths of the satin-smooth cunt of one's beloved daughter, above all if, courageously stirring her ass to and fro, she discharges copiously. Happy, oh thrice happy he who steals the prize from any future son-in-law detested by both concerned...

Conquette Ingénue's menstrual period came a week after the historic night of her first discharge: thus, she was perfectly nubile, but while in a waking state I could not obtain any essential favor from her. My sister Marie, who was thoroughly acquainted with my character, placed her as an apprentice in a women's dress and jewelry shop run by an attractive person whose husband had a functionary's post. Offering herself in the place of my spectacular daughter, although unable to console me for her loss, Madame Comprenant, the dressmaker, undertook to distract me; I also went back to stuffing my niece Beauconin, then married to her cousin: but would this double activity be able to prevent me from insulting the virtue of the eternally provocative Ingénue? Hopelessly in love with her and not daring in daylight to have at her darling downy cuntlet, and deprived of access to her during the night, I had to be content with gazing at her from the street. There she would be—the window was so disposed that I was permitted the view of an exquisitely-shod foot, part of a lovely leg... and if I bent down, when she made certain movements I could see her thigh and her cunt, or at least picture them in my imagination, which always beheld her unclothed. A mere glimpse of her would put my prick in the air, I would enter the house and at the crucial moment invariably find either Ingénue's mistress or the pretty Mademoiselle Beauconin; just before threading the needle of the one or the other, I would half open the door so as, while fucking either her mistress or her cousin, I would be able to see the delicate foot or the voluptuous leg of that divine creature who was exclusively responsible for my erection.

Four years passed in this manner. During that

period Conquette Ingénue and I never once came to grips. Finally, not one whit less eager to have her—and she was magnificent at eighteen—I resolved somehow to arrange for her to sleep in my house: I hit upon the expedient of detaining her until a late hour and to keep her by me for the night use, pretexting a sudden illness. She slept just as soundly as she used to years before; and so it was I fell to tonguing her directly she had closed her eyes: her discharge had the proportions of a river in flood. Her mons Veneris was superb, it was upholstered with a bush of jet black hair, soft and fine; I burned with desire to stopper her cunt, but, as usual, her ejaculation had awakened her. "How odd it is," she said; "whenever I stay the night under your roof I have the strangest dreams which do the strangest things to me!" I limited myself simply to asking permission to kiss her slippered foot; or sometimes her leg; by dint of much wheedling, I once went so far as to get her to allow me to touch the velvety hair which embellished her trick; but the sensation so alarmed her and made her so skitterish that, fearing lest I succeed in deflowering her before she became a married woman, aided by her mistress, Madame Comprenant, she rushed precipitately into wedlock with, as it proved, a dreadful rotter of a fellow. It was that rash step I had the greatest trouble forgiving her, but the poor child suffered so much from her hasty decision, she had so much opportunity to repent of it, and her charming cunt was subsequently to serve me so well, that I was more than willing to let bygones be bygones and forget the errors committed by youth and inexperience. I had yet another motive for compassion: I owe that execrable marriage a host of indescribable delights (as shall be seen in the pages to follow) as well as my present comfortable circumstances.

CHAPTER VIII

Conditions of marriage.

The next Sunday, Conquette Ingénue, being at my home as on week-ends she costomarily was, she could not avoid noticing that my prick was hard and upright as ever prick can be. She trembled for her virginity; I had kissed her feet, her legs, but she had fended me clear of her cunt... Of a sudden, I get to my feet, go round behind the chair she is sitting in and from behind slip my two hands under her bodice and seize her bubs... Ah, how pretty they were, small but firm, and so fair, so ripe!... There was no way for her to elude me... It was then she declared in all seriousness that she wished to marry; I went and stood before her, my prick in the air and as solid as a mace: she blushed to her eyes. My spirits were in a prodigious ferment, I was in every nerve inflamed by love and lust; I announced that I would sign no marriage contact save upon condition she first let me depucelate her; she said that would never do. By main force I took hold of her cunt; she tried to back away. "Is that not enough? You have touched me, now will you not give your consent?" "I have to get my tongue into you..." "Your tongue?"—she seemed not to understand; I explained. "My tongue indeed, and I propose to keep it there until you discharge..." She pondered the matter, then sighed: "Oh, all the things you've done to me! You were the cause of my dreams."

Lying down upon the bed, she resigned herself. "Satisfy yourself," said she, "and do not deceive me. I wish to be a maid upon my wedding day : Monsieur Vitnègre is a widower and Madame Comprenant says he knows all about these articles, whether they're new or used." During this speech I was feasting my eyes upon that ravishing article, upon the sight of a belly modeled like Aphrodite's and as white as ivory, of an alabaster thigh, of a satin-smooth ass. "Make haste," said she. "I'm composing an inventory of all the goods we are to deliver to your Monsieur Vitnègre, and everything appears to be in first-rate condition, except for one thing I'll tell you about... But let's suck..." I was completely carried away... I licked her furiously, keeping a sharp eye open for the gushing descent of her virginal liquor, awaiting that instant to hurl myself upon her and encunt her : she came with the sixth thrust of my tongue, but came with a well nigh unbelievable abundance; could this be fuck? I wondered. However, the merry jig she danced convinced me it could be nothing else : wherewith, abandoning her cunt, I leapt upon her, mad with pleasure. I am fully certain she would have given me a free´rein, but her unpracticed cunt, although well wetted by her fuck and my saliva, was not to be penetrated. I had not yet acquired the skill needed to make one's way into certain virgins whose cracks require to be greased with pommade or fresh butter. At last, she seized my prick, attempting to oust me; gripped in her soft white hand, my prick spat forth its charge and I soaked her fingers, her cunt, her belly, her thighs with a spray of fuck. A tidy thing—she always kept herself spick and span—she broke free of me and ran off to wash herself.

"Who would ever suppose," I exclaimed as I watched her rinse and wipe her ass, thighs and cuntlet, "that I'd been futtering you?" "If," Conquette Ingénue retorted, "if you were only reasonable you'd give me that pleasant licking as often as you wish, for, upon my soul, it does delight me." "Well said," I declared and, fondling her cunt, I had her dart her tongue into my mouth. "But," she went on, "no more of that other thing which left a mess in what I've just washed; I want to be an honest woman." "You owe your pretty cunt to your father," I observed to my charming daughter. "If you were rich, I'd give up my plans to marry and I'd devote myself to your pleasures. But I must have a husband if I am to cease to be a burden to you."

Touched by her words, I showered her with kisses from head to toe: slippered feet, legs, forehead, eyes mouth, nipples, thighs, ass, I kept relentlessly at it until she discharged. That done, I affixed my signature to every paper she brought before me; I adored her.

She went off and married and for three months avoided seeing me; such conduct infuriated me, and I swore I'd fuck her and make her fuck if I were ever to get my hands upon her again—I'd fuck her a thousand and one times over before I'd forgive her for abandoning me so monstrously, so unnaturally. But little did I know that she was already unhappy.

CHAPTER IX

I am compensated for the loss of Ingénue.

Victoire Conquette, my second daughter, since her mother's death had been living in the country with her Aunt Genovefette, at the time married to her latest keeper. Having no cunt to which to devote myself, I wrote to have Victoire sent home without delay. While awaiting her arrival, I made myself comfortable with a pair of little and still unbearded, or at best downy-haired, cunts which I succeeded in perforating with the help of some pommade: these fetching targets belonged to the sister and the mistress of my secretary, an excellent lad who himself put them at my disposal, in such wise as shall be seen in due time; he and I had hitherto been fucking his elderly mother-in-law, preferring not to resort to whores.

Directly Victoire returned, I ordered shoes made for her as I had done for Ingénue: shoes with slender high heels, and this child, who had attained the age of fifteen, caused me as stout an erection as her sister had. But I was not interested in deflowering her; I simply employed her as a hors-d'œuvre, to whet my palate and put me in form for heavier undertakings: the encuntment, more vigorously executed thanks to Victoire's ministry, of Minonne and Connette, respectively the sister and mistress of Trait-d'Amour, my secretary, or of Trait-d'Amour's mother-in-law. To prepare myself for these enterprises I would have Victoire, gaily clothed and of course shod, enter the room, I would seize her by the skirts and seat her on my knees, being myself nude, if circumstances permitted; my trousers down, if trousers I was wearing, I would have myself caressed, given a few licks of the tongue; if I chanced to be naked, my prick would wedge itself between her thighs and commence to waggle up and down, to left and right; if she were fully dressed, I would have her fist my prick and, she being exceedingly innocent, say to her: "Eh, my pretty one, squeeze my finger tight, tighter still!" Minonne, Connette or the mother-in-law, one of the three, would always arrive: Trait-d'Amour would go off to summon one of them as soon as he saw me encloset myself with Victoire. Hearing their approach, I would, by a hidden door, convey the charming little one to her room, I'd return for a delicious fuck in which Trait-d'Amour would participate by tickling my balls. Once I was done, he would straightaway encunt whomever I had possessed, and in my turn I would tickle his balls.

This life would have suited me for a long time— even though it was a life led without my beloved Conquette Ingénue who had become Madame Vitnègre—had my sisters Genovefette and Marie not decided that it was indecent for me to keep Victoire alone with me in the house; they joined forces and obliged me to apprentice her to a lingerie merchant and his wife, perhaps the most virtuous and God-fearing couple in Paris; Madame Beauconin led little Victoire away to her new guardians.

Fortunately the good Fanfan, a few days before, had introduced me to a superb woman who was separated from her husband and hence wildly amorous; Victoire knew nothing of my latest acquisition, and this lovely woman, supposing that my heart belonged to Victoire, fucked beneath me like a she-devil, calling me her papa and bidding me "Stuff her, stuff your beloved Victoire, your passionate and tender daughter."

CHAPTER X

Concerning the villainous husband.

But the moment was approaching when I was to recover Conquette Ingénue; my keenest desire, even as I lay in the arms of Madame Maresquin (Victoire's friend) was to make a cuckold of Vitnègre.

᛫ There came a day when I encountered my Conquette on the Pont Notre-Dame. She was most
distraught, very tearful, and she cast herself into my
arms; I was deeply moved and all my former anger
evaporated at once. Although aggrieved, my delicious
daughter was still beautiful, perhaps the more so for
her unhappiness. My first impulse was to lay firm
hold of her cunt, but I checked myself, for we were in
the street. I went to see her the next evening, at
the hour she had told me her husband, or rather her
monster, was never at home; I did indeed find her
alone and in the course of that first visit she con-
fessed to me she had taken a lover. Infinitely pleased
by this avowal, which proclaimed Vitnègre's
cuckoldry, I flattered her, spoke sweet nothings,
coaxed her, got her to agree to open her cunt to
Timon, her beau; but soon after I gathered this was
a purely Platonic attachment wherein Conquette
found consolation for the brutalities of a thorough-
going debauchee by recounting her woes to a soft-
pricked but sincere and spiritual poet: she liked to
speak of her undemanding and patient lover, and
as I was the only one with whom she could safely
discuss these questions, I promised her I would
arrange secret interviews for them: she was in
seventh heaven.

I paid her a second visit: Conquette mentioned
some of Vitnègre's recent infamies. Upon one occasion, stooping down to pick up something from the
floor, he had one of his friends seize her cunt. She
had protested. "Why, it's merely a cunt you've got
there in your hand," Vitnègre said coolly to his colleague; "didn't I tell you her cunt-hair is softer than
silk? Well, old man, would you believe it? the inside
is softer still." Conquette wished to leave the room;
he caught her brutally by the arm, had her climb
aboard him, drew her skirts high up above her

thighs and clutched her cunt in his hand, bringing it into clear view of his friend and frigging her betimes. While all this was going on he described how much pleasure she was able to give her partner when she chose to be agreeable. "But," he added, "she's like every other whore: you've got to give her a good thrashing to make her do her duty." Next, he attempted to expose her breasts, but she broke away from him; whereupon he swung his booted foot and bestowed a lusty kick upon her ass. Some few days later the same friend having dined with them, Vitnègre, noticing that after coffee his wife had gone off to piss and then paid a visit to the bidet, said to his cohort, Culant by name: "There we have a damned clean cunt, and were we to employ a little dexterity, or if need be a little force, we might both be able to give it a lick or two. However, if it's to be by force, don't be startled if you hear somewhat of an uproar; but if by milder means we are to obtain our way, here before you is the key; it opens the door which yields entrance to the corridor; you will step in when, weary myself, I shall say in a loud tone: 'Come, Madame, show me a smiling cunt and let's begin again'—and then advance boldly, my dear chap, smite unsparingly, for I'd as soon have the whole wide world fuck this bitch: her path's still insufficiently trod—needs widening!" Conquette was called back into the room, the husband had her sit down before the fire; he deployed his prick, discovered his large brown balls, recommended that his friend do the same that he be completely at his ease, and as the latter hesitated: "Untrouser him this very instant, buggress," said he to his wife, "or I'll tear out your cunt-hair by the handful!" He did indeed reach forth his hand, Conquette uttered a cry; Culant immediately brought his prick and balls to light, in so doing asking Vitnègre to deal gently with her.

"Look sharp there, buggress, frig us both, one with each hand. I am her master," went on that scoundrel, addressing Culant, "she does just what I tell her—how can she help but obey?" Conquette was weeping; Culant sought to intercede in her behalf. "Very well, then, let her suck my prick, there, that way, on her knees, for I think I'd like to squirt into her mouth. I used to discharge into my first wife's—she died, you know, and perhaps from over-drinking, who knows? it used to be my greatest delight to slake her thirst!" Culant remarked to the effect that thus to use it would be to spoil the prettiest of mouths. "My God! Objections, objections, always objections! then I'll employ my own mouth—" "The sight would make me come, I fear," Culant said. "Why then, my sly one, pray go into this little room." Vitnègre thrust Conquette into a dimly-lit cabinet and then urged Culant in after her; wherewith the wicked fellow adjusted his dress and left his house for another, where he had the habit of gambling. Culant, left to his own devices, sucked and licked Conquette but dared not fuck her, having so diminutive a prick he was certain she would recognize that it did not belong to her master. Nevertheless, Culant discharged six times and Conquette did twice as well. When sate and spent, he gave her a blow of his fist, that she might persist in mistaking him for Vitnègre. But that evening, returning from his adventures, the monster said to his wife: "Well, buggress, were you adequately tongued this afternoon? 'Twasn't I toiled over you, I'd surely not have done you the honor of half-a-dozen discharges—my friend doubtless has taken a liking to you. But can you have failed to recognize him? For I hear you blew off twelve times in a row, and you never stiffen with me. And the blow he gave you—a stout one, eh? You felt it, I trust?" And thereupon the wretch burst into laughter. "Well, there you are, bitch of a lawyer's bastard, there you are, a whore to the teeth, I've nothing to do now but cash in on your cunt." Terrified, Conquette then and there formed the resolution to leave him; it was the following day we met on the bridge, and having taken her decision, she intended to carry it out and be rid of that monster.

My daughter's tale, although related in rather more subdued terms than in the version I have given, had revolted me; I assured her of speedy aid—but, at the same time and as I sought to comfort her, my prick held a fine consistency and threatful slope, for all stories of libidinous brutality excite my prick into an erection.

I solicited her favors; my request was answered with blushes, but I was permitted to kiss the pretty green slipper she was wearing. I went no further, wishing to start things aright. However, during the visit I paid her on the morrow, I laughingly slid a hand between her blouse and her back, then came gradually round to her bubs which, to be sure, she undertook to protect, but which remained in my possession all the same; shortly after achieving this success, I set out for another and began to stroke her hair. Then, eager to see to what point I could carry matters without encountering a determined resistance, I teased her about having a little tuft of coarse hair amidst the silky hairs upon her cunt... which she gave me to fondle, all the while trembling lest her husband interrupt us. In order to put her at ease, I had her talk about her lover, and while she prattled on, I proceeded from one liberty to another, finally inserting three fingers three inches into her cunt... She was so engrossed in her subject that indeed I do believe she fancied it was Timon who was cheering her up. As I rubbed away, I told her I had located a pension for her and that she could go there directly she left

Vitnègre: she reddened with pleasure and threw her arms about me. I darted my tongue into her mouth, then felt hers enter mine. Furiously happy, I was on the point of asking her to tell me in what manner she had been depucelated when, Vitnègre's step sounding outside the door, I dashed into the same cabinet Culant had used thinking I would be able to get away through the door to the hallway, but what was my surprise to see a monk enter by that same door. I retreated and hid behind a large sofa; he failed to notice me. Vitnègre entered by the door leading from the room I had just left. "Salutations, my most reverend father. Will you fuck her before dinner, or after?" The monk, appearing to meditate over his reply and squinting through a glass panel which afforded him a view of Conquette, licked his lips and finally said:

CHAPTER XI

A maidenhead intended for a thick prick blasted by a small one.

"No, my son, no, 'twill be as priorly we agreed: go into the room, increase the light therein so that I shall have excellent opportunity to see all that comes to pass: amuse yourself with her: teats, asshole, cunt. I shall reserve my best for the night." "Nonsense," said the generous husband with a large gesture, "I'm quite willing to throw this one into the bargain." But the man of God remained adamant. "No, I say, I only like bedtime fucking—you know; to suck tongue and bub, to encunt, to embugger, to be suckled, etc., etc., to sink a good tooth into a pretty tit, to nip its extremities... Proceed, dear boy, go into the other room with your prick aloft, warm her up, and, I beseech you, brutalize her just a little..."

Vitnègre, his loins bare, returned to his wife who, as always, trembled at his approach. "Mark you, buggress, the condition my prick is in? It's because of that neat little foot I see before me. It's pleasure I'm searching after... the other day I overheard some poor sod behind you say he'd like to get his tool in you... get that kerchief away from your chest, I've got to see your dugs... pretty things they are, by God, white, firm... Ah, my little slut, I'd tear off these pink buttons if I weren't afraid of damaging the merchandise. What a fuckable shape to those buttocks!... Up with your petticoats, whore, up with them, above your waist, above the navel, let me see that mechanism... Very nice... now walk, presenting your cunt... now turn around, and let's have a look at your ass... excellent, capital... a very graceful movement you've got, bitch, wiggle your ass, do you hear me? And wiggle your cunt too, agitate it, by God, and keep it up till I tell you to stop." She toured at least a hundred times around the room, alternately exhibiting her ass and her cunt. His eyes fixed upon the spectacle I heard the monk say : "That bugger's prick isn't as stout as mine... he wasn't able to depucelate her. Ah, dear Jesus, how she'll screech tonight! But I mustn't have that. Screech ? Then there'll be a scandal, the neighbors will come running," reasoned the ecclesiastic, "they'll think someone is killing her and who knows? maybe I shall. Shall I? Ha! why not? What? But I'd best go now," and the odd fellow did go, murmuring as he left on tip-toe : "She's someone it'd be a delight to kill, that's clear, and killed she'll be." At the same instant Vitnègre gave

Conquette the signal to stop parading: "Whoa there, bitch. Stand still a minute." He entered the cabinet. "What do you think of her?" he demanded. "Like to have a go at her now?" My prick was as hard as a rock; attempting to simulate the monk's voice, I said in a hoarse whisper that yes, I might try her after all. Vitnègre went to fetch his wife and, driving her brutally ahead of him: "Get along with you, bitch, whore, or I'll fuck your ass!... ah, but you're going to howl like a crowning cat—but see to it, you bloody-cunted slut, see to it you don't wake the neighbors, for if you do I'll bring every blessed one of them in here, that wouldn't bother me one damned bit, I'd keep your cunt corked even though all of Paris were here to watch me operating." With these words he pitched her head over heels onto the couch which had been placed in the cabinet, then disappeared; I leapt atop my daughter who, feeling herself being almost painlessly probed, refrained from raising a fuss. "Scream!" I said to her in a low voice. And scream she did, she screamed to wake the dead upon discovering she had some stranger's member in her trick. As soon as I had discharged, and discharged deliciously, by having her oscillate her cunt, I made my escape just before the neighbors put in their appearance, and as she kept up the disturbance, I sent them in to rescue her. She was found standing on her feet. "'Tis only my wife," said Vitnègre with an apologetic smile, "we were making love, a mere nothing don't you know. Look at the silly creature, she's still soaking wet with pleasure, but she's got the temperament of a wildcat: she bites and howls whenever you show her any kindness at all." Agreeing that Vitnègre was a very witty fellow indeed, the neighbors all laughed and withdrew.

Vitnègre dined and comported himself with a degree of politeness; he wondered whether his wife had identified her fucker as a monk and feared that she might chatter about what had happened. I took supper in a cabaret opposite Vitnègre's house; I saw him leave, and when I had finished my meal I returned to my daughter, who related everything that had passed. I said not a word.

I induced her to describe the circumstances of her depucelation—for she believed she was a maid no more—because I had a strong taste for such narrative and hoped hers would sufficiently restore my vigor to enable me to fuck her once again; she launched into the story as soon as I had put her in the right mood by speaking of her lover.

"Our first night and the three succeeding ones each netted Vitnègre five hundred *louis*, or so I subsequently learned from him. Directly we reached the house in which we we were to dwell together, he lit four candles and disposed them around the bed. He had me lie down with my skirts raised above my waist. He turned me this way and that way, examining and kissing me everywhere; he had me lift my legs in the air and then stand up on the bed. 'Wiggle your ass,' said he, 'no this way, the way I'm doing it'—he showed me how— 'as if I were busy fucking you.' I pointed out to him that this was indecent... 'Indecent! Bah! a wife is her husband's whore,' he observed philosophically and fell to licking my cunt and then bawled at the top of his lungs: 'She's discharging! look at her squirt!'... and he had me grasp his thick member, as heavy as a horse's and of the same color... 'Down on your back,' he cried, 'I'm going to fuck you now.' He flung himself upon my belly, but could accomplish nothing. 'They who say your father popped your cherry are a pack of bloody liars; you're as mint as a six-months-old babe. Would that all of Europe were here to bear witness to this marvel... into which a knitting needle couldn't go.'

He lubricated me with some preparation, oiling me before and behind, extinguished the candles (my maidenhead had been sold) and pretented to climb into bed; actually, it was someone else who lay down beside me. For all night long I was harassed by a fat member which got nowhere in the face of my narrow avenues."

At that point in her story when she had quoted Vitnègre's exclamation, "She's discharging!" I had slid a hand between her thighs; she felt it there but offered no resistance; I sank a finger into her cunt. "Ah, papa," said she, "you'll be just as hard on me as the others when the day comes that I am depucelated—" "How's that? Depucelated? Is this true, my heavenly child?" "Never has anyone entered into what you are holding with your hand at this minute." "O adorable girl, I am a god, not a mortal man!... But you've given me too fierce an erection! I must have your precious favor, else I'll have a frightful spermatic colic..." and without further ado I picked her up in my arms and carried her into the adjoining cabinet.

CHAPTER XII

Wherein the most delicious of incestuous unions is recounted.

"You are all of you alike," she sighed, "and even my own papa cares for me only on account of that hole." "And on account also of your breasts, your nipples, your mouth, your eyes, your voluptuous figure, your inspiring curves, your legs, your prick-lifting feet, your soul, naive and virginal still despite all that has been done to make a whore of you." As I pronounced these words, I raised her skirts from behind—she was bent forward over the couch placed in the cabinet for purposes of fuckery—and I readied myself to attack her from the rear, but pommade was necessary to effect the introduction. "It's all my own fault," she continued, "if these stories I tell inflame every man who listens to them; Timon only once threatened my virtue and that was after he had heard the same tale, although I didn't go into all the particulars." She sprang away from me, for my device was hovering within an inch of success. "And so you wish to make me ill, downright ill," I said in the most plaintive accents. They melted her, her lovely blue eyes became moist, she came back and leaned forward and inserted my prick herself, and aiding me despite some sharp pains which the pommade only partially lessened, she said: "Whenever my sister and I would watch you stick it into Mother—and we saw you doing it all the time—you used to roar with pleasure, but you must not roar now, Vitnègre might walk in." I promised to labor in silence... ah what delights were mine! I encunted her, my beloved partner's trick twitched and gripped my prick; never was satin so smooth as that celestial ,cuntlet's interior, the cuntlet yet unfledged is not narrower. "Ah, if that rascal of a husband of yours had really known what your cunt is worth, he'd have battled his way into it even at the price of dying in the attempt." "No, his member is too thick, you see, he was afraid of spoiling me. He frigs himself, or has me frig him, while holding me by the hair or a buttock and when he discharges he swears and blasphemes." She contracted; she discharged... whereupon I too

came, deliciously, ecstatically, crying aloud notwithstanding my promise. "Move, move, shake, stir your
ass," I said again and again, "squeeze your cunt, my
angel, good... good... choke it to death... ah again...
and again!" and she wrung my spouting prick and
herself discharged repeatedly; I felt the last depths
of her cunt pinch and suck the end of my prick!...
I discharged three times running without budging
from her cunt, and she shot off perhaps ten ejacula-
tions, which I could sense from her convulsive shud-
derings, her spasms, her jerking up and down; at
last she was spent, panting for breath... I disencunted
as soon as I felt she had ceased to emit; she washed
herself at once, for Vitnègre had the whimsical habit,
upon his return and even in the presence of anyone
he brought home with him, of seizing and sniffing
her cunt.

We went into the salon to rest ourselves and to
talk. I divulged the entire adventure of the monk
in whose interests Vitnègre had made her display her
breasts, her ass, her cunt... I described the huge
proportions of the monk's engine, assuring her that
it was twice the size of her husband's, I provided her
with a picture of the barbarous joy of the ecclesiastic
near whom I had laid in hiding, and who in the most
unequivocal language had expressed his desire to split
her open like a ripe melon with that massive prick of
his. Shuddering, Conquette cast herself into my arms
upon hearing of all this. "Oh save me, dearest papa,
only save me and I shall be devoted to you forever!"
"I shall save you," I affirmed. I explained how and
why the beastly monk had gone, swearing that, had
he remained and tried to violate her, I would have
stabbed him to death without hesitation. I explained
also how her abominable husband had surrendered
her to me, thinking he was giving her to the monk
who had paid for her. "You know, O adorable child,

how I put it in you... 'Tis I who, contrary to all hope and all likelihood, 'tis I who snatched your maidenhead from the clutches of our enemies."

Conquette kissed me prettily upon the lips. "But how are you going to rescue me?" she wanted to know. "I shall come to fetch you an hour from now, I'll lead you away, you'll stay at your pension; as soon as you are safe and sound, I'll introduce an attractive and talented whore into the cabinet—I've got your key to it and I've already found the whore and she's agreed—as if I were going to fuck with her: I'll make a noise immediately I hear Vitnègre and the monk arriving, I'll skip out, I'll listen to what goes on, and tomorrow we'll see what's to be done." This scheme delighted my daughter, who saw her sufferings about to be brought to an end; I ought to have take her away without wasting an instant, but instead I amused myself by having her tell me what had befallen upon the second and third nights of her marriage.

CHAPTER XIII

The rental of Conquette's ass and cunt.

My matchless daughter resumed her woeful story in these terms:

"Vitnègre repeated the same things the second night. Taking light hold of my breasts: 'These seem of an admirable firmness,' he commented and stationed me as though he were exhibiting me on the auctioneer's block to a crowd of imaginary buyers (one of whom was only real). After having placed my fur in view, he turned me around and showed my buttocks. 'Still a virgin,' said he, as if speaking to himself. 'In order to perforate her you'll have to grease her like a pig and dip your own prick in butter.' He sucked and violently pumped my cunt and when I was wet enough to satisfy him he let me catch my breath.

"After a brief nap I woke to find that I was lying on my belly, and that astride me sat a man who was struggling to drive his exceedingly massive member into my fundament, but although he cared not a whit for my groans and sighs, he failed over and over again to open a passage through my anal rosebud (that was his expression as he spoke in a low whisper to someone nearby). I next heard someone else in this room say: "Well, I'm not the one to be of much help: my prick's far too heavy to blaze the trail... Here, have a look. Much too thick, isn't it?" I understood nothing, fell back to sleep and did not awake again.

"The next day, towards noon, having first buttered my rosebud and steeped his member in olive oil, Vitnègre bade me lie down upon my belly and pull my skirts up, then he mounted into the saddle. 'I've got to try out this buggering club on you,' he muttered. I reminded him he had spent the whole night trying me out. 'That will be enough from you,' said he. 'All we need to do is enlarge the vent... Ah, by God, what a fortune these two gems are going to bring me once the rumor gets abroad!' He strove with might and main, tortured me for a good two hours, and all for nothing; he had to suspend his experiment, a copious discharge depriving him of rigidity and strength.

"And the third night he once again repeated what he had done on each of the previous ones. Upon awakening and while still sleepy, I found myself lying upon my back; above me was a man frantically attack-

ing my gem with everything in his power; I uttered
a protest... 'Are you discharging, my dear?' inquired
Vitnègre. My rider dismounted, and he added:
"Beware lest you cry wolf the moment you see something hairy coming your way. Buck up, my heart, fist
this prick of mine, I've a yearn to discharge. Tickle
my balls with your free hand, that's it, do what I'm
doing to your cunt... fine... splendid... ah!' (It was
not before we had been married six weeks that he
began to call me bitch and whore.) But 'twasn't he
I fondled, I discovered that afterwards. Someone
discharged no less than six times in succession, I serviced that man steadily for more than an hour, and
he devoted another to tonguing me; I was at the end
of my strength. And then he had me piss into his
mouth and he lost not a drop: he swallowed it all;
he left me at last."

I restiffened despite my four discharges and said
to my daughter: "I can bear it not another second,
oh, divinely becunted angel. I'll not try to hide it
from you, my delicious little friend: apart from my
passion for you, quite as inexplicable as your beauty,
something else powerfully stimulates me: 'tis the
desire to cuckold Vitnègre. Wouldst, were such a
thing possible without obliterating your heavenly
charms, wouldst that all the men in the world could
make use of your cunt that he might be universally
cornute! Come, come give me my happiness," and
I was bearing her towards the divan when we heard
a key turn in the door. I immediately hid myself
in the obscure cabinet. Vitnègre appeared with a
young man in tow; we clearly heard him say before
entering: "You've got the sort of prick that should
fill the bill, and that's why for six bumfucked *louis*
I'm letting you have a pucelage that's worth a
thousand. Here's the way we'll go about it: I'll pre-
cede you and make as if to kill her; you'll beg me to

spare her, and I'll only let her off if she seconds you in wishing to be encunted by you. My big-pricked clients are all annoyed not to be able to fuck or embugger her; they pay like the devil, you know. We get on very well from what she earns... I feed her excellent dinners; look at her; chubby, wouldn't you say? But first of all you're to encunt her, that's a matter of pressing urgency; and tomorrow you'll stick it into her ass, which is an operation of secondary importance. Mind you, I adore her; I treat her a little roughly, that's only to make her pliable, so that she'll bend to my will. I've earned three thousand francs from her and we've not been married longer than three months. Let's go in now. She'll ravish you. But show her no pity." Such was the monstrous Vitnègre's speech.

We did not wait to greet them. I pushed Conquette ahead of me, we emerged from the house, went straight to the pension. She wished however to accompany me; we went to get Connilette the whore, an appetizing, well-decked specimen. Conquette preceded us; fortified by my presence, she opened the door to the obscure cabinet, entered, we followed her; I told Connilette to stretch out fuckably on the bed. My daughter received the two libertines; they found her in superior form. The young man—he went by the name of L'Enfonceur—and Vitnègre himself vied with one another in praising her. Vitnègre, who was mad about her feet thus shod in high-heeled shoes, kissed her nether extremities, saying: "Ah, that's it, my dearie, let's go softly to work. I'd be the world's most unhappy man if I had to give up the idea of fucking you. You've got to be trimmed to measure, or rather enlarged: my prick's too stout. Unprepared, it would do you damage: here's a better-proportioned device which without discharging is going to perforate you, and thus pierced, you'll manage to accommodate my weightier instrument tonight—and I intend to bury it deep. Here, look at what I've brought you," and he pulled L'Enfonceur's prick out of hiding. L'Enfonceur? Or was it Timon, the modestly-furnished poet? Yes, it seemed as though Vitnègre had, I have no idea how, discovered his wife's predilection for that handsome taffy-haired youth, and he employed him in the following manner.

CHAPTER XIV

The young man, the whore and the monk.

Upon recognizing her lover in the man her husband was bringing home to encunt her, my daughter blushed with modesty and desire; she found an opportunity to whisper in my ear: "Tell the whore to leave, we shan't be needing her tonight." I saw very clearly that Conquette was in a lather to be fucked by her gallant; I did not send away but concealed the whore; and there follows an account of what took place next.

Just as soon as Connilette was installed out of sight behind the large sofa in the cabinet, Conquette went in to join the two men who conveyed her to the locale selected for sport and had her sit bare-assed down upon their clasped hands. "Well, my little harlot of a wife, you're going to be depucelated at long last, thoroughly fucked upon this occasion," declared Vitnègre, "but never fear... when later on tonight you have to cope with a thick prick..." He disposed her skirts and adjusted her. "Excellent. Now, L'Enfonceur, let me put your prick into the works... no, better still, my little helpmeet will insert it herself: she must become accustomed to performing these chores." Vitnègre quit the room. I remarked however that he left the door ajar: whence I augured some villainous stunt, but I was there in case of need. Speaking in a muffled voice, Timon said to my daughter: "Shall I put it in you?" "No, no, he's gone off to get some listeners"—this word sent a chill through Timon. "But he'll maim you, you'll end up a cripple!" "I don't sleep here anymore." Satisfied by her short reply, the lover set forthwith to tonguing her cunt with great gentleness; the voluptuous girl discharged nonetheless... she was beside herself when I heard Vitnègre return, I supposed with the monk; he entered rapidly, followed by three neighbors. "I'm going to show you precisely what I mean," said he and indeed he showed them something in his room.

At this point, however, my love-smitten daughter, yet impaled by her lover's vibrant tongue, pronounced a deep sigh; the three neighbors pricked up their ears. "Why, that must be my wife," said Vitnègre; "I didn't realize she was in the house: I've purchased that cloth for her." "Oh, but she must see it, you must fetch her in," chorused the three neighbors. The monster bade them wait a moment—one of the neighbors indeed was about to go in search of Conquette—he took a candle, saying that he would find out first whether she were asleep. He reached the door, halted and feigned a look of scorn and anger. He drew back, but over his shoulder the three neighbors had seen quite as well and as much as he: Conquette half-naked, stretched out on her back upon the bed, a man's head nestled between her thighs. Vitnègre ushered the neighbors out by the corridor, all the while striking his forehead and uttering confused sentences.

He had attained his object: if during the night his wife were to scream and weep, the three neighbors would now know the reason why and would explain it to anyone else; if Madame Vitnègre were to perish, rent asunder by the monk's claymore (the monk, who was very rich, was to pay sixty thousand francs for his victim, several others of whom he had killed, since he always chose narrow-cunted prey), then it would be she who was in the wrong.

And now Vitnègre returned to the two lovers who had altered their position. L'Enfonceur, after having spilled his seed upon the floor, had remounted upon my daughter's belly. "Ha!" said the infamous husband, "have you run your peg all the way into her? Encunted her solidly?... Have you discharged, and has she?" "We have both discharged," replied Timon L'Enfonceur. "I am going out now," said Vitnègre, "keep raking her out while I'm gone—I'll be away for a half-hour. Don't be alarmed by what you are going to hear: I have my reasons for all this." He went into the hallway, opened the door quietly and began to shout as if he were kicking his wife about like a football: "Bitch! slut! whore! You fuck when I'm abroad, do you! Slime! Fuck-bibbler! Asswipe! You screw, eh!... Well, I'm going to the police, do you understand? I've had enough of this." He noisily opened the door, then slammed it, but before departing he whispered to the impassioned couple: "Wiggle your ass, bounce it, my dearie: courage, L'Enfonceur, dig in, scrape the barrel clean." L'Enfonceur, puzzled, watched Vitnègre go. "A nasty ruse, that one," I whispered to my daughter; "the monk plans to kill you, and Vitnègre is neglecting nothing to motivate your death." "Save us," she said, terror in her voice. "No, we're numerous enough to protect you. Pretend to Timon that I'm about to arrive here."

Timon re-entered the boudoir. "Here is papa," said Conquette, "he's just come, thank heaven." "Ah, yes," said Timon, "his presence will shield us, for I was about to propose that we flee from this place. But let's wait and see what happens." Timon and I conferred; I pointed to where Connilette lay hiding and outlined our scheme, which he thought marvelous. However, time was rushing by. Timon carried the light back into the boudoir, my daughter and I hid ourselves while the young man and Connilette adopted an intimate posture upon the bed. "Be careful," she warned him, "keep your prick at a distance, for I'm in bad shape, my boy, don't let your balls touch my hair, I've got crabs..."

Wherewith Vitnègre and the monk made their entry. The neighbors clustered at the window took the holy man for the chief of police.

CHAPTER XV

In which there figures a fucker à la Justine.

First, the monk removed his gown. Then he produced and brandished a prick of such colossal, nay, outrageous dimensions that my affrighted daughter hugged me in her arms. "Ah, but you carry a bludgeon under your belly," said Vitnègre in a flattering tone. "It's killed two nuns each of whom had previously borne two children to our abbot; I believe I've never encunted a woman without killing her, never, that is to say, but once: my own mother escaped being disembowelled, God knows how, but fucking her gave me no pleasure, the old bitch was slack-sprung and bled hardly at all... As for your wife, ah! this is going to be a festival! she's as good as fucked and finished already: she'll be dead before I'm done encunting her, and I'll embugger her corpse!... By the way, here's the money: sixty thousand in bank-notes..." Vitnègre counted them, put them in his pocket. "If only," said he, "if only I could encunt her just once—" "Are you jesting?" roared the monk. "Afterwards, after I'm done... the body will still be warm." I shuddered and as I had a brace of loaded pistols with me, I was tempted that instant to blow the monster's brains out... but no, I held back, thinking of the pox which was going to consume him. "Before they're in rags and tatters would you like to see her cunt, her pretty face?" "No, that would soften my prick; lead me to her: I prefer to dispense with light." They crept towards the bed, feeling their way along in the darkness.

Intending to remove L'Enfonceur from bed so that space would be cleared for the monk, Vitnègre preceded the latter. Finding only a partially unclothed woman there, he was fair to dip his wick in her cunt, which desire he signalled to her by bringing his mouth to that dangerous orifice. She was fending him off when the monk all but crushed him by hurling himself upon the girl. Vitnègre was obliged to beat a retreat on all fours.

Father Fout-à-Mort—as Vitnègre called him—was accustomed to begin his operations chewing his mount's nipples as he at the same moment effected his devastating entry into the cunt, but cast as this one was, and yet further widened by a sponge the girl had just removed, his engine was vaster and would not enter. Connilette emitted a piercing shriek as she felt her cunt being torn; she struggled to get away, scratching and fighting with both hands. Knowing she could not escape her fate, Fout-à-Mort, whose pleasure was in direct proportion to the beauty of the woman he was killing and the straitness of her cunt, only forged the more resolutely ahead; while holding her legs wide apart, he bit off first one and then the other of her nipples. Connilette's cries were ended by a deep swoon or death. I regretted not having made use of my pistols—the monk's head was at the most a yard away—but upon hearing the shot the neighbors would probably have broken down the door, and it was that which restrained me. Having battled to the bottom of the mangled girl's cunt, Fout-à-Mort finally discharged, shouting and bellowing and thrashing like a lunatic. "Have a fuck," said he to Vitnègre, "before I plumb the bitch's ass." The scoundrel drew near, but feeling what resembled a blood-soaked cadaver on the bed, he recoiled.

"She's dead!" he exclaimed. Fout-à-Mort felt her pulse... "No... the heart's still beating... quick, then, I've got to embugger her." Connilette's asshole was far narrower than her cunt, the monk had to toil like one of the damned; however, thanks to a mighty effort he achieved the thing and was heard to say to Vitnègre: "Where there were formerly two holes, there is now but one," and he discharged horribly...

Quivering with dread, my daughter grasped me around the waist. Vitnègre was weeping: "Oh, my poor wife, I have surrendered you to your judge, you are undone..." "But I paid for her, did I not?" demanded the awful monk, "and so she belongs to me. Now get out of here, go to bed and go fuck your sixty thousand francs. You are in my way, you bother me; I'm going to get my money's worth while she's still warm, why not? I'm going to fuck my whore's asshole and cunt another five or six times." The cringing Vitnègre did as he as told, retiring to a little chamber and getting into bed.

Fout-à-Mort worried his defunct victim's broken body indefatigably. At last, himself grown weary of the work, he went in search of a light so as to feast his cruel eyes upon what he had done... (I said that the girl was pretty.) "She's still lovely to see," quoth the monster, "but the whore's face is rather distorted: she no longer looks her old self." He peered at her cunt, raising her up by the ass... and let her fall again, bursting into savage laughter. "In faith, the slut's got either a damned big cunt or a damned big asshole... I don't know which... But... is she truly dead, I wonder? He took off the few clothes left on her body and carried it, naked, into the other room, deposited it on a large table, fetched a great salad-bowl, drew forth a surgeon's scalpel and lancet... (Through the windowed door we were able to see what he was doing.) "Off with the fleshy excrescences, for a beginning." He hacked away most of her breasts, scalped her mons Veneris, sliced steaks from her thighs, split open her belly, tore out her heart, her lungs, her liver, her womb, turned her over, removed her buttocks, severed her slippered feet, which he put in one of his pockets, severed her hands, which he crammed into another, turned her over again, cut out her tongue, cut off her head, stripped the flesh from her arms; next, he took a sheet from the bed and found her nightgown. "A royal dinner there for my brethren at the monastery and myself." The terrible cannibal wrapped the salad-bowl in the nightgown and the torso in the sheet, called to Vitnègre, said he was through with his work and was leaving, then told him to publish news on the following day that his wife was dying: "Have her put in a coffin and I'll look after her burial." And having recommended that he take care to remove all traces of blood from the floor and furnishings, he bade Vitnègre adieu and left, taking with him his salad-bowl of human flesh. It was three o'clock in the morning. Vitnègre wept, but hearing our movements as we were preparing to leave, the cowardly dog was so terrified that he fled and locked himself in his little chamber.

We encountered no one as we left; crossing the court, we heard the neighbors muttering to each other: "He didn't kill her after all. D'ye see? He's taking her along with him." As soon as we were outside, afraid lest we be pursued, we ran, threading our way through back streets and ruelles, and we were wise to do so: we heard running footsteeps, but they were in adjoining streets and we were not stopped. I took my daughter to her pension having left Timon behind to watch and promising to come back within thirty minutes.

"You saw what my fate would have been," said Conquette, "had I not delayed your going by according you my favors." "Quite," I said. "O dear papa, my whole body is yours... do with it whatever you like." I asked for her room. I told her to go to bed. "No," said she, "I'd never be able to sleep. What of my belongings? my clothes and jewels... do you suppose we'll manage to get them back?"

I applauded her lucid presence of mind. The hour was nearly five. I rushed back to join Timon, whom I found pacing in front of Vitnègre's door. "Nothing so far," said he; but the next instant we saw Vitnègre emerge: Timon followed him and I went to get my daughter: her being there was now necessary to us. Some officious neighbors halted us; upon returning with Conquette and two hangers-on I came upon Timon, who informed us that Vitnègre has walked to the boulevard and beyond. Conquette opened the door. We loaded four trunks which had been readied but kept hidden; we left unseen and went to the house where one of my trusty servants dwelt. Only then was Conquette at her ease; she retired for the night and Timon and I each went home for some rest.

CHAPTER XVI

Fucking-couch, storeroom, burial, love-making.

Now we are coming to some first-rate fuckeries, those in which my delicious Conquette Ingénue and my ravishing Victoire Conquette are to show their true mettle and whence they are to emerge seasoned veterans, making their fortunes and mine thereby, and losing thereunto a false delicacy and over nice scruple which always bar the road to prosperity. The régime I chose for the education of those dazzling creatures and their companions may perhaps startle the reader, but, as in all other things, he would best suspend his criticism and judge only by the outcome.

Let us take up once again the thread of this charming story and turn to a few preparatory love-bouts which will usher in the main ones; I may however advise the reader that in this work he will come across no further Sadean horrors. 'Tis the painting of sweet voluptuousness constitutes genius' masterpiece.

The first visit Conquette received on the day following her inhumation and at the same hour was paid her by Timon. He found her at her pension. He recounted how, after having died two nights before, she had just been buried, but he was inhibited from speaking freely by the presence of the master and mistress of the house. Now, in this same building, only a few steps from where I lived, I had a small room where I hid the copies of each number of my *Annales* (1), whose printing was at the time forbidden by the government: my daughter was to have her bed in this secluded place and was to sleep there that night—she would have been there already had it not been that she had recently arisen. The bed I had installed—for my own use, for my secretary's, for his sister's, mistress' and mother-in-law's—was a comfortable and generous fucking-couch beneath whose thick coverlets one could nestle very agreeably. Vitnègre had one just like it: he used to hide in it when one or another of his clients came to exercise the cunt or ass of his wife (he called her his golden-egg-laying goose): he didn't like to miss anything of the spectacle and was, furthermore, afraid that a client might spirit her away from him; apart from that, his lust was flattered by watching: he was mad about his wife's feet; while she was being feelingly tongued by one of those buggers (they all adored her and were keenly to regret her loss), he would draw off one of her slippers: they were narrow and he used them the way another might employ a cunt. "Friends," he was wont to confide to his colleagues, "I have never fucked anything belonging to my wife but her shoes."

Sensing that Timon had a quantity of things to tell her, and that he was unable to talk where they presently were, Conquette pretended she had left a letter in my storeroom and that she wished to show it to him; having a key, they went down together.

I had just arrived there; I heard my daughter's step, her muted voice and Timon's; I hid myself in

---

(1) Rétif published *L'Anti-Justine*, it will be recalled, under the name of Linguet, editor of that famous newspaper, *Les Annales Politiques et Littéraires* (1770-1790).

the capacious bed. They entered. Conquette carefully closed and locked the door, covered it with the mattress padding which prevented noise from being overheard outside, and they seated themselves near to where I lay.

"Ah, Madame," began that sensitive youth, "what scenes we've had!... He discovered, I know not by what means, that I loved you—perhaps my glances betrayed me—or because one day when I was with him at your home, and one of your purchasers was caressing you with his leave and his guise, he saw me shower kisses in one of your slippers—I thought I did so unnoticed... but he seemed until then to have been totally unaware that you loved me, or that you and I were ever acquainted... And then came the terrible day. He called at my lodgings; I was having coffee; it was three in the afternoon. 'I'll never be able to depucelate my wife,' he told me, 'my prick's too large; you're a handsome lad, I've chosen you to handsell her, 'twill be this very day... I simply ask six *louis* for her hire... I'll give them to her as a gift... she likes to buy herself trinkets.' I produced the money on the spot and we set out... you know the rest.

"After leaving you on that fatal night, I slept until ten in the morning. I went to my office but on the way stopped at your husband's door. I knocked and heard to neighbors whispering to each other: 'It's the confessor... so it couldn't have been Madame they took away last night.' The wicked fellow opened the door—that atrocious monk was with him; a friar had brought the coffin, it contained something swathed in shrouds, and he was reciting prayers aloud beside the body, which lay in the obscure cabinet... 'He's a friend,' Vitnègre explained to the monk; then, to me: 'My poor wife has passed away.' 'Passed away?' said I. 'She died in the arms of this reverend father.' The expression made me shudder. The monk spoke:

'I did all in my power... we have taken all the necessary steps: she shall be buried quietly, permission has been granted us to carry out the little ceremony: it will take place at about four.' I left. After my mid-day meal, towards three-thirty I called again at Vitnègre's house: two priests, four pall-bearers, the monk and the friar carried out the body. There was no chanting. It was buried. We'll see what happens next; I plan to watch developments. You are thought dead, my beloved; will you accord me your favors? For you are free."

"My friend," was Conquette's modest reply, "let me begin by thanking you for the important services you have rendered me; but there is someone else who has rendered me yet greater ones: but for him I should have been doomed... Where I still in possession of my favors, I should bestow them upon you, but they are now the rightful property of my first lover who, lying in concealment, discovered the plot they were hatching; he has just deflowered me, he made love to me once again after doing so, he is your single rival, but I adore him: his name, which I am going to disclose to you, shall prove in what high esteem I hold you, for, truly, this is a confidence to be guarded faithfully: he is my papa." Upon hearing these words Timon fell at his mistress's feet... "Angelic girl, divine girl," he said, "I discern therein all your filial piety and the beauty of your soul! Fuck your father, yes; may he be alone to encunt you: you would be worthy to be fucked by a god, if the gods still fucked these days... but I ask but one thing: to lick out your cunt, my precious, and, with your father's noble permission, to sodomize you." "My most amiable friend," Conquette said to him, stroking his hand and smiling with infinite sympathy, "you are an eminently reasonable individual."

Timon shed his trousers, deposited in her hands

a depucelating instrument, yet more meagerly constructed than my fine prick, had her caress his little globes and requested leave to frig her; she refused; wherewith Timon lay her upon the bed, hoisted her petticoats and voraciously, but fastidiously, sucked her cunt.

No indeed, never were such joyous sighs pronounced. "Ah, Timon! your tongue's even better than a prick," the young bard was told. She had ejaculated with the third lick of his gifted tongue, and in her delirium she raised her legs high in the air, clicking her heels, elevating her ass to favor the application of her pumper's mouth and the intromission of the tongue with which he was exciting her clitoris.

She was the image of her mother in this heel-clicking, for I never rogered that lamented woman save in daytime, for, whether having at her cuntwardly, bumwise, or orally, I wished to be inspired by the best part of her: I am referring to her leg and foot; I used to ask her to click her heels, because that reminded me of a woman walking—and that would always give me an erection.

When my daughter had her fill of discharging, she thrust Timon away from her swimming cunt.

CHAPTER XVII

The asshole handselled. The cunt-fucking father.

The celestial Conquette Ingénue was as always her fair-minded and clear-thinking self: the reader will be not in the least surprised by the speech she uttered now. Turning over on her belly, "My next-to-best friend," said she, "lubricate me: my foremost friend depucelated my gem, justice demands that to you be offered the first use of my rosebud—papa would surely approve my decision." "O goddess!" exclaimed Timon as he inserted pommade in her anus by means of a simple piece of apparatus, "what a tranquil judgment you have, what unfailing wisdom! He shall have the cuntlet and I the rosy vent, each of us shall enjoy the privilege of exclusive fuckery." Timon burst through the narrow gate despite one or two little squeals and titters from my cherished daughter, and after some lively thumps and rattlings, he discharged. "Fuck!" he roared in his cultured voice, "fuck!... what an ass! Why, this is the very pleasure of Olympean Zeus!" and he slumped forward drained of sperm and short of wind after that single stroke of lightning; and it also occurred to him, to my measureless satisfaction, that he had an appointment at seven. Rolling her upon her back so as to be able to give her a farewell kiss in the form of a few stabs of the tongue aimed into her cunt, Timon left the amorous Conquette Ingénue stretched out upon the bed. He lit his candle, opened the door and shut it behind him.

He was no sooner gone than I sprang from hiding and landed upon my adorable daughter, who had been moved by, and whose cunt was oscillating vibrantly from those three nips Timon had bestowed in going. "Why, gracious! Are you there?..." "Of course, my beloved: he embuggers, I encunt! you are at the origin of this shattering erection you see me wearing..." "O dearest papa! Fuck me, do... fuck your devoted daughter, fuck her" (it was the first time in her life she had used this word; she repeated it thrice, being by no means blind to its singular potency), "you'll have to do the fucking, for I'm perfectly exhausted."

She grasped my prick, plunged it into her cuntlet.

"Push," she cried, "push, divine prick, paternal prick, squirt fuck into your daughter's cunt!" While holding forth in this strain, she flung her ass about with such energy I was soon lodged in the depths of her cunt... Long live common everyday cunt-fuckery! Of the forty manners of being rid of one's load, 'tis by far the best. I had my daughter's mouth, her tongue, her white breasts, the view of her charming countenance, always made doubly attractive when the woman's being fucked... her sweet phrases: "Dear, most beloved prick, divine prick, oh how it itches my cunt. Thrust, drive deep, bugger, deeper... I'm coming... I'm dis... charging... fuck, fuck a river of fuck... your tongue, dear cunt-fucker, dear lover... oh, I'm dis—charging again, fuck, bloody bugger, suck, bite my tits..." In tune with Conquette's second emission, I discharged, shooting my seed to the last recesses of the wrung-tight cunt gripping me like a mailed fist. And I felt myself adorably needled by what the vulgar call the clitoris, and more polished persons the finger of heaven; and some other interior organ, the cervix, attained only by lengthy pricks, avidly sucked the end of my engine. Discharging with this delicious idea in my brain—picturing myself wedged in the most beautiful of women, her back arched, her flanks heaving, solidly stoppered, sweating with joy—I fucked the child of my loins, I frotched into her cunt... what, I thought, our mingled seed may create a new child!... I'm cuckolding that bounder, that bleeder Vitnègre! I'm fucking the wife he thinks dead!... the wife he's never fucked... we're fucking her, Timon and I, he her ass, I her cunt, while that base, vile dog is frigging himself at the thought of her; he believes her cut to pieces, quartered by her damned monk's member, and what! her cunt streams like a princess's being futtered by a regiment of the royal guard!... Those ideas, rapidly turning over in my imagination, doubled, quadrupled my delight.

My daughter squeezed me out. "I'm full to the gills," said she, "my cunt and my ass too, I've got to wash."

I ran in search of warm water, climbing up to the kitchen where I found Madame Brideconin, the lady of the house, seated by the hearth, her snow-white breasts lazing in plain view. I kissed them, took the kettle which she had set to heat on the hob for her own use. Monsieur Brideconin said: "I've just given her a plumbing in honor of your daughter, Madame Poilsoyeux" (the name I had given her so that she'd not have to bear her infamous husband's). I went back down to the storeroom, I myself sponged clean my divine girl's secret charms: I noticed a few traces of blood near the rosebud and also, indeed, in the cunt. "What have we here? Have I hurt you?" "Yes, ever so slightly, my darling tormentor, but pain made my pleasure the greater... even in my ass." Cleansed, Conquette Ingénue regarded me for a moment. "I was in such a hurry to make love with you, O guardian angel, that I did not even have the time to ask your opinion on what has taken place between Timon and myself." "I too have things to say on that head, but we are going now to have supper: you need rest, we'll chat tomorrow." I gave her my tongue, she gave me hers, they entwined; I kissed her pink nipples and we set off to eat.

During supper I related to Madame Brideconin that much of Madame Poilsoyeux' alleged death she and her husband had to know in order that they avoid compromising her.

While we supped, my daughter's host carried her bed down to the storeroom; when everything had been arranged she and I went back down together. "I think I'll be afraid all alone in here; ask Madame

Brideconin to spend the night with me." "I'll stay, my lovely." "Oh, I'd prefer that!... not for love-making, but so that my loving papa will sleep with his head pillowed on the breasts of Vitnègre's wife while Vitnègre passes the night boring himself or fucking one of my old shoes." "Heavenly child," I said, "I am going to tell you tonight what I had planned to postpone until tomorrow." As might a newlywed husband, I undressed my goddess, kissing everything I brought to light; when both of us were in bed, I set her on my lap and began my discourse.

CHAPTER XVIII

Fatherly advice delivered
to the daughter while encunting her.

O affable reader, I am able still to feel throbbings of the most exquisite voluptuousness as I recall to mind those enchanting moments that were mine thanks to Conquette Ingénue.

"Lower yourself slowly, my queen, and with care, that I may insert the tenon without scraping the mortise." She followed instructions... When perfectly encunted, she bade me speak. "You know, my dearest, that I have seen everything, heard everything. Your divine sentiments in my regard have penetrated me with gratitude and admiration. I wholly approve your gesture in awarding to Timon the handselling of your sublime ass; with transports of greatest joy I welcome and accept your devotion to me. However, my dear daughter, 'tis in your interest and for your welfare and happiness I employ it as I see fit. I am older, wiser than you; but unlike a sultan, subject to foolish jealousies and alarms. I have no intention of preserving you for my exclusively personal pleasures; you will have a buyer... which would you prefer amongst the three men to whom your pucelage was sold?" "The best-mannered, O incomparable papa, but he was also the one with the biggest prick." "I shall therefore have your gem widened by a stoutly furnished gentleman of my acquaintance; he is not particularly lovable nor lovely, but some better-favored personage might weary you by making you discharge too frequently, or, worse, might win your heart, and that must not be allowed to happen. A preparatory fucker ought to gain possession of nothing but your cunt. Neither Timon nor I have the sturdy construction required for the job, we're merely equipped for depucelatory exercises, but are no cunt-stretchers; however, a number of possibilities come to mind. I'll talk the problem over with the individual you prefer, then with the two others if he proves unwilling to cooperate. I have spied upon those three, I know their addresses; I'll not compromise you, as your father, I ask of you nothing but submissiveness and obedience." "They are yours entire, dear papa." She squirmed about for an instant and discharged. "Should, as I judge likely to happen, should a significant rise occur in your essential temperature, I shall take good care—and you may rely upon me—that you will not lack for pricks... 'twill be an unending succession of homages. Maturity in years deprives me of the capacity to sate your young lust—should it be a question of lust—and so I propose to bring you a series of nice clean youths, steadily increasing the diameter of the prick." My provocative daughter began again to stir at this juncture. "Dear fucking-father, I want to be cunt-fucked by Timon, my ass-fucker; will you allow it? You have converted me, he'll encunt me, but only in your presence." "Yes, yes, very well." I strained upwards with a heave of my back; she burst into song: "Dig deep, dig deep into my cunt, far-darting prick, make me come!... Oh buggerfuck!... Fuck, screw me, screw right and deep and harder!... I'm discharging (and so she did, suddenly freezing her body as though electrified) ah!... ah!... O darling papa... ah! ah! ah!... (with a sigh) ...never before have I discharged like that!"

I lit a lamp; my daughter repaired to the bidet to polish her gem whilst I dipped prick and balls in soothing cool water in order to relax my enfuriated machinery. I enquired, where had my daughter learned the expressions she had employed upon discharging?

"During the third week of my marriage," she answered, "Vitnègre went to bed with his god-daughter, the wife of a police spy. By her god-father's orders, this woman pretented to enter a delirium when he rogered her, and those were the words she uttered—and there were others, too, which would sound less musical upon my lips and in your ears: for example: fuck-puker, bleeding bull's pizzle, butter churn, fuck-to-death ramrod seer swab, cunt-scraper, and many more." We got back into bed and fell asleep in each other's arms.

The next morning I repeated my instructions to Conquette; we heard a knock... it was Madame Bride-conin who was calling to my daughter; I hid under the bed-clothes. "They're looking for a whore from the Port aux Blés," she said when Conquette opened the door; "she vanished the other evening. One of her companions says that she was going off to sleep with a man she had described as a lawyer, but, so this companion would have it, he turned out to be a surgeon who, with a friend to help him, killed her during the night and dissected her. They're probably talking about you—you know how stories get distorted. My husband's going out to find out what's what." She left and later Conquette and I went up to take breakfast. I left her, promising to join her for dinner at noon.

I returned promptly at twelve. Brideconin had left the house. It was indeed about Connilette the hue and cry had been raised. The police and their informers had searched every house in the street but discovered nothing. By way of precaution, I changed my clothes, went out and came back in the late afternoon, but did not stay for the night. Sleeping at home, I rested myself for three nights and let Conquette Ingénue rest also. I loved my daughter for her own sake as much as for my pleasure's and had no desire to impose the measure of my middle-aged forces upon the appetite proper to her nineteen years. And I had other reasons as well; I behaved in accordance with them.

CHAPTER XIX

The elderly rake with the grey-tinted pubic hair.

What you are about now read will, in view of the sentiments I have just professed, probably surprise you; but, bold reader, refrain from beforehand estimations; if you must pass judgment, wait a little till you know me better.

I knew one of those pleasure gourmets, a large, vigorous man, extremely lewd and lustful: his name

was Montencon; I had often dined at his house in the
rue Trousse-Vache; upon a number of occasions,
dinner over, he had persuaded me to encunt little
Vitsucette, his mistress, whom he was pleased to hold
down while I toiled in her hole. He had even procured me his landlady's daughter, a regular little
jewel seduced by her mother's lover, a noble by the
name of Foutanes, who had finally turned her into
a whore; she amused us all of an evening. Montencon, having made the pretty Adelaide Hochepine
tipsy on wine and brandy, he had the courtesy to
send me first into the fray after his mistress had
given my balls a hearty manualizing by way of pre-
lude; I encunted and then he embuggered her, he too
having initially had his pearls rubbed by Vitsucette;
she washed my member and I then had a second shot
at Adelaide. Montencon bade Vitsucette wash me
again. "I have my reasons, my dear chap; I've a
fondness for having my prick sucked." He hopped his
device into Adelaide's mouth, was pumped, discharged, and had her swallow his seed; I was repelled
by this performance and by its duplication, effected
immediately afterward with Vitsucette. Having
found all this fuck-quaffing eminently disageeable,
I never went back to Montencon's for another soirée.
But he was the personage I invited to dine with us
in the storeroom, and whom I had selected to begin
the amplification of my daughter's cunt and her
training in battle: the work had to be done; for I had
individually promised each of Vitnègre's thick-
pricked clients that she would soon be back in active
service.

Montencon was not unknown to Conquette, whose
mother he had fucked prior to the syphilitic days;
he was nothing if not eager to slip it to the daughter.
I found him halfway up the stairs as I myself returned
home. I introduced them; he stood motionless,

struck with admiration and full of joy to behold so beautiful a woman.... I had business to attend to; I stayed no longer than a minute, saying I would leave my daughter to keep him company. He went with me to the door, stammering excitedly. "Ravishing creature! faultless taste in clothes! remarkable footwear, especially the footwear! A damned pity Vitnègre made off with that pucelage!" "Vitnègre?... hardly, my dear Montencon. She's a maid." "No!" "Indeed she is." "My good Linguet, may I go and try to put at least one horn on that fool's head?" "Do the best you can," I replied, "but with your grey hair... I'm not so sure you'll succeed. Only a jaded bitch who's generally fed up with all the rest is apt to be willing to spar with a healthy greybeard libertine; with well-behaved maidens, you know, one must be tender and gentle, and what with your face of a satyr or a reprobate... I don't know. But try it."

Directly I was gone Montencon addressed himself to the task. He experimented first with gallantry and compliments... and got nowhere. At the end of his patience, he hurled Conquette onto the fucking-couch and being a vigorous fellow, he brought his prick nigh to the lips of her cunt, holding her struggling body with one hand. However, he was unable to advance further; she contrived to kick him in the behind, the blow undid what little he had accomplished; he was at his wit's end and might have threatened her with a knife when I reappeared. Conquette adjused her clothes without showing a hint of ill-humor; I whispered to Montencon: " How did it go?" "She's a devil and it went damned poorly. I'll doubtless have to finish by frigging myself." "Courage, my friend, you'll fuck her yet."

We sat down at the table; Conquette talked to Montencon just as if nothing had happened—and nothing had—and even laughed at his jests; he asked why she'd not let him encunt her. "Bless me!" she replied, "why did I not submit? Why should I?" "Because," he retorted, "I was as stiff as a bleeding mule." "You sound like Vitnègre." That however did not prevent Montencon from recounting his enterprise in the most savoury language; he praised the beauty of her cunt, the silky quality of its hair, the plump fairness of her buttocks, the firmness of her bubs, the pinkness of her asshole, the ivory-colored elasticity of her belly, her thighs; he exalted her foot and leg and in brief declared a general enthusiasm for all of her. Thus approved, Conquette blushed and was only the more modest in her triumph. I explained that I alone had fucked my daughter whose life I had saved and whom I had deflowered a week before, and I related the entire story. "You fuck her?" "And who has a greater right to? I am twice her father." Montencon bit his lip, Conquette embraced me.

Throughout the meal we admired Madame Poilsoyeux's voluptuously moulded buttocks, whose splendid lines proclaimed themselves whenever she rose to ask for a plate or hand one around; she was wearing pretty green shoes with slender green heels, her silk stocking had a pink tint; I enquired whether she was wearing a garter-belt. "Certainly," said she, "I always do." "In that case, show us more of the world's prettiest legs." She refused my request, but we besought her with such insistence that, to put an end to our importuning, she placed one foot upon a chair and lifting her skirts, exhibited a leg sufficient to send a dying man to hell.

We were, Montencon and I, beginning to lose our heads, but did our best to keep a grip upon ourselves. The ribald old fogey, during a moment when Conquette was in the kitchen, suggested we get her drunk by pouring champagne (he had brought me a bottle

of it) into her red wine instead of water; I feigned
assent, but before Conquette came back in I joined
her in the kitchen and told her what we were up to.
"My judicious, most reasonable girl," I added, "you're
going to have to be stuffed; that's what I brought him
here for, but I didn't know how to proceed. I was
pondering ways and means when he made his suggestion: you'll pretend to get drunk, so shall I, and
thus he'll never be able to get the upper hand. His
engine's rather stout, although of medium length;
after him, I'll get you Trait-d'Amour, my former
secretary, a pretty lad who'll carry on with the enlarg-
ing process; he should be able to prepare your cunt
for whichever client you prefer. Trait-d'Amour
knows about you; I've asked him to wait a few weeks
before I place you and him in the ring together. Let
me handle the business, my beloved, I'll be there
to put a stop to anything unseemly." "I am your
servant, dispose of me," she said, "in any way you
like. The situation from which you rescued me was
so dreadful that I cannot disobey you." We returned
to the dining-room; an instant before entering it, she
pulled one bub from her bodice and had me kiss it...
Montencon had completed preparations, pouring
champagne into the decanter of wine; Conquette,
warned, discerned the trick and unobserved slyly
managed to fill her glass with water, reserving the
wine to besot Montencon himself; but the bawd was
not to be made drunk on anything but the lovely eyes
and other charming features of my delicious Conquette Ingénue.

CHAPTER XX

"How that girl was fucked!"

When at last Madame Poilsoyeux, who affected a convivial tipsiness, appeared to be in the state Montencon esteemed desirable, he signalled to me and, waiting for the first opportunity, I caught her round the waist with one arm and with my free hand seized her cunt (apart from a strong desire to possess her at once, I wished to embolden her and prepare her cunt for the admission of a member more sizable than mine). I thrust her upon the bed, calling to Montencon to bring me what there was left of the butter we had eaten during our meal; I deposited a lump the size of a walnut in her orifice and pushed it in out of sight... "I'll do that, please leave it to me," she said in the calmest of voices; however, her ass was moving with an admirable rhythm and the couch was creaking a marvelous tune; I discharged thanks to these effects, and myself emitted many musical cries of delight. "Well, bugger," said I, "it's your turn now."

Standing by the bed, holding his stoutly risen prick in his hand, Montencon gazed down at us; I had no sooner disengaged than he leapt bravely upon my daughter whose wet cunt was still aquiver, and doubly resplendent with its garnishing of butter-and-fuck sauce. Montencon lunged, penetrated... Conquette screamed... I stepped forward, alarmed and ready to fly to her aid, but she was already smiling brightly. "Are you well bedded in?" I asked her fucker. "Jesus Christ, yes! and delightfully... she's nipping my prick; but what a cunt she's got... it's like satin in there... ah! ...ah! I'm fucking her... Shake your ass, heavenly harlot, throw it about, buggress... O delicious cunt, dance under my balls!... jump, do you hear!... I'm com-ing... I'm dis-charging!... ah!... ah!... ah!" The greybeard sank fainting down upon my daughter's breasts; she was swimming in fuck and joy! I'd feared that she might be shy with a stranger and lie stock-still instead of answering her antagonist blow for blow, but immediately she had felt Montencon's prick's scrape in, she had thrashed about like a captive panther, roared like a young lioness, and discharged like a thoroughbred mare. Montencon, without decunting, began to fence with her again, shouting, weeping with lust, and periodically murmuring: "Divine bitch... play the whore... I guarantee your efforts will be rewarded." Three times over the battle was renewed; neither gave quarter; finally, dry from extreme toil, both desisted.

"That was a fuck worth ten of the everyday variety, and that cunt's worth a thousand of the sort I used to have you stick, Linguet, even my little land-lady's. One leaves it for a moment, but regrets having to do so; but I say, my friend, dig in again, why don't you? A woman's a match for sixteen men in this game, let's not allow her to cool off nor suffer from idleness." Whereupon Conquette Ingénue, having lain motionless, save for her cunt, which she kept contracting as though a member were still stuffing it, jumped off the couch and ran to wash herself.

She found warm water ready for her; Montencon and I cast ourselves upon our knees before our divinity and one of us cleaned her ass, the other her cunt, then her buttocks and her thighs, for she was awash with fuck and even bleeding slightly; taking care to wet neither her nightgown nor her stockings, we had her stand with her clothing drawn up above her waist. After a scrupulous ablution, we admired her, for she was ravishing with her ass and cunt thus exposed; we had her walk to and fro and we stared adoringly at the magic of her shifting hips and buttocks. "What enchants me," said the oldster as he watched her move toward us, "is that black cunt against a ground of lily-white skin, that silken cunt-hair and that line of coral dividing it down the middle." The lovely creature turned about and exhibited further charms. "Ah!" exclaimed Montencon, transported, "what an ass!... it is not one jot inferior to that peerless cunt." She came back. "Unspeakably beautiful cunt! 'tis worthy of that divine ass..." When Conquette came close to us, he kissed her fur, then, getting to his feet (for we had remained kneeling the better to appreciate the drama), he carried her to the couch, begging my permission to tongue and suck all those charms before I refucked her... Great God! how she was tongued and sucked... he tickled her rosebud with his nose and tongue until her teeth chattered, then he concentrated upon her cunt: the beautiful girl shivered and trembled beneath this treatment and then, ejaculating, she neighed like a little horse into whose vulva one inserts for the first time the awe-inspiring and deep-driving engine of a vigorous stallion. The untupped mare's dimpled, superbly-fleshed buttocks shook; a groan rose from her very soul and was answered by the geyser sprung from her sperm-spewing stud's prick.

All that, I say, and my voluptuous daughter had been merely tickled by a tongue!... Montencon abandoned her bubbling well and I, leaping upon my Conquette's heaving belly, holding her ass three inches above the bed, dived brutally into the abyss;

she did naught but seem to sway gently before that onslaught, my lustful impatience required more. "Pull off one of her shoes," I said to Montencon, "and tickle the soles of her feet with it." He removed a shoe, but the scoundrel amused himself by sniffing it. "'Tis Cypris," quoth he, "and within her shoes have the scent of ambrosia." "Tickle her feet, I tell you!" I roared. He did and at her second twitch I discharged like Vesuvius in eruption. In my ecstatic joy I gave thanks to fate for having blessed me with so perfect a daughter, whose twitching cunt procured me such intense pleasures. "I am discharging again..." Conquette stammered; "my father's prayer drove his prick deeper into me." "O, what a worthy father! what a pious daughter!" exclaimed Montencon... I decunted. "But tell me why," said the energetic old bawd, stretching out upon my daughter again and reencunting her without having washed, "why did you have me tickle the soles of your celestial fuckeress's feet?" "I obtained the recipe from a printer who was wont to fuck the wife of his confrère with the latter's enthusiastic cooperation. 'But,' my printer friend asked the fellow he cuckolded, 'what in heaven's name did you do to her to make her give me such pleasure?' 'You saw, didn't you, that her feet were bare? Well, someone told me that the sons of Mesdames Quillenpoche and Radball, both eight years old, having chanced into the room where a barrister and a pimp were cuntstuffing their mothers, the little youngsters, loath to disturb the party, removed a delicate slipper from each lady's foot and therewith tickled their soles, the which caused those ladies to skip in a very lively fashion and to receive from their own sudden movements quite as much satisfaction, as they simultaneously gave their operators; and so, since that day, in like circumstances they always have their feet tickled." "Kindly do the same for me," said

Montencon. He began his coming and going in Conquette's cunt. "Astonishing!" he remarked; "your own father's fuck—the fuck whereof you were created—amalgamed with yours in your sacred cunt, should, it seems to me, serve as pommade... but I can hardly get into you!" From the crimson color of my daughter's cheeks I saw he was hurting her. "Decunt, bugger," said I to her plumber, " your mule's prick is giving that little hole mouthfuls it can't possibly swallow." He did withdraw his shaft, I popped a gobbèt of fresh Normandy butter into her crack. "Ah," said the complacent child, "that ought to loosen the hinges..." Montencon reencunted wrathfully, he entered with veritable majesty and struck bottom. Conquette jerked her ass. "There 'tis," cried the lecher, "I feel your darling little nipper—well, go to it, let's clap another horn on that fuck-in-the-ass Vitnègre; pinch your ass and fling it about, my precious bitch..." This coarse language hurled me into an erotic furor, unpityingly I tickled my daughter's bare feet, the while saying: "Fuck, my love, fuck like a goddess, show us you know how to fuck... and you bugger, flood her cunt; have you ever sunk your line in a cunt to equal my celestial, my divine whore's?" Conquette thrashed on the bed as if she were bent on breaking her back and her encunter's too (as did Mademoiselle Timon under that great personage, Mirabeau), but Montencon resisted with steadfast muscle and bone; however, Conquette's ensuing discharge was so violent that the explosion nearly blasted the stopper from her hole—but, as subsiding she fell back, his prick, rasped by the velvety cunt, discharged with ravishing effects.

He shivered four lances without quitting the lists and at the last, after I'd tickled his balls, he ejaculated quite as abundantly as he had at the first. But he was weary. "Now, by God, that Vitnègre's properly cornute," he said, parting with his seed, "for his fuckeress wife's shot off three times as often as I." Conquette smiled. "How many?" I enquired. "Oh, ten times, twenty, I've no idea," she explained with becoming modesty, "for it's not polite to keep count after the first score." I kissed her forehead, she retired to the bidet. I saw with ample clarity that she had a taste and a talent for the sport, and so I decided to take some of the sting out of her before surrendering her to her heavy-pricked favorite.

Wishing to soothe her well-tried cunt in the bidet's cool water, with the most gracious air and sweetest blush Madame Vitnègre begged us to leave her for a time. Saluting her respectfully, as befits a beneficient goddess, we bowed and left the room.

"I humble myself before such a man," Montencon said to me, "I'd consider it a greater glory to be her father than Marie Antoinette's. She is just as superior to ordinary fuckeresses as Mademoiselle Contat and Mademoiselle Lange are superior to a working-class whore who frigs pricks behind the carts on the Quai du Louvre."

Upon which words we bade one another farewell. "Ah," Montencon murmured as he walked away, "how that girl was fucked!"

CHAPTER XXI

Fout-à-mort's last hour.

Your purists must surely have raised a squawl over the preceding chapter!... Purists, eh? may they go to the devil.

I expected a little chilliness, or a pout, or a serious

air the next day, but no, my Conquette chatted with me as usually she did... A week passed during which I made no effort to stuff her. On Saturday, thoroughly recovered from the worrying Montencon had given it, her gem began to itch again; she remembered what I had told her; that she could let Timon encunt her. She took the greatest pains with her toilette, donned a shawl and went out that evening. But I was watching her and having Madame Bideconin—or, as I jokingly called her, Madame Conbridé—keep a sharp eye on her. I was warned in time, I followed her to protect her from mishap; she entered a house, mounted a flight of stairs, I listened at the door and was able to peek through the crack. Conquette cast herself into Timon's arms. But he was ill. Hence, the lovely thing got no more than a tonguing; instead of caressing her in the way she would certainly have preferred, Timon fell to narrating the rest of the events concerning Vitnègre, Fout-à-mort and Connilette.

"Rather than going straight to my office—for I was feeling badly—I went to pay Vitnègre a visit; I found him in poor sorts also, this as a result of the monk's terrifying threats—they had an interview yesterday. The monk had sent someone to fetch him. Vitnègre ran to the monastery and found the entire brotherhood in the infirmary, standing by Fout-à-mort's bedside he had listened to the enraged monk's speech. 'You snivelling wretch, you dog!' the discourse began. 'If I had the strength I'd throttle you. But as it looks as though I were going to die of this—so at least they tell me—I'm going to inform the lieutenant of police of everything. They'll hang you. D'ye hear that? A bloody shame, eh? You sold your wife to me, you did—a lovely creature, and I took an infinite pleasure in killing her with pains far worse than those of childbirth; a lovely creature—I wanted to eat her; I carried home some of her with me: cunt, womb, lungs, head, and so forth. I disguised them. My fellow-monks, without knowing to whom they belonged, consumed her ass, her buttocks, thighs, calves, feet, arms, hands, shoulders, liver, et cetera— in a word, everything and all of us, including myself, have caught the pox... Well, your wife—young, heathy, still a maid—didn't have it. I know damned well what you did. A false compassion moved you to spare your wife for whom I paid good money to fuck to death; you substituted a whore in her place. A filthy, scurvy trick, that, a villainous stunt, do you hear? Were I to recover, I'd have your wife, never fear; and if I die, it's the rope for you...' Vitnègre swore by every devil in hell that 'twas you he had on the bed; the monk, who had just been given a rubbing with mercury and whose tongue was swollen, nodded in sign of disbelief. Then the doctor drew Vitnègre aside: 'Have you business to conclude with that rascal? Judging by his tongue I calculate he has no more than two hours to live. He has so terrible a case of syphilis that I've been forced to give him three times the dose I've given the others you see over there in those beds, and they're beginning to salivate. I know this fellow, though: a monster. The world will be better off when rid of him... wait a while and he'll cease being able to speak.' 'We've got to prevent him from writing!' 'Never fear, his eyes have already started to go... he can barely see, his tongue's beginning to emerge from his mouth.' The doctor took the monk's pulse. 'He's suffering the tortures of the damned... thirty minutes more and he's done for.'

"Grown bolder, Vitnègre spoke to the monk: 'Infamous swine, I gave you Connilette, the whore —she's the one you fed your friends, 'twas her infected womb you ate.' The monk raised himself upon an elbow and aimed a tremendous blow of his fist at Vitnègre who, had he not been saved by the intervening bedpost, against which the monk's raking hand struck, would probably have been killed. As it was, Vitnègre was knocked down and taken from the infirmary; but this morning he learned from the doctor that the monk's inflamed tongue had choked him to death a quarter of an hour afterwards. They burned everything he wrote while on his sickbed.

"Calmer now, Vitnègre has just told me the whole story. The hour is late. I can't take you home. You'd best go, my darling friend."

Such was the tale Timon recounted to my daughter, which I overheard and which later she repeated in entirety to me. She returned home, her mind occupied by gloomy thoughts. I followed twenty paces behind her, glancing left and right to guard her from any misencounter. My prick rose like a pikestaff at the sight of her moving haunches.

She entered the pension and lingered in the kitchen; I went directly down to the storeroom and hid myself. Down she came, carrying a lamp in one hand and a kettle of warm water in the other; she washed her fur, sighing all the while, and saying to herself: "Even though the villain's dead, I'm still afraid..." I tapped on the bed. Conquette raised her eyes and saw me; I recounted everything she had been doing. That caused her a fright, but it was a salutary one and cured her of the desire to go to see Timon by herself. I told her I had met Vitnègre on the Quai des Ormes, adding: "You went there for a fuck. You'll be fucked, too. I'm going to spend the night with you." She sought to beg off, protesting that Timon's story had banished all desire out of her; I refused to listen to such nonsense and got into bed. She soon lay down at my side.

CHAPTER XXII

The fuckeress's appetite restored.

"The appetite is restored by eating," says the proverb, and we shall see how well it applies to Conquette.

Once we were in bed together and my daughter within range, I frolicked with her breasts, sucked her teats and encunted her. For I know not what reason —whether because put out or stubborn—my divine child lay there unstirring, inert like a slaughtered calf; I also ceased to move and remained with my sword in the scabbard; later, having slid over upon my side, I fell asleep, my weapon still sheathed. Conquette, who had passively submitted to everything, probably went to sleep also for, when I awoke, I found I was still lodged in her trick; I began to move a little. She hugged me, squeezed her cunt, shifted her flanks, said: "Push harder, dearest lover!" and began to jolt me with all the strength of her loins, belly and thighs: she discharged, so did I... "Who's thy chosen fucker, O goddess?" "Ah, for such things as these, there's no one but you... I'll resist your will no longer, for you are wiser than I... I have had pleasure—and owe it to you only... Begin again, dear papa, for I would discharge in your honor... I adore you..." Vigorously reencunting her, "Prithee fuck now," said I, "as not long ago you fucked with your lover." She shook her buttocks as in olden times did Cleopatra or Messalina

and between leaps and bounds, "Oh bugger-fuck!"
she exclaimed, "fuck, fuck, fuck me, fuck your slut...
cuckold my sweetballocked sire whose wife I am...
whose mistress... whose whore!... Ah, I feel your
prick deep withon my cunt! your tongue... give me
your tongue... oh, I'm coming... com—ing... com—
ing... fuck me!... oh! oh! oh!... no more, I can bear
no more!" and that over with, she went off to wash
her cunt.

No sooner did she return than I mounted the
ramparts again. Off we started. "Fling your ass
about, beat me with your cunt," I exhorted her,
"make it dance... I can feel your nipper biting my
prick's end... ah, creature of my own prick, you fuck
mightily well for a novice... Now accelerate your
movements... more rapid yet... good, excellent... what
flexible loins!" She leapt thrice and discharged
like a musket. "Oh!" she cried, "I wish my father's
balls were freighted with a ton of fuck, and that he'd
shoot it all into the bottom of my cunt!" Her prayer
was answered, for I emitted straightaway, and our
rains of fuck met in ecstatic confluence; she per-
formed a copious ablution; I refreshed my weary
fucking tackle, then we got back into bed... and had
at each other a third time. The tourney lasted above
an hour, I sucked her nipples and tongue and gave her
mine to suck, I had her discharge now and again,
finger me constantly and stimulate my balls...
I simply had not the heart to decunt... Of a sudden,
my daughter, whom I fancied thoroughly done up,
fell to wiggling her ass, to convulsing her cunt as in
days bygone her mother used to, but even better...
My prick adopted the most resolute slope, but I was
not within sight of a discharge... and was able to ream
her barrel as much as she liked. "I'll not bother to
speak of a Vitnègre," said Conquette, "whose pleasure
when aboard a woman depends upon the degree to

which he brutalizes her, but you, dear papa, you fuck with greater tenderness and more deliciously than Timon caresses me, you ply your peg like a god... This discharge is for you... a gift for papa... papa... drive deep, you're in your daughter's cunt, forge ahead, papa, strike with your ass, fuck me, papa... you're in my cunt, so fuck, bugger, fuck... fuck your daughter, you incestuous pig... drive, drive deeper... into your girl's cuntlet..." She sweated and lay as though dead while her fuck streamed out of her entrails.

I began again to heat the tube, wishing also to discharge before calling a halt to the night's games; the spark was soon aglow in her: "Fuck, dearest pimp, I'm your whore, your breadwinner, your bloody cunt-for-hire... your devoted fuckeress, your loving child. Fatten me"—agitating her ass with fury—"stuff a boy or a wench into my cunt... if 'tis a girl, her maidenhead will be yours, if a boy, he'll be mine to fuck!..." "Here!" I cried, "here, my darling daughter, is the fuck you yearn for!" I released it deliciously, and my fuckeress discharged with even more pleasure.

"Ah, what a night!" she murmured, " Timon would never have entertained me so sumptuously." She washed, then I did, and we fell asleep.

CHAPTER XXIII

Filial tenderness, fatherly love.

To be reserved and dignified, modest and voluptuous and an accomplished fuckeress too—that is character in a woman.

And it is rare. Such things are not to be taken

lightly. Montencon, at first, failed in his attempt to stuff Madame Poilsoyeux; she was quite as modest, quite as restrained after he succeeded in fucking her as before. She carefully followed the advice I had given her not to allow him to take her accorded or extorted favors for granted. One day, as she bent forward to stir up the fire, Montencon laid hands on her cunt; she wheeled around and slapped him. "I who know her very well," I said to Montencon, "never touch her buttocks or tug at her cunt hair without first asking permission. To be sure, she usually gives it, telling me to be quick about my business. When she is dressed and got up like one of the Graces, I begin by requesting leave to kiss her foot; then, gliding my hand up along her leg, I say: "You've such a pretty leg... let me kiss it." I advance to the thigh : "What satin-smooth skin!" I say. I delicately raise my hand to her fur and exclaim: "You know, simply to see you walking in the street and shaking your ass in the charming way you have, is enough to give any man an erection, make every woman turn green with envy; and I am able to say to myself: 'I've just fondled and kissed those tempting, incredibly fuckable delights.' I follow you, I overhear men saying: 'By God, I'd fuck her silly!' I can tell from their expressions what women are thinking 'What a coquette! That gait, that posture, those clothes, that air signify: "I want to be fucked! Come along, all of you, fuck me!'" Buggeresses, my prick stands up for nothing but the magnificent cunt which arouses your jealousy. My daughter smiles when she hears these remarks, yields to my fondling, then gives her bubs, buttocks and cunt to be kissed."

Montencon stared admiringly at me and asked Conquette's forgiveness: he had been listening to what I said, and her cheeks were suffused by a chaste blush.

Some time later, having conducted her to the home of a friend, having then returned in the evening to bring her home, as I was walking several paces behind her, the sublime contours of her buttocks gave me so solid an erection that, once back at Madame Brideconin's, I made a bee-line for her cunt. She demurred, for the landlady was stirring about in the vicinity. "At this particular moment, my adorable goddess, I am so inflamed by lubricity—it was the way you walked that provoked this commotion in me— that I could very easily fuck you in front of everyone in Paris." I gritted my teeth, still holding tight to her cunt hair, that silky hair which formed a long and superb peruke in the Louis XIV style. "Well, then," she replied, "let's go to work, for you mustn't spoil my curls." "In the nude, my queen." Without relaxing my grip on her cunt I followed her with every step she took. She gave me a pretty kiss—her tongue featured therein—by way of thanking me for allowing her to get undressed. "Don't let go of my hair," she added, "that helps put me in form." Such agreeableness only made me adore her the more. An instant later she was down to her corset. "Do my shoes suit you? Or would you prefer me to put on slipers and other stockings?" "Slippers." With one hand I removed her shoes, the while tickling her cunt. "Oh, that white leg! how neat and tidily made you are!" She donned her slippers standing up, I released her cunt, she proceeded to wash it; next, she walked several times around the room that way to increase my excitement. "I'm going to drink you dry," she promised, observing I had virtually lost control of myself. While I stripped off my breeches she sat with her legs crossed, wiggling her tantalizing pink-slippered foot.

I could contain myself no longer; seeing me about to leap upon her, Conquette walked towards me, had me hold her skirts up, leaned her elbows upon my shoulders and, without touching my prick with her delicate hand, impaled herself gently. She gradually descended until I thoroughly stoppered her dear little prick-squeezer. "Don't move," she said, "I want to do the fucking by myself." When she felt pleasure surge up in her, the divine fuckeress, overwhelmed, let go and fell upon me with the whole weight of her body. "Dearest prick... in you go." She glued her burning lips to mine, contracted the muscles of her cunt, darted her tongue into my mouth, and squirted, giving vent to all her soul contained... I discharged with a prolonged shudder of joy... she kept on with her fucking for ten wonderful minutes. "Oh, fuckery I adore, the lightning-flash of joy remains in the sky all the while I fuck with you..." 'Twas then I felt the emotion that had assailed me long ago when, as a boy unleashing his spring-tide discharges, I used to lose consciousness, and I thought now I might expire from happiness in this unique cunt. I said so as I ejaculated. She whom I held on my spear only fluttered the more energetically. "A son, a daughter, or both niched deep in my womb," she said, "impregnate me, dear fatherly prick..." I swore, I cursed, I called my daughter by divine titles: "Celestial cunt, majestic cunt, cunt of the gods, cunt of my prick... Was it I... or a king, or a prince, or indeed the strapping young attorney's clerk who fucked you into your whore of a mother's cunt? Who knows? But this prick of mine makes you my true daughter by mingling my fuck with yours. Divine, sacred slut, adorable embuggered buggeress, I've got absolutely to embugger you too... No, on the other hand, your fuck is too precious for me to consent to lose a drop of it." "Fuck me as much as you like, and wherever—in my ass, my mouth, between my breasts." I said I would respect her wishes and then explained why I had

followed in her tracks to and from Madame Brideconin's pension: "My purpose was, firstly, to be there
in case of danger and, secondly, to hear whatever
was said to you by the men and youths whose pricks
you made stiff. One said: 'What play in the hips,
what appaling movements of the ass! Ah, by Christ,
my sweet bitch, were we alone I'd make your cunt
bubble'!" "I too heard him," said Madame Poilsoyeux with a smile. "Another—it was tonight—
took one look at you and began to twiddle his member
in the middle of the street. 'Little mother,' he said,
'I frig myself and I'm going to discharge all because
of you'." "I heard that one also, I smiled at him and
he added: 'Oh, if you are a whore, a divine whore!
fifty *louis* for you: three screws, 'twill take no more
than an hour, either at your place or at mine... I live
at number 16, rue de Buci, third floor, the door on
the left'." "A pretty fop," I resumed, "muttered
aloud: 'My prick in her mouth and my tongue in her
cunt... aye, 'twould do nicely,' and he frigged himself,
frigged, frigged!" "I saw him, I gave his prick a
little tap with my fan; I felt very sorry for him
indeed, I thought about him afterward... Perhaps
that was why I seemed a bit testy when you seized
my cunt upon our arrival here." These words gone
out of her mouth and we staged a scene much like
those I have already described, except that this time
I laid my daughter on her back. "Dreadful papa," she
pouted, "you're pretending you are the fop... 'tis he
fucking me now... you have me fucked by everyone
who desires me... and so I'm going to discharge in the
fop's honor, sir, with his prick in my mouth, his
balls dandling on my bubs and my father's prick eight
inches deep in my cunt... I'll swallow... your sweet
fuck... (convulsive movements within her cunt)
I discharge! I'm coming!..." Never had she mani-
fested so much passion.

She was thinking clearly, for between a brace of discharges she said: "I like your lips, they go with mine, and I don't like Montencon's... I don't want him to encunt me any more," she said, flailing her body spasmodically, "with his tongue in my mouth... ah! ah! ah!... if I had that buck with the fifty *louis* —and you know I'm not a saucy creature—I think I'd play the whore, but I'd insist upon the money in advance—Vitnègre told me girls always do—and only then would I pull down his breeches and let my cunt be martyrized for pay."

"Quite right," said I.

CHAPTER XXIV

A masterpiece of paternal affection.

Conquette was, as I say, naturally self-contained; she was only subject to libertinage's frenzied exaggerations during lovemaking's ecstasies, which with her, owing to her vigorous temperament, were overpoweringly strong.

Two wholehearted fuckings, a mere nothing for a younger man, left me exhausted; and yet, upon opening my eyes, I beheld a Conquette breathless with lust and eager for more. I dashed round to the rue de Buci, found No. 16, gained the third floor; I found the young man with the fifty *louis* to spend: he recognized me, I began at once to speak. "I am the father of the young lady you offered fifty *louis*." "The offer's still good. Three fucks, an hour in all and cash on the spot." "In my presence?" "In yours and all France's if you like. But no trouble, my good man. I'm not anxious to be rolled." "Of course not. And for my part I don't want any noise. She's yours for an hour—a quiet hour." "By Jesus! let's be off..." He placed fifty *louis* in his purse.

We arrived a few minutes later. "Here's the gentleman who caught your fancy," I said to my daughter, "you need fifty *louis*, he's got them for you in his pocket. Now you must earn them." The color mounted into Conquette's cheeks. But she said not a word. The gentleman removed his breeches, approached her, seized her breasts, her cunt, then said to me: "Take the money. This satin-smooth cunt, these velvety breasts are worth the prize." I took his purse; he toppled Conquette upon the fucking-couch; she emitted a cry. "Oh, sir, my kind sir, please don't do me any harm..." "Have we a maid here?" "Alas!" she sighed, "yes..." He encunted her like a shot. She sighed some more, made timid sounds, and discharged. "She's adorable," declared the embattled fucker, for he was fucking and refucking her without pity and without withdrawing; 'twas thus he exploded three times in a row.

My daughter now caressed him, now begged quarter, but went on discharging uninterruptedly. He decunted in the finest humor and, spying several drops of blood shed as a consequence of his furious fencing, "Yes, you are honest people," he affirmed, "a depucelage of that order is downright cheap at fifty *louis*; I'll send you fifty more." (My daughter had left the room to straighten herself out.) "Indeed, were I not already married," he added in a gentler tone, "I'd marry her for both her cunt and her affections... You'll receive fifty additional *louis*. I'll always remember her—but shall see her again." He departed; my daughter thanked me and told me she was satisfied; I turned her earnings over to her. "No, dearest papa, that must go for our expenses." A little later, the ramaining fifty arrived; of that sum I could not prevail upon her to accept more than six *louis*. I left the other ninety-four in my storeroom and bade her use them if need arose.

When on the following day I appeared in the room, Conquette announced that she was afire. "Do you know where the fop lives?" she enquired. "The one who pulled his prick from his breeches?" "Yes," she said, "that one." "He's of no interest. That sort always proves a fool." "Fool or not, I'm ablaze. Let's go out. We'll find someone and you'll follow after me." "Divine child, although I weary my feeble self in your heavenly cunt, my desires remain unimpaired—and if I were to die of pleasure in pleasure, I'd beg you to give your ass yet another jerk and let me expire in the depths of your exquisite trick." "We'll have a fuck, then—but just one. You are too dear and too necessary to me for me to neglect your welfare." I climbed into the saddle. While she adjusted my prick at the gates of heaven, I said: "This outing you propose strikes me as dangerous." And as she lay still, I continued: "No need to treat me with kid gloves... move your ass, my sweet, jump, d'ye hear? skip, screw! discharge!... there's only one shot in the pistol, but it's of a generous calibre. And before you come to grips with some heavy prick or other, you need to be exercised a little." That inspired her. Her electrified ass and cunt vibrated like Marie Antoinette's being fucked by a rascal of a gendarme in the Conciergerie. We discharged, Conquette and I, she like a queen, I like a stalwart revolutionary... I decunted, she washed.

CHAPTER XXV

How the good father had his daughter fucked.

On with the task, 'tis that and naught else which counts; we've a cunt to enlarge, and so there's nothing for it, it's got to be fucked.

The reader will recall the name of a certain Trait-d'Amour, formerly my secretary, Minonne's brother and the lover of Connette whom he, too thick-pricked himself, had me depucelate for him. He was a vigorous lad of twenty; he lived a stone's-throw away, I went in search of him. "Well, my boy, how would you like to give a charming woman four of five substantial fuckings? I'm anxious to do her a kind turn, and think with your aid she'll have the highest opinion of me. You'll have to work in the dark; but I'll arrange for you to get a glimpse of her before then. One glimpse, my good fellow, and you'll serve her royally well." "Excellent, excellent, it's been a fortnight since I dipped my engine in either Connette or my sister, and I haven't anyone else at hand to fuck."

We reached the front of the house. Conquette was seated in the salon, and visible through the window. "Ah ah! But she is a provocative lass! charming... eminently fuckable..."

I entered alone. "Unlimber your bubs," I said to Madame Poilsoyeux, " raise your skirts, a young man is watching you from the street... a handsome, splendid lad of twenty." "My fop?" "No other... he's named Trait-d'Amour. That's it, show your cunt while washing it; I'm going out to join him."

"Now look sharp," I said to my young stallion once I stood at his side again, "she's about to rinse her ass and scrub her cunt..." My new-found son-in-law's soul stood up in his eyes... Conquette discovered her breasts, lighty sprinkled rose-water over their pink extremities; next, she lifted her clothing above her midriff, annointed her ass and cunt with perfume, arched her neck, stroked her breasts, rubbed her cunt languorously, and finally, before drawing the curtains, lay down full length upon a couch. I recommended to Trait-d'Amour that he follow me in a moment, and went in to prepare Madame Poilsoyeux for her visitor. I stretched out and encunted her, Trait-d'Amour made his entrance and set to tickling my balls. I discharged like a field-piece; my fuckeress uttered exclamations of voluptuous joy and I hastened to decunt. Trait-d'Amour had been waiting in readiness, his prick deployed, his breeches removed; he leapt aboard my daughter. Bending low over the encunter's head, "Stir yourself, my beloved," I whispered, "flex your muscles for me. I'm far from done with you." However, Trait-d'Amour was scarce able to bury his massy device in that strait cunt, even though my fuck, liberally distributed thereabouts, served him as pommade; Conquette, jolly well jammed, intermittently gasped, whimpered and sighed but nevertheless met each forward thrust of the prick with a doughty heave of her loins. I had a new erection, but without once deserting his post, Trait-d'Amour ran off three emphatic fucks characterized by three copious discharges. I had virtually to drag him away from work. "Rest yourself," I whispered in his ear; "I'm going to join the party." "I'll stay," he replied, "for you'll need me: your prick's not what it used to be, you know, and this cunt deserves the best. It's presently full of fuck; if she doesn't wash she'll never even feel your little prick inside her." Conquette did indeed repair to the bidet and at the sight of her snowy thighs, her marvellous legs and perfect feet, her ass, her cunt, her belly of ivory, her sweet navel, her proud firm breasts, my prick hardened considerably and lengthened a little. "Noble fucker," I intoned in a voice loud enough for her to hear, "reveal yourself, that my goddess may behold the superb prick I have placed at her disposal."

Trait-d'Amour appeared, his spear in hand; he was not the hoped-for fop, but was more handsome, doubtless better furnished, and my daughter smiled contentedly; then, lowering her gaze upon that upstanding masterpiece at his groin, the lovely girl, having taken it in her fair hand, said with a sigh: "'Tis then this princely object has given me such trouble and so much pleasure too." Trait-d'Amour thrust her towards me, spread her thighs wide, lay me down upon her and clapped my engine into her cunt. "Your beloved has too gentle a hand," said he; "she's got to put you in a sweat. One must encunt stiff-limbed; thrust, my good master, spur with both heels, the steed's a fine one. And you, my fairly encunted goddess, make your ass fly, lift your cunt; 'tis a lively fellow of much virtue who's about to moisten your cunt with an honorable liquor." This harangue brought a smile to the befucked's face. She, to disguise the source of her amusement, replied: "Ah, Monsieur Vitnègre, how many horns you wear today!" "Come, come, my nymph," Trait-d'Amour continued, "think now that 'tis for you to bear three-quarters of the burden... we require movement here... fine! that has the look of something done in friend-ship, and you have the ass-play of a princess. The

flanks now, the hips, I say, fling them about... With
your satin-smooth cunt you're putting your fucker in
seventh heaven... Courage, master be stiff, go
squarely at it, there's joy to be had there, a splendid
ride is yours if you'll deal firmly with your mount...
Ah! what a breakneck pace, how she capers!... my
stars, 'tis a discharge on the mare's part... ply your
spurs!... how she rolls her ass, the dear creature is
all in a lather... but likes a free gallop, 'tis plain...
Here, I'll tickle your balls, for you must keep up
with her... you're discharging too? Well done, I say;
what action, what verve! and now she returns blow
for blow..."

My modest daughter never swore save when pro-
foundly moved and when fast-gripped in lust's delirium; but the present goings-on loosened her tongue:
"Bugger!" she cried, "oh fuck me for Christ's sweet
sake! Fuck my cunt to pieces... fuck my soul out of
my body... I'm melting... melting into fuck... I'm
discharging!... oh, but what I'd do to have two pricks
in this bloody cunt!..." "'Twould never do, my dear,
you're too narrowly constructed," Trait-d'Amour
explained; "otherwise we'd find some way of giving
you that pleasure... But someday perhaps we'll fit a
prick into your ass while a second stuffs your cunt."
I was weary after a delicious discharge; I decunted in
a trice, in another Trait-d'Amour took over my sta-
tion: Conquette was still in a ferment and Trait-
d'Amour speedily filled her hungry cunt. "You," he
said to me, "you fucked my younger sister, and
I fucked her after you; you depucelated Connette for
me: tell me now, do their cunts match the one which
by your kindness is giving my prick a squeeze at this
very minute? No sir, no. This one's of satin and
velvet. However, to judge by its silken fledging,
I dare fancy the interior of the cunt of my pretty
hatmaker in the rue Bordet will approach it... Am

I hurting you, my queen?" "Yes, and delighting me... go on, go on, more... fuck, good friend—" "Ah, what satin! what sweet humidity! I'm well in, eh? I'm fucking aright, am I not? And I'm coming!... leap, twitch, jerk, wring my prick, O divine, O sacred, O heavenly cunt of my life!... A dear, a darling little nipper she has deep inside her... squeeze, bite, pinch me, beloved little one... make me convulse in your pretty cunt... Do you like fucking G goddess? Have you a taste for fuck?... Four discharges are going to flood this dear hole... go drown, go drown— there's my second!" "Fuck me a third, screw!" cried Conquette, "don't fail me, don't falter, dear love-stick!" "Don't leave her until well after your discharge," I told my former secretary, "let her relish the final pulsations of your goad... How beautiful she is thus befucked... the sight arouses me afresh... She looks a very goddess, let her have her fill... hammer it home, rub her raw and ragged, she's still yearning for it... Good, good, she's squirting! What a picture of joy as she discharges!... I believe she's dry, my lad—" "Dry? I think not. She burst four times running, that makes seven all told," said Trait-d'Amour, washing the ecstatic child's cunt, "but she's got a furious talent for this. Refuck her while I catch my breath. I'm going to try to make it an even dozen." "You will injure your health," Conquette said to him; "you've encunted me seven times already today—" "Never fear," said Trait-d'Amour. "Twelve for you then," said she, "and that will come to sixteen for me." I went into prompt action, she darted her tongue into my mouth, I slid my rock-hard prick into her cunt. Trait-d'Amour took her when I was done and did not let her go, despite her pleadings, until, good as his word, he had sprayed her five more times and brought the count to twelve.

She rose gloriously up directly he decunted. "Take

this pitiless young man away from me," she said, "leave me by myself; I need rest, believe me, and at least thirty minutes on the bidet; my poor fur is in tatters..."

We left her; we went to Madame Brideconin's kitchen and had each a good plate of bouillon. I asked the landlady to keep some soup hot for Madame Poilsoyeux.

Set to rights, Conquette arrived and appeared as demure, as decent, as modest as if she had never been fucked in her life. Trait-d'Amour left the house, well satisfied but not better informed. Madame Brideconin, very discreet in these matters, told him nothing of my relations with my daughter.

END OF THE FIRST PART

EPILOGUE TO THE FIRST PART

I hesitated a long time before deciding to publish this posthumous work of the only too famous Linguet, generally renowned as an important lawyer. The typesetting having been once started, I resolved to have only a few copies printed, thinking to put them in the hands of two or three enlightened friends and as many women intelligent enough to provide me with a sound opinion upon its effect, for I was eager to discover whether it would, if broadly circulated, have an evil influence as great as the infernal fiction against which I had hopes it would act as a counter-poison. I am not indeed so witless as to suppose *The Anti-Justine* is harmless and non-toxic; that however is not the question. Rather, it is this: will it effect-ively combat the baneful *Justine*? That is what I wish to learn from disinterested men and women who will judge the book's impact upon themselves.

The author declared his intention to steer clear of cruelty, bloodthirstiness and murder of the woman possessed; has he avoided these atrocious, dramatic devices? He declared he wished to inspirit jaded husbands and bring them back to the happy and wholesome enjoyment of their wives; he affirmed his belief that the reading of but half a chapter of his work would be enough to bring about a reconciliation; was he right? Has he succeeded? The reader will decide.

A glimpse at the table of contents indicates the salacious character of this book, but nothing else would have sufficed to produce the desired effect. So 'tis then for you, my friends, to judge and do not deceive me.

The Anti-Justine will have in all five or six parts like the foregoing one.

I will pass to the second volume or part of this production designed to awaken amorous sentiments in gentlemen whose ladies presently inspire none in them: such is the object and whole purpose *ne quiesces* of this excellent labor, clearly of love, by which Linguet's name will be rendered immortal.

THE SECOND PART

CHAPTER XXVI

Some very useful advice
to the reader and to the author as well.

At long last we have reached the epoch, so frequently alluded to, of the first magnitude fuckeries.
Instead of preparing for them, had I chosen abruptly
to introduce them now, they would surely have
bewildered the most widely experienced reader.

When I opened this broadened phase of my enterprise I was sure of having not only the two or three
buyers Vitnègre solicited for Conquette, but several
girls as well, amongst whom the attractive rue Bordet
hat-maker who was usually sent forth in the van: she
would be let out to clients of whose proportions I was
uncertain, and from her reports I could gauge whether
it were safe to expose my less generously cunted girls
to any given prick. It was nonetheless essential, in
order to avoid their suffering grave injury, to have all
my girl's cunts prodigiously stretched; but I had at
the same time to keep them away from too many dis-
chargers. The reader will discover how I managed
in these delicate affairs.

The reader will also find a brief story inserted in
each of the scenes to follow—this so as to vary a bill
of fare which otherwise might prove monotonous, to
give the reader's imagination a periodic rest, and also
to put down a number of adventures I thought I ought
to omit from the earlier part of my tale; each little

story will sort properly with the context and larger scheme of the work. For nothing would be more out of place than a philosophical dissertation in a book like this; it would become insipid were it to be made heavy, and the reader's taste for philosophy, moreover, would be spoiled: my moral purpose—and mine is as good as any other—is to give those who have some spirit in them an *erotikon*, well-spiced and lively, which will encourage them to put a no longer lovely wife to the best possible use. But not by any means to the same use suggested by that cruel and dangerous book, *Justine ou les Malheurs de la Vertu*, which of late has enjoyed such a regrettable popularity.

I have thus still another important intention: I wish to preserve women from cruelty's delirious excesses. *The Anti-Justine*, no less highly seasoned, no less ambitious in its situations than Sade's novel, but altogether unbarbarous, will henceforth prevent men from resorting to barbarity. The publication of this antidote is a matter of urgency, and if dishonor in the eyes of purists, fools and thoughtless censors is to be my lot, I accept it willingly in order to come to the aid of my countrymen.

The work shall have two parts: after the narrative constituting the first will come a series of letters, written with equal vivacity and forming the second.

Cupidonnet's girls recount to him the pleasure-parties their keepers have made them take a hand in, carousings in whose delirious, drunken course their keepers would sometimes have them possessed by a dozen men in succession. But not all of these letters are erotic; some will interest for other reasons; amongst them will be found an account of a resurrection and the important discovery of the origin of Conquette Ingénue and Victoire Conquette, two girls my own daughters have since replaced; and that will

justify one aspect of my behaviour which has probably caused the reader some disquiet—I need say no
more.

There remains much that might be said about the
scenes I am going to bring before the reader's eye,
hoping to make him forget what he saw in *Justine*
and prefer *The Anti-Justine*. My book must just as
much surpass the other in voluptuousness as it yields
to *Justine* in cruelty; the reading of but one chapter
must be enough to move a man to the proper exploita-
tion of his wife, young or old, pretty or ill-favored,
provided the lady has a hygienic acquaintance with
the bidet and a well-developed taste in footwear.

CHAPTER XXVII

The first magnitude fuckeries begin.

After such an evening of gay disporting, my daughter needed to repose herself: the next morning her
gem was so fatigued she could not comfortably get
up from her chair. She stayed within a short distance
of Madame Brideconin, fearing lest someone might
come to cross swords with her. Although cured of
her aches and pains by the third day, she also avoided
being alone with me all the rest of the week: meanwhile, her natural cravings must have accumulated
and increased, since she never frigged herself.

On Sunday, at one o'clock, she went to her pro-
tectress' kitchen for the last time; before leaving the
storeroom, she presented me with her pretty foot,

which I kissed, and without a sign of squeamishness
surrendered her cunt-hair to my affectionate fingers.
I led her as far as the door, promising to come to get
her by five—this made her flush but I observed that,
as she mounted the steps, she smiled, thinking I had
gone. I was on time; we went for a stroll; I had her
walk ahead of me, noticing she was being watched by
a man I guessed to be one of Vitnègre's clients, but
she being wrapped up in a shawl, he was able to recognize nothing but her shapely behind and interesting
gait. I overtook Conquette and asked if 'twas he she
preferred. "Yes," was her simple reply. Wherewith,
speaking in a louder tone, I addressed her as my
daughter. The man moved off. I had forewarned
Trait-d'Amour; he had a key to my storeroom; we
returned there and found him waiting for us. I supposed he was alone, although I had suggested he fetch
along four other actors, two of each sex. Laughing,
I told him my prick was stiff and longing to burrow
into a cunt. "What!" said Conquette, "are we to have
double-fuckery again? I must assure you that I'm not
in the mood for a crowd." "We'll put you in the
mood for one," Trait-d'Amour said ironically, for
he thought she was my whore. "Deign to glance at
this prick I have here," and he exhibited a superb
one. "Allow me first to give your cunt a licking,
Mademoiselle, my master will encunt you when you
have a fancy for something more substantial than a
tongue. I've made complete arrangements to afford
him, and you too, a royal entertainment." He thrust
her brutally down upon the bed and lodged his head
'twixt her thighs, as he licked her, saying, in the
manner of a threat: "Don't resist me, else I'll hurt
you." But, like all other high-spirited women,
Madame Poilsoyeux appreciated a shade of roughness
in fuckery and its accessory activities. Thus, thinking
he was forcing her to do his will, he was admirably

flattering hers... the lovely creature began to discharge.

Whilst I stiffened vibrantly at the sight of my daughter's glistening cunt and buttocks in decisive and swift movement, I perceived something stirring behind the curtain of the alcove. I went to see what it was: there were Minonne and Connette having their cunts licked by two lads, Trait-d'Amour's friends. By signs I bade them make no noise, and with a gesture encouraged them to enjoy themselves.

Meanwhile, Trait-d'Amour was nipping and sucking Madame Poilsoyeux' cunt; when she had sufficiently entered into the spirit of things, he retreated from the breach, drew me towards her and inserted my militant prick in that cuntlet reempucelated by seven days of inactivity. "What," he demanded of the encuntee, "what have you to give me to suck?" She tendered him the index finger of her right hand which he did indeed fall to sucking after having nevertheless called to this sister and his mistress: "Hither, buggeresses, and show your abilities!" One, Minonne, whose hand was as soft as my daughter's cunt, tickled my balls; the other, Connette, rummaged with a buttered finger in my fuckeress' asshole so as make her quiver beneath me. Madame Poilsoyeux was sweating with pleasure; she shot her tongue into my mouth, calling me her fop... her dear hundred-*louis* cunt-stuffer... her beloved thick-pricked client... her peerless Trait-d'Amour... At last, drunk with erotic fury, she cried: "Vitnègre, you fuck-in-the-ass sod, screw me! fuck me... put your fat black prick into me, let it split me like a melon and embugger me!" and she discharged like a she-devil. At this crucial moment, my mouth contained my encunted daughter's trembling tongue, one of the two girls was massaging my testicles, the other was licking my back and spine. Hitherto I had discharged upon many a fair occasion and thought I knew what it was to release a packet of well-warmed seed, but never had I sensed anything to equal what now I experienced... this all but rent me asunder... What delight! Trait-d'Amour raised me from my daughter and flung himself into her fuck-drenched cunt. "There's a cunt!" said he, forging ahead, then retreating, each time progressing further and with a jolt. "The difference between this cunt and others is like that between satin and sackcloth!" The young ladies had no need to fondle the hard-fucking Trait-d'Amour; he was by nature blazing hot and soon had his partner afire. I beckoned to the two lads, Brisemotte and Cordaboyau, and had them lay out the two girls, one upon a sofa, the other upon my cot covered with a simple mattress, and I bade them fuck away within plain view of the silken-cunted beauty. By an exceptional stroke of luck, my daughter ejaculated for the second time beneath Trait-d'Amour, and the two encunted girls discharged at the same instant as did all three of the men then at work: a six-gun salvo! incredible. The lovely Poilsoyeux's knees drew stiff: "Oh my God!" she cried three times over. "Aïe! aïe! aïe!" Minonne: "Ah! ah! ah!" Connette: "Oh! oh! oh!" the three men spoke in chorus: Trait-d'Amour: "Ah, my goddess, fling your ass at me!" Brisemotte: "Shake your ass, bitch!" And Cordaboyau: "Stir it, whore, stir your ass!" Upon discharging, each exclaimed: "Fuck! fuck! fuck!" Trait-d'Amour: "Ah, my divine one!" Brisemotte: "Ah, my sacred slut!" Cordaboyau: "Oh glorious buggeress!" Each in his character and according to his peculiar manner. But all of them together.

Madame Poilsoyeux, much practiced by now, prolonged her discharging beyond anything like an ordinary term: the two others had been unstoppered and had already washed long before she was done ejaculat-

ing; the outpouring finally came to an end. Trait-
d'Amour washed her, and seeing my prick restiffened:
"You'll doubtless wish to fuck her as much this time
as you did the last?" "To be sure," I replied; "my
vigor returns to me with no one but this young beauty,
I'd fuck her until my prick was reduced to a splinter
and my balls as dry as sand; you'll see how well I can
manage when skirmishing with a peer; I simply ask
to have a double encuntery in view: 'twill give me
heart for the good fight."

CHAPTER XXVIII

Pertaining to embuggero-encuntery.

My response brought a smile to Trait-d'Amour's
lips; in all likehood he doubted of my capacity to
match deed to word. "Very well," said he, "I'm
going to give you a pleasure you've never had before,
nor these other buggers either. I learned this exercise
from the Abbé Chonauche, formerly a member of the
Order of Ste Geneviève, who used frequently to
embugger me in the days before I had a beard on my
chin or hair on my balls. Once, noticing I was
getting tired of his sodomistical incursions, he told
me to go and bring him the little Culfraisé, young in
years, pretty as Cupid and not yet sold to an English
lord. He had me take twelve francs to her mother
and a message saying the girl would receive twelve
more in addition. The Abbé had her lean with one
elbow upon a low table, he got behind her and
embuggered while I, in front, encunted her: we

marched in simultaneously, our two pricks felt each other, either that or the little slut wiggled her ass in such a way as we fancied we felt one another. Chonauche would now and then let her drive her cunt down around my prick and then, his prick halfway dislodged, he enjoyed the possibility of reembuggering her; while she assfucked with him, I partially decunted, and would then reencunt: this intriguing game lasted as long as Chonauche could hold back his seed: usually, he'd not discharge at all, reserving all he could muster for my asshole. And so he would have little Culfraisé lie down on her back, I'd encunt her; meanwhile, the Abbé would embugger me, and we used all three to discharge with one peal of thunder. We'll not adopt the Abbé's scheme, 'tis too fatiguing a way to fuck... but he used to pay the pretty buggeress... Are you paid, Madame? No, surely not, she's an honest woman, I can tell it from her style of fucking: no whore fucks like Madame. Such being the case, I'm going to give you a physical demonstration with one of the other two girls... Step forth, Minonne, come along, Connette; whichever of you would like to be embuggered and encunted simultaneously, let her present herself, skirts in the air!"

During this speech, which allowed her some respite, Conquette had covered her cunt and breast, and the two girls, bubs flying free, had sat down beside her; she had kissed their nipples and then calmly covered their breasts with their kerchiefs. (Madame Poilsoyeux always became modest again directly she ceased to be fucked.) The two girls replied as one: "I!" "I would!" "Very well," said Trait-d'Amour, "first one, then the other. Have we any pommade or butter at hand?" "We do," replied the lovely Satin-cunt, blushing. "Here is a jar of pommade, you will find butter in that dish on the table." "We'll save the butter for you, my lovely lady—as lovely about the ass and cunt as in the face," resumed Trait-d'Amour. Minonne was industriously greasing her rose-bud. "And so you're to be the first, little sister?" "Aye, and 'twill be you who will depucelate my ass." "I'm a maid in that sector too," cried Connette. "No, no," said Trait-d'Amour, "I'll not take these grave responsibilities upon myself; I am today entirely at Madame's disposal. Although bumstuffing, whether active or passive, has always frightened me somewhat, Madame's smooth behind tempts me as much as the narrow scabbard she has beforewards and which in a week's time, if left unused, or in an hour, if rinsed with cool water, will righten to such a degree, one would think her a virgin again; I am convinced Madame has never been bumfucked"—kneeling, he peered at her asshole—"no, she looks chaste in this quarter too." Conquette smiled dreamily.

Trait-d'Amour's two comrades drew cards to settle who would depucelate Minonne's ass, for both were eager to have her; fate chose Cordaboyau (moderately pricked) to do the work; he oiled his tool to the root. Trait-d'Amour had Minonne lie on her side, he situated Cordaboyau before her ass and Brisemotte (largely and splendidly pricked) before her cunt. The two youths closed in, each striving to his utmost to wreak havoc, which vigorous bilateral penetration gave Minonne such pleasure that she exclaimed: "Good God! what delight! 'tis a fuckery fit for a princess!..." They say the Queen fucked sandwiched by d'Artois and Vaudreuil... the latter would sound her vent... "Come along," said Trait-d'Amour, "endeavor all three of you to discharge at the same time." Cordaboyau clutched the wench's haunches so as to drive the deeper into her; Brisemotte did the same; so that, immobilized, she was buffeted about in every direction. "Pay close attention," I told Conquette Ingénue, "and you'll be able to do likewise when your turn arrives, and arrive it shall, for you must become acquainted with every variety of fuckery." Although covering her face with her fan, she turned in such a way as to be able to watch the game through it. Minonne was panting... Connette, stupefied and tongue-tied, lay motionless, staring at her. "What are you doing there, buggeress?" demanded Trait-d'Amour, our master of ceremonies, "come to our aid, Madame, suck her nipples, lick her cunt, it's as tidy and clean as a bride's sunny countenance." These energetic words brought the queen of the festival into the dance.

Whilst Minonne labored and whilst Connette was being labored over, the latter unveiled her breasts and Madame Poilsoyeux', she sucked their extremities, she had hers sucked; the titillations procured her by Conquette's mouth, as satin-soft as her cunt, hurled the young Connette into an amorous fury; she pulled up Poilsoyeux' petticoats, inserted her tongue in her cunt, tickled her clitoris; however much in a frenzy, the lovely Conquette's eyes were fixed upon Minonne who, at this point, was announcing to her fuckers that she was readying to discharge: they redoubled their thumping and thwacking, she cried: "Divine prick!" and opened the sluices... the embuggerer and encunter caught her in a crossfire of fuck; it streamed from both ends of her. My daughter, poignantly tongued by Connette, was beside herself and that demure beauty said to the young girl: "Get out of my hole, slut!... give me a fucker!... ho! I say, fucker!... two hundred of them!" Trait-d'Amour hears the call, he draws the toiling Connette aside, pulling her away by the pretty blonde goatee growing on her cunt. He anoints Madame Vitnègre's splendid asshole with butter, rubs some on his towering prick, lies belly down upon her buttocks, nips into the rosebud heedless of the embuggered goddess' faint protests, grips her with powerful hands, turns himself and her over so that now he is on his back and his prick still buried to the hilt in her ass; her cunt yawning at the ceiling, Trait-d'Amour calls to her father: "A sublime cunt longs for your kind attentions; stuff it with something stiff. Don't spare the rod—the slut's ass is full of me and I'll give you a little movement. Forgive me, goddess, I'm a bit giddy... Connette, fiddle with our friend's balls, give 'em a spin..." I encunted my delicious daughter and felt Trait-d'Amour's ponderous weapon throbbing nearby, further constricting her passage and causing her cunt to oscillate as never cunt oscillated before. I was delirious as I shouted: "There 'tis, bastard of a Vitnègre, thoroughly a cuckold, cunt-and-asswise!..." The idea inflamed me, and its brutality prevented me from discharging too soon. I attained the charming nipper at the bottom of her cunt, it suckled my prick and Trait-d'Amour communicated all his movements to me, causing my adorable fuckeress, already prepared by Connette's tongue, to make some truly startling ones. "Ah!..." exclaimed Conquette, "screw... oh, screw me... I am dis—char—ging... f-f-fuck!" "There's a cunt full of fuck for you, queen of pricks and gods!" bellowed Trait-d'Amour, and I felt the spasmodic twitching of his thick prick disgorging a cupful of semen. Then I too unburdened myself. My daughter, inundated by fuck, squirmed and thrashed. "Oh satiny cunt of my prick," I cried, "how delicious you are!..." Madame Vitnègre was still emitting when Trait-d'Amour emerged from her anus: his withdrawal made her discharge again... Conquette, in whose cunt I left my prick to tremble after its eruption, stammered, wept, laughed, shook beneath me; Connette had abandoned my balls; his prick still erect, Trait-d'Amour had returned to us. "Fuck her for me while she's hot," I said, "she's still leaking... And you," I said to Connette, "go lick that rosebud all covered now with nectar." She obeyed me; but Minonne, her cunt and asshole unstoppered and scrubbed, had nothing to keep her busy; she took Connette's place, asking me whether indeed it were not impertinent to tickle her brother's balls while he was fucking his mistress.

In the meantime Cordaboyau and Brisemotte had laid hands on Connette, the former now encunting while the other embuggered her so as to provide my daughter with an inspiring example. But everything was drawing to an end. Madame Vitnègre ceased her discharging, Trait-d'Amour decunted and guided her to the bidet. She tactfully covered her cunt and breast, then said to the girls: "My dear friends, go help my landlady prepare us a fine supper." They ran to do her bidding. "If," my daughter said, "you only asked for our ordinary supper, there'll not be half enough," and she suggested I confer with Madame Brideconin who, as it turned out, had prepared the usual meal. "Then go quickly to the butcher across the way," said I, "and get some good wine too, for we'll not be drinking water." Then we all gathered together in the storeroom.

"Prick up again?" asked Trait-d'Amour; "mine is. We ought not let these cunts pine away simply because we are waiting for the meal to be served." "I'm not stiff, in truth," I answered, but the sight of my goddess' behind and of her foot sets me afire." "Why, then, I've something in mind to put a little backbone in your sausage."

CHAPTER XXIX

A new actress; the dance of the blacks.

"Look sharp, wenches," Trait-d'Amour said to his sister and mistress; "be quick, off with your clothes! and, as for you buggers, take off yours too." He removed all he was wearing. "But we need another actress. I've just seen an engaging creature pass by." "That was Madame Brideconin, our good friend's landlady," Connette explained. "No, no, my dear, that was a little brunette who lives at the other end of the court; she's the younger sister of a tall blonde we'll perhaps someday persuade to join us and whose name is Conindoré. The little one's named Rose-Mauve, and they say she's a clever creature and as amorous as a cat, although for all I know she's still a virgin, for her mother keeps a close eye on her; however, when a man kisses her he has no trouble getting her to stick out her tongue at him." "I know her," the lovely Poilsoyeux said in her well-modulated voice, "and she... she... Trait-d'Amour—" "Yes, my goddess?" "Put her pretty tongue in my mouth and..." "And what?" "Tongued my fur clean." "Go fetch her, Connette." "No," Conquette said with decision, "I'll go for her myself." She left and having encountered Rose-Mauve, who was coming back down the stairs because she'd found at home that wealthy old uncle of hers whose impotent lubricity she used to stimulate by tickling his scrotum and testicles, wich would get him limply up, Conquette told her what was afoot, obtained her consent, and brought her to the storeroom. The two girls and the three young men were as naked as the day they were born; without addressing a word to her, they all five set to work removing her clothes, all of which, save her underslip, disappeared in a trice; next, her ass, her cunt, thighs and feet were washed... Then Trait-d'Amour said to her: "You must do everything in imitation of my sister and my mistress." There and then the dance of the blacks began: each girl made all the movements of an ardent negress who first flees from the prick she is dying to have in her cunt, who is then caught by the prick, and who finally wiggles and slithers her hips and ass just as if the prick were gliding into her. The boys chased after the girls with their pricks in their fists and directly they had seized them, they were turned round for encuntment and stuck from behind; the boys squirmed, writhed, snapped, bit and fought as though they were tearing the cunts to pieces; the girl took the prick in her hand, the boy the girl's cunt-hair, etc., etc.

I had a thundering erection; I raised my daughter's negligee above her waist: "Cunt of Venus!" I said, "copy all those ass- and cunt-movements you see..." She was definitely aroused, ran into the center of the dance, and began rapidly to execute the various steps. Seeing my prick aloft and his companions also in a cheery disposition, Trait-d'Amour sounded the trumpet: "To the couch!" He abandoned Rose-Mauve, his dancing partner, who appeared most chagrined; however, "Your turn will come, my sweet," he told her as he lay Conquette on the sofa and adjusted pillows under her ass. "Come, if you like," he called to Rose-Mauve, "come lick this cuntlet while I stuff you from behind, or embugger you, whichever you prefer." "A virgin ought not to be depucelated.

from behind," she replied in a lively fashion; "so embugger me, do, while I tongue this delightful love-crack." She sucked the dazzling cunt that belonged to Monsieur Vitnègre's dazzling wife, and Trait-d'Amour forged ahead stubbornly into the charming cunt-sucker's asshole. Madame Poilsoyeux cried aloud for aid: "The prick!" she said, "the prick!" I could restrain myself no longer, I swept Rose-Mauve out of my way and pitched headlong into the cunt of my daughter, then panting with lust.

I was in the midst of a vigorous encuntment when I had the delicious surprise of feeling my asshole and my balls too being laved by Rose-Mauve's velvet mouth and tongue; I cuckolded the blessed Vitnègre as copiously as if I'd had the balls of a god. Ablutions followed. "With my goddess' permission," said I, "I must settle a debt with Rose-Mauve." "No!" everyone chorused, "no! wait until Sunday..." I paid no attention to them; I thrust my lance into the maid, she swept, sobbed, shrieked and bled in ecstasy, and they were all witness to a resounding victory... But Conquette scolded me as we went to supper.

Conversation was sober, temperate; Brideconin and his wife were edified by what they heard (they shall soon be seen collaborating in our pleasures). At dessert, Trait-d'Amour asked me to tell a story in keeping with our amusements; I gave him a letter sent to Vitnègre by one of his three clients—I'd found the letter in one of my daughter's trunks, and I invited him to read it to the company.

CHAPTER XXX

A family arrangement.

"One of our well-to-do colleagues had a mistress of sixteen; he used to enjoy her in the same manner for which I have a preference. Let me tell you the story of how he got her—I like writing such tales, they give me an erection, and I dare say reading them has a similar effect upon you.

"This girl's father had formerly been rich and had brought her up with all possible care and delicacy; but now he had fallen upon hard times, and was so sorely reduced he was unable to feed either her or his twelve-year-old son. My colleague having found the girl pleasing, he asked to buy her; the father sold her to him for 12,000 pounds; but as Piocheneuil (my colleague's name) is a jaded rake, he requires a real pepper-pot stew to whet his appetite: his favorite stunt is to have the father undress and wash his own daughter before he, Piocheneuil, takes his pleasure with her; the father then catches up the fucker's prick and directs it into the pretty Piochée's unfledged cunt. Her father had oiled it the first time. During the act, he exhorts her to wiggle her ass, to hug the fucker in her arms, and so forth, and when Piocheneuil decunts, the father washes his prick, his daughter's ass and cunt, and dries them. In the course of their conversation, Piocheneuil soon learned that Piochée had a brother, a veritable Adonis, that is to say, the perfect image of his mother, who had been a most beautiful woman. My colleague hears of the boy's existence and successfully negotiates for him too; he is greased by his father and embuggered by the capitalist. A few days later, wishing to fuck the sister more vigorously, he had the father wash her, the younger brother suck her, and he encunts her when she is within an ace of a discharge. Thereafter, he gave up sodomizing the little lad. 'Bugger!' said he to the father, 'the sight of your daughter's cunt leaves me cold; I need to be stimulated; do me the kindness of embuggering your young son, that ought to stiffen me.' It was to the father's interest to flatter the libertine's whims; and so the father set to work and aroused the old satyr to such a point that he encunted and even embuggered the little girl.

"That has been going on for five or six years. When the boy reached fifteen, Piocheneuil had him encunt his sister. He fucked her immediately afterward while the father embuggered the lad; at other times the brother embuggers his sister while the old rascal encunts her... That's the life my colleague leads, and he find it delicious at his age. The girl is delicate and pretty, the boy is handsome, the father's a horror. The girl has become pregnant; my friend is probably correct in ascribing her state to the boy. I hope she bears a daughter—the children of incest are commonly very beautiful—and I should add that this attractive boy is the son of an elder brother who fell madly in love with his mother. He devised a scheme whereby, mixing some ingredient in his father's soup at dinner-time, he caused him an enduring and recurrent diarrhea. Obliged constantly to get up from bed, the father would unknowingly cede his place to his son who, every time his father went out to the toilet, used to encunt his mother... six times a night, as a rule. Those, then, are the origins of this handsome mother that, dressed in her clothes, he is taken for her. So it was that a former lover of that beautiful woman kept the young man as his mistress, requiring of him only that he array himself as once she dressed, borrow her name—Madame Broutevit—speak in her lisping low voice, say 'my cunt' instead of 'my ass', whilst he, Vitacon, the lover, would allude to the past by saying to his 'mistress': "Come, my dearest, I'm going to futter you from behind.'"

CHAPTER XXXI

Further arranging of the same familiy— ten years later.

"I'll give you the rest of this story. Piochée did indeed have a daughter who, today, is fourteen and who is quite as lovely as her grandmother; she serves my old friend's pleasures; no longer able to encunt, he has the child caress him while Piochée, her mother, sucks his prick. 'Tis while in the throes of this drawn-out and difficult pleasure, caused by the sensations quickened in his paralyzed prick by the four-teen-year-old Piochée's palate, that he says to Piochée the Adonis, little Piochée's father and uncle whom the girl once loved incestuously: 'Get stiff, bugger, but don't discharge! You'll depucelate your little slut of a daughter as soon as your grandfather pulls his prick out of your ass.' The little one was cunt-sucked by the old scoundrel, then pommaded by her mother; her father, his asshole unencumbered, approached her and darted his prick into her cuntlet whose lips

her mother held drawn apart—but the fucker made
no headway at all. Wounded, the little one raised a
squall; touched by the scene, the old satyr's prick
stirred pathetically, and he cried: 'But, what the
devil are you about? Push, why don't you, push,
damn your eyes! push, you bugger, in with you, get
out of sight, split the girl's cunt wide open if need
be, blow it to bits, what do I care? In with you and
may she conceive a little wench whom we'll deflower
in her turn some fine day.' And the skinny old ape,
thanks to some strange phenomenon, emitted a few
drops of fuck which fell into Piochée's mouth; at the
same moment Adonis, forcing the last barricades,
heedless of his daughter's outcries, discharged well
within the battered fort. The old bounder was so
delighted by this performance, he straightaway wrote
out annuities of a thousand crowns for both Piochette
and Piochée—this above and beyond what he had
already conferred upon them. His great joy, while
using the mother's mouth as an envelope for his
defunct, ancient prick which has long since ceased to
discharge, is to witness Piochette being probed in
either cunt or asshole, and also at the same time to
have the father embuggered while fucking the daughter of the grandfather, who, in his turn, embuggers
a lackey upon whose ass sits Piochée being fucked
by yet another lackey... In a word, he enjoys seeing
everyone simultaneously in action. It is, believe me,
a veritable three-ring circus. He sees to it that the
old Piochard is kept in the best possible health: he is
fed an invigorating diet so as to preserve that frightful
monster's capacity to encunt his daughter and embugger his son... During this tumultuous scene, the
ribald old impotent fondles the dainty young lass'
bubs or cunt, or sometimes snaps his tongue into that
latter part of her, and licks. And sometimes his
weary old head fairly reels when he has the mother

encunted and Adonis embuggered by a dozen or score of his friends, all these penetrations occurring, be it understood, at a single sitting; the little girl, at such times, is always nude and placed within plain sight of the embuggerers and encunters. 'Tis old Piochard's chore to insert the pricks in the appropriate cunts or assholes.

"The foregoing account ought to give you some approximate idea of the excellent use we can make of your wife once you have depucelated her: you'll not be deprived of anything, never fear; you will yourself fit the pricks into Madame's asshole and cunt, you'll be her pimp and when both her holes are adequately enlarged, you'll perhaps, my dear fellow, be allowed to fuck her in each of them.

"My fraternal salutations and heartiest best wishes,

"L'Elargisseur.

"P.S. In the course of my most recent visit, I discovered that Piochette has indeed brought the prettiest imaginable little daughter into the world; Piocheneuil showed her to me: she's three years old now. But by way of a crowning detail, let me tell you this: the old libertine has already got his prick into her mouth—yes, quite, into the infant's. When he give it to be sucked, he has the young mother toy with his balls. I asked why he felt in such great haste, why he had to employ a mere babe for these purposes. 'Ah,' he replied, 'they're capital at that tender age: they understand nothing, hence are disgusted by nothing. And that counts. Do you suppose,' he went on, 'do you suppose any rational being would want to suck this poor old prick of mine? Ha, 'tis to be doubted.' "

CHAPTER XXXII

Wherein figures much encuntery.

"Such, dear Madame," I said to Conquette, "would certainly have been your fate had you not had the good fortune to die and cease to be Vitnègre's wife." My remark astonished everyone, including my daughter and the Brideconins.

This letter, read to the company after we had put away a quantity of champagne, elevated the spirits of the younger members of our group. While the Brideconins tidied up after the meal, the rest of us repaired to the storeroom. There, half tipsy, Trait-d'Amour took me aside and, pointing to his comrades: "How the devil can these buggers have an inkling of our happiness and of what your mistress' cunt is like if they don't handle it for themselves? I'm not suggesting that they ought to discharge into it, surely not, but simply that they take a quick experimental dip to sample its smoothness. As soon as they've all had a plunge and are out again, you or I—depending upon which of us two is in the better state to do the job—will finish off the work and make Madame discharge." "Agreed," I answered. Cordaboyau, stiff as a mule, presented himself first. We had Conquette repose upon the fucking-couch, adjusted her clothing and declared we'd stand by to pluck him from the breech as soon as he'd obtained a notion of the narrow cunt's incredible geography and

velvet-like texture, and when the fluttering of his
eyelids indicated an imminent eruption of fuck.
"Well, in that case," said the bugger, "have one of
our sluts lie down near at hand. Tell her to grease
her cunt : I'll sound it when I feel my prick convulsing
for a discharge." Rose-Mauve was pommaded and
stationed within convenient reach of Cordaboyau.
He slowly encunted Conquette, the remarkable qual-
ities of whose cunt elicited exclamations from him,
but he sank down to the bottom. We watched him
carefully... he winked ; Brisemotte and Trait-d'Amour
instantly picked him up. "The blasted scoundrel,"
they cried, "he's about to come !" And they deposited
him upon Rose-Mauve, whose legs were well-spread
and waiting ; Connette guided his prick to the mark.
Rose-Mauve, most passionate of the ladies at our
disposal—with, of course, the notable exception of
that incredible Madame Vitnègre—swallowed the
prick with three speedy jerks of her ass ; Cordaboyau
accompanied his discharges with howls and shouts of
lust ; Rose-Mauve's legs wrapped round his waist with
a perfectly delicious fury.

What I was watching brought my prick aloft and
I plunged into my daughter's wet cunt ; sufficiently
exercised, she discharged twice by the time I'd
moistened her with my paternal seed. She giggled,
sighed, twitched and rolled and kicked. "Ah! ha!"
said Trait-d'Amour, "you are her cunt's very soul, my
dear master ! it melts into love-juice when you perforate it. Fuck him, divine creature, and discharge !"
Next came Brisemotte's turn ; lubricated, Conquette
was stretched out upon the couch ; he plugged her
gap. The bulkiness of the prick and its rigidity
fetched muffled groans from her breast ; she labored
with all the best in her, but the formidable engine
lay three inches from home. All of a sudden we
perceived that the treacherous Brisemotte was about

drench in a torrent of sperm the cuntlet he was martyrizing; we were unable to pry him loose; his prick was lodged tight, inextricably wedged, like a great mastiff's would be in the vulva of a bitch of that same breed. In this moment of peril, we, Trait-d'Amour and I, addressed ourselves imploringly to Conquette's sense of propriety. Faithful to our pricks, that adorable fuckeress lunged her ass powerfully backwards and disloged Brisemotte's member. Without a moment's hesitation, Trait-d'Amour, all asweat, drove his hanger into the gaping cunt. Enraged, Brisemotte hurled himself upon Rose-Mauve, who was expecting nothing of the sort; he fucked her from the rear, and with such brutality he made her cry out as much from pain as from pleasure. Seeing Connette getting to her feet, "Stay where you are, slut!" he roared, "I'm in such a rage over that velvet-lined cunt Trait-d'Amour's fucking that I'd encunt the Place de la Concorde." Once through with Rose-Mauve, he did indeed fuck Connette, brought shrieks from her, then without pausing had wildly at Minonne, and resumed: "Rose-Mauve, why have I not got that infernal landlady under my belly? The old girl limps gracefully about, she's got fair dugs, call her hither!" We prepared Rose-Mauve for him, he embuggered her. Meanwhile, Trait-d'Amour was fighting it out with Madame Vitnègre, who complained tenderly of his roughness and discharged uninterruptedly, for her encunter did not once decunt. "Let any buggeress who's got nothing else to do," said he, "come here and tickle my goddess' teats; that will make her give me a jolt or two." "Very well," I joined in, "Minonne, go tickle her clitoris; Connette, employ your soft hands to dangle your cruel cunt-splitter's balls, and I'll tickle my beloved's delicate feet." All this was done. Violent leaps and starts, cries, exclamations of lewd delight: "Divine fuck!... divine cunt!" "Divine prick!" By these tokens our two co-workers gave evidence of their frenzy.

However, Cordaboyau's nose caught the scent of Conquette's sweet little shoe, and he went like a shot to put his prick into it. "Don't bother over that thing," said Rose-Mauve, solidly embuggered as at the moment she happened to be. "That's silly. My cunt is idle, why don't you give it a fucking?" She thrust her belly into the air and while Brisemotte continued to tunnel into her ass, Cordaboyau took possession of her cunt.

I had such a blinding erection, thanks to what I saw and heard going on, that I was ready to encunt Minonne or Connette; my daughter, then busily discharging, spoke softly to me: "Can it then be... that you are tempted by some... some cunt other than mine?..." This example of filial devotion touched my heart: "Off with you," I said to Trait-d'Amour, "you must have discharged by now." He decunted and I, stirred by an unlimited fatherly affection, encunted my daughter without even washing her flooded cunt. "We'll mix our three fucks," I said as I burrowed in. "May your daughterly cunt engulf the paternal prick and delight therein! Move your ass to and fro, my adorable child, give me back all the fuck I spat into your mother's womb so as to beget you. Ah! how the wench writhed, shook her ass and vibrated her cunt the day I stuffed her with you! She was wearing her shoes, her clothes, they were somewhat askew, she was so furiously hot she got astride me and encunted her own self in order to excite me the more. While she was posting up and down, she said: 'Push it in, my chick... bury it completely... my cunt's oiled and ready for anything, I've just been fucked by that handsome law-office clerk you're so jealous of.' And she squirmed and twisted. As for myself, I fucked her then with the same religious zeal wherewith I am fucking you now; 'twas I who engendred you in her slithery cunt... although you bear a likeness to Louis XV who, so they say, used to fuck your mother." "Oh dear father! heaven-sent, thrice-blessed prick!" was Ingénue's reply, "overwhelmed by fuck and tenderness, I feel by my insatiable cunt that I am truly your daughter, I sense it when I am gripped by the pleasure that is mine when the celestial thought enters my mind that I am being fucked by my father!... Let us discharge in unison, dearest papa... I have more fuck when... fucking you than anyone else... Ah! ah! burrow, dig in, dig in, father-prick... My fuck's long in arriving... for I've done a lot of fucking, you know, but while waiting I have all the more pleasure... Ah, fuck! oh joy!... Vitnègre, monster who would tear me to bits without even trying to tupper me, why are you not on my belly now? Why is your black prick not gouging my cunt? And Fout-à-Mort, rend me in twain!... Dear papa," the delirious girl continued, "divine fucker, I'm coming... I'm c-c-coming... for Fout-à-Mort's sake!..." And she gave vent to a tide of fuck; her eyes rolled, she babbed, she foamed at the mouth. She had locked her legs around my waist and with her cunt and thighs she beat out a fine paradiddle upon my belly; I said, I believe, that someone had put her shoes on her feet and with each jolt of her ass she clicked her high heels together, as her mother used to so as to remind me, while we fucked, of the beauty of her feet. This spectacle looked so delicious to my three droll companions-at-arms that, carried away altogether, they fell to encunting: Trait-d'Amour stuffed Rose-Mauve, Cordaboyau Connette, and Brisemotte Minonne; those lads made the girls screech like so many virgins.

When at last I had ejaculated, I told my one-time secretary to decunt, lift me, and put me down in an armchair; he did so. My daughter was palpitating; she was tickling her cunt with three fingers. Trait-d'Amour stiffened afresh, with lunatic celerity he leapt upon her. "Embugger me, if you would be so kind, sir," she murmured; "I believe that would better serve to make me discharge." "Ah, yes!" cried the bugger, "your cunt's too weary," and he pierced her asshole dry. "I'm going to discharge again," she announced, continuing to frig herself. "Wait, wait an instant," her young perforator said, "I'll frig you while embuggering." Embuggered and frigged, Con-quette's teeth chattered with pleasure. At this point, Brisemotte, finished with Minonne, sprang upon Rose-Mauve whom Trait-d'Amour had abandoned for my daughter; Rose-Mauve got herself embuggered and frigged to boot; Cordaboyau turned Connette over and dealt likewise with her; free, Minonne tongued Conquette's cunt while her brother was sodomizing Conquette; and I frigged Minonne. The three bug-geresses declared that friggery joined to embuggery was divine.

As for myself, I sat slumped down in my arm-chair, a listless finger in Minonne's cunt, for I had scarcely the strength to frig her, was toppling over with drowsiness and yet stiff as the devil and lusting for all four of them. It made no difference to me whom I encunted, I must confess. Brisemotte steered Rose-Mauve towards me, his prick lodged in her asshole: I encunted her; the lively Minonne turned her alabaster buttocks around and presented me with her cunt, and I was about to sound it too when I heard Conquette exclaim: "I see what you're doing!" She snapped Trait-d'Amour's prick from her ass and rushed my way. "If Cupidonnet's going to die from over-taxing his prick, 'twill be in my cunt he expires."

She caught me in her arms and engulfed my weary weapon. We ended up in a heap and each quietly squeezed out his last drops of sperm.

Thus concluded that memorable soirée; the following Sunday was fixed as the date for the next party. After having given herself a scrupulous washing, Conquette went modestly, indeed shyly to bed. I was unable to walk. My three gay colleagues remunerated their little partners and then picked me up bodily and carried me home, where they tucked me into bed.

CHAPTER XXXIII

The sensible fuckeress.

The following day, after I had completed my work, I went to visit my daughter; she was in the storeroom and embraced me directly I arrived. "In heaven's name, dear papa, look out for your health. My need for your paternal kindness is greater than ever. What would become of me were I to lose you? You are the best of fathers, you give me all my necessities and much pleasure besides. I have an insatiable gem, but your Trait-d'Amour appeases it and satisfies me wonderfully well. I am well aware of the gift you have given me, and am grateful for it: my gratitude and tenderness belong entirely to you, I give no one else anything but fuck." "My adorable daughter, you are always so faultlessly modest." "I am also obliged to Trait-d'Amour for having brought along his little sister and his pretty mistress, especially for having turned them over to his two comrades so that he was able to devote all his attentions to me and relieve you in the hour of need, for I was very hot indeed. The girls are dear little creatures and are at least as accomplished as Rose-Mauve who, I must say, is not without her merits. But you must be careful not to overdo it, papa; stay close to me, I'll keep you busy enough. And no more than one party a week—I'm thinking of your capacities now, not of mine. Trait-d'Amour will give me most of what I need between parties. By only making love on Sundays, the boys and girls will find their appetite increased and their pleasure greater; we'll devote half the day to the games and it will be delightful. But I'm jealous of you and Trait-d'Amour; don't put it in anyone but me, tell them all you don't want any cunt but mine. I am jealous by nature; and then again, where will you find a wife or a girl better than the one you have? I'm always clean and neat, whenever I do pee-pee I wash as much for the fun of it as for fastidiousness' sake, since this part of me, which you are so generous as to find charming, is always so hot that I never bring water into its neighborhood without feeling voluptuous sensations approaching those of love-making. And so don't put it in me during the week, wait until Sunday, your pleasure will be greater and you'll avoid killing yourself. Touch neither my fur nor my bubbies." "You're quite right," I admitted; "during the week I'll kiss nothing other than your pretty feet, and I want constantly to have one of your slippers on my mantelpiece at home." "By all means. There's nothing more flattering than thus to be worshipped even down to one's least articles of apparel; and because you adore them, I take the very best care of my feet. I wash them in rose-water twice each day, morning and evening, and whenever I come back from a walk." "Ah, celestial fuckeress, let me kiss them! let me kiss them!" "None of that during the week: it arouses you. Kiss your idol, my face is as sensitive as most other parts of me. But go no further. Apart from that, I'm yours, do with me what you like, sell me, surrender me whenever you wish: I'd give myself with pleasure, knowing it is for you."

Despite my inclinations, I fasted dutifully; I kept control over myself because it was necessary to do so. But there on my mantel lay her slipper, pink with green heels. I rendered it a daily homage in honor of my daughter, the most pious and most devoted child any man ever had. On Saturday I told Conquette of this ritual; she was transported with joy. She darted her tongue into my mouth, gave me her nipples to suck, her silken cunt-hair to fondle, and said lovingly: "I thank heaven for having given me such a good father; he took the best care of me during my childhood and I am happy now to be able to make some return for his kindness by giving him a little pleasure; I am the charm and delight of his life, he is the charm and delight of mine. In love, and this I know by experience, nothing equals the voluptuousness of incest." A few minutes later, at eight o'clock, the whole of our little society—Trait-d'Amour, his sister Minonne, his mistress Connette, Rose-Mauve, Cordaboyau, Brisemotte—came to talk over the next day's get-together. I gave them the password and asked them to stay for supper; we had a fine eight-pound roast leg of lamb and quantities of Burgundy with hot pâté; after the meal, eager to inject a little fire into them and into myself too, I related, in the Brideconins' presence, the following story.

CHAPTER XXXIV

The man with the tail.

"You enjoy stories," I said, pushing aside the plate containing my pâté, which I did not wish to eat. "We'll have very different business on our hands tomorrow; while you are finishing your supper I propose to entertain you with a tale." My friends laughed merrily and then fell silent and listened.

"There was in the city of Sens a widow, still beautiful although the mother of six girls, eldest of whom was nearing twenty and was named Adelaïde; the second, Sophie, was less than nineteen; Julie, the third, was almost eighteen; Justine seventeen, Aglaé sixteen, and finally, the youngest, Emilie, fifteen. As for the mother, brought to bed with her first child at only fourteen, she was consequently thirty-four. Madame Linars—that was her name—had as well two nieces, one of fifteen, the other of twenty-two, Lucie and Annette Baco; also in the household were a pretty chambermaid of eighteen and the cook, a tall and handsome girl of twenty years. The hushad mismanaged his financial affairs before he died; his widow had only the income from her dowry, roughly five or six thousand pounds, with which to support her numerous entourage; the nieces had, between the two of them, only fifteen hundred pounds a year: thus there were eleven persons to maintain on at the most seven thousand five hundred pounds.

"There then appeared. in Sens a large and handsome man whose face indicated an age of thirty, whereas he was actually ten years younger than that. He was said to be exceedingly rich, and indeed he was. His arms and chest were covered with a thicket of hair; his regard was direct, penetrating, even fierce, but his smile was sweet and gave him a mild aspect. And it was often he smiled, and unfailingly when he saw a pretty woman.

"The eldest of the Linars girls was charming. Fysistère, ravished, fell head over heels in love with her even though in his seraglio he already had at the time a married woman whom he'd spirited away from Paris with her husband's consent; he had also this unfortunate lady's sister, sold him by her father; thirdly, he had a superb Carmelite nun, their cousin, who had given herself of her own accord to him, because (doubtless) she was hysterical or, if you prefer, a nymphomaniac. But all his mistresses were pregnant at the time: Fysistère employed them exclusively for the begetting of children. He went to Madame Linar's house to ask for Adelaïde's hand.

"The hairy rascal, discovering no fewer than eleven women in the establishment, fairly trembled, so at home did he feel. He produced an inventory of his goods, reckoned up his fortune, and proposed to marry the eldest. An annual income of thirty thousand francs and documents he exhibited induced Madame Linars to accept without having to be asked a second time; thereafter, appearing the perfect gentleman, he paid the family visits until the marriage, and he distributed presents, not only to his intended, but to her mother, the sisters-in-law, to Lucie and Annette, the two nieces, as well as to Géoline and Mariette, the servants. 'Twas by means of these gifts he laid siege to their virtue.

"But a few details are required to be better acquainted with this personage.

"Fysistère was one of those hirsute men who have descended from a mingling of our species with that of the strange men with tails who dwell in the isthmus of Panama and upon the island of Borneo. He had the vigor of ten ordinary men, that is to say he might have beaten ten if they'd fought with the same weapons and on an equal footing, and he needed all for himself as many women as ten men would require. At Paris, he had bought the wife of a person named Guac, a scoundrel who'd sold and surrendered her to him. Fysistère had since then been keeping her under lock and key; he took his pleasure with this luckless creature (the most enticing woman imaginable and one furnished with a passionate temper) ten or twelve times each day, which usage so fatigued her that she had recommended he consult her father and arrange to buy her sister too, Doucette by name, who would share her work with her. He did as she suggested, but these two women were soon worn to a frazzle; happily, a nuns' confessor at about the same period located the hysterical nun for our satyr. She was the two sisters' cousin; the confessor got her from her convent by a ruse, saying he planned to take her to a health resort: he delivered her instead to Fysistère: she serviced him alone for a fortnight; her two cousins thereby got some much needed rest.

"'Twas at this period the man with the tail came to Sens and met the Linars family. Before he had acquired Madame Guac, he had been brought three dressmaker's apprentices every morning, but the precautions he was obliged to take for the sake of his health when dealing with creatures who, after having seen him, circulated freely about town, these safety measures, I say, annoyed and hampered him no end and spoiled the pleasure he took with the girls he had procured. Moreover, as he had decided upon a plan to increase the size of the race of tailed men and to populate all of Borneo (his native island) with them, he was eager to be able to keep an eye on the children he sired. His three women were gravid, he preferred not to fatigue them further for the time being. As soon as he gained entry into the Linars home, he would have undertaken without delay to deflower his future wife, or stuff one of the nieces, or the cook or the maid, had he not noticed that this would have brought on complications; he decided to postpone this supplementary recruiting until after his marriage. The first whom he assailed was his mother-in-law-to-be. He gave her a gift of two thousand crowns in cash one day, and, she flying into an ecstasy of gratitude, he slid his hand under her skirt: 'You'll have an identical sum every six months,' said he, 'if you let me put it in you now; nor need you worry lest your submission prove prejudicial to your daughter: there's more than enough left for her.' As he was uncommonly powerful, he stirred and stuffed her all the while he was talking. The lady found herself caught; she'd been very far from expecting this: she was fucked at least ten times over, so vigorous was her opponent. At last, released, she gasped: 'My stars! what a man!' 'I am indeed an uncommon one,' said he, 'and when both you and your daughter shall have had to do with me, of your own accord you'll go scouting after mistresses for me. I am excessively demanding.' The lady, who was fond of love-sport, blushed to the eyes with anticipation and pleasure. She was exploited every day while they waited for that upon which the wedding was to be celebrated. When this day arrived, seriously worried about her virginal daughter's inexperience, she besought the tireless Fysistère to treat her gently. 'Six times,' he replied, 'no more, provided you promise to receive me immediately afterwards or to give me the elder of your nieces.' 'No, but I'll give you Géoline or Mariette, whichever of the two is more willing.' On the evening of the wedding-day, Fysistère, although he had been furnishing Madame Linars regularly every night, was on pins and needles with impatience to have at his bride. Immediately after the supper, he picked her up like a feather, bore her to the marital couch, and attacked her without further ceremony. She uttered dreadful screams. The mother, alarmed, ran in with Géoline in tow at the very moment Fysistère, largely unconcerned about the young woman's groans, was preparing to begin afresh. The mother let him finish, then, heeding her daughter's urgent pleas, she took her from the bed to wash out the blood and semen with which her wounded cunt was brimming. No sooner were they gone from the room than Fysistère laid hands on Géoline and raped her despite her loud remonstrances. He repeated his prodigious performance four or five times; she took advantage of an interval to break away from him; but Fysistère threatened Madame Linars, saying that if she did not offer herself in her daughter's place, he'd torment Adelaïde till daybreak. The lady was tired; she went in search of Mariette whom she locked into the nuptial chamber; Fysistère violated her and kept his seat until he'd discharged four times. Then he allowed her to get some sleep.

"The next morning he soothed the young domestics' injured feelings and even won them over by awarding each of them an income of twelve hundred pounds a year, but they insisted upon having the following night off. That evening, Fysistère reencunted his new wife six times; she was beginning to conceive somewhat of a taste for the game; then, her mother, rested, was in her turn reamed clean and dry

six times in a row; and that sufficed the man with
the tail. Came the evening of the third day: he
reencunted his wife only once, for she begged quarter:
After her, he had Géoline six times, then Mariette
five, which made the round dozen he was accustomed
to. The fourth night he had his wife once, his
mother-in-law four times, Géoline three, Mariette
four: twelve all told. And so it went for two months.
'But, my dear boy!' Madame Linars exclaimed,
'you're wearing yourself out! What is the good of
doing it so often?' 'My aim is to beget children:
I intend to populate an island in the Indies where the
men of my race originally come from. When I find
you are pregnant, I'll cease tuppering you, you'll
bring me other women, especially your daughters
and your nieces, because the blood in your family
is distinguished. Every member of it you bring me
will receive an annuity of six thousand pounds; I'll
give only twelve hundred for those not of your line.'
Madame Linars was amazed at this proposition, but
she was tempted by the six thousand pounds for her
daughters and nieces. Six weeks later, Madame
Linars, the bride and the two servants, Géoline and
Mariette, were all pregnant; Fysistère declared he'd
have nothing more to do with them until after they'd
given birth, and he pressed Madame Linars to bring
him her nieces and two of her other daughters. She
was obliged to consent. She led them in herself,
after having explained what was expected of them,
and she assisted at their deflowering, quieting their
fears and stilling their cries by her words and
caresses. 'My reasonable child,' she said to Lucie who
was lying on her back and being readied for the
operation, ' tis pleasant indeed to have six thousand
pounds a year... That comes to five hundred a
month,' she added while pommading her, 'think of
it! Five hundred all for yourself!' and she directed

the stout device into her crack; although a virgin, the lovely Lucie made no outcry thanks to her mother's sustained and effective prattle. Then up stepped Annette, the second; her aunt exhorted her, pommaded her, inserted an index finger as deep as possible into her cunt, so as to clear the way. She introduced the member into the thus readied trick. Nevertheless, once perforated, Annette uttered shrill cries, but they had not the slightest effect upon Fysistère, whose hairy tail, quivering, with animation, Madame Linars was stroking. 'Ah, mother dear,' said he to her, 'get on top of me and bury it in your cunt, you'll find it is agreeable.' She did so and was so delighted she called in her eldest daughter and the two servants to procure them the same pleasure.

"Annette having been sufficiently often encunted and pleading for respite, Géoline took her away to wash the blood and sperm from her muddied gem, and Madame Linars went in quest of Sophie, her second oldest daughter. Adelaïde refused to submit to a skewering, so Céline popped the tail into her cunt. Sophie moaned very little when exposed to the initial onslaught; she gave back a few blows during the two succeeding ones, even though she was bleeding. Géoline scraped herself with the tail throughout the whole séance. Fysistère had discharged a mere nine times; he had still three more shots in his chamber. Julie was sent for: she was the third daughter and seventeen years old. Her mother oiled her, which did not prevent her from screeching, since she was very narrowly constructed. Neither Julie nor her cousin took significant pleasure in coitus for the first fortnight. Lucie was impregnated at once, three days later Sophie was too, but they held their tongues, and went on tasting pleasure which they were fond of. As for Julie and Annette, three months passed before they became pregnant,

Annette warming herself with the tail while Julie weathered the prick's attacks.

"When it became plainly evident that the four beauties' bellies were laden, Madame Linars was required to supply her three last daughters and a first cousin, named Naturelle Linars. They were surrendered, both Justine and Aglaé, and so was Emilie, although only fourteen: they were all deflowered in a single nigh notwithstanding their screams and the damage sustained by their delicate machinery. Naturelle was twenty-one: here was a superb morsel the man with the tail had kept in store for the end of the feast. She was impregnated straight off, and the three others, young though they were, did not get through the month empty-bellied: they were stuffed, each of them, three times a night, but whether because they lacked spirit or zest, or because they were too narrowly made, they suffered upon every encounter and were thoroughly delighted when they were pronounced gravid.

"The tailed man was mightily pleased with himself: to date, he had fecundated fourteen females who held out the promise of at least fourteen children. 'Twas at this period Madame Linars gave birth to a girl; a month later, Adelaïde, or Madame Betoiled, also brought a girl into the world, then Géoline and Mariette each produced a boy, and Annette and Lucie each a daughter. All six wished to nurse their offspring, and so they were packed off to an estate in the vicinity of Seignelai, considerably removed from the main-traveled roads in the Yonne, but situated by a little stream called the Serin.

"What with some of them nursing children and others in confinement, Fysistère needed new women. He asked Madame Linars' permission to fecundate his three earliest concubines—Madame Guac, her sister Doucette and the Carmelite whose hysterics had quieted down since her child-birth. The good woman agreed most heartily, for she was having a difficult time finding fecundable material for her son-in-law. She had already cast an appraising eye upon the four least ugly maidens in the village and even upon a fifth, the prettiest of them all, a married woman who had had no success in attempting to get a child by her husband. Madame Linars had virtually won them all over by means of the twelve hundred pounds per year, but she was not yet sure of their discretion.

"The three concubines were sommoned to headquarters; they arrived late the same evening and were all three placed in a huge bed large enough to accommodate five. Fysistère lay down in the midst of his harem; he palpated them all, then selected Madame Guac, the most voluptuous, and fucked her furiously three times over. He next fastened upon Doucette, whose timid sighs and little moans transformed his prick into a pile-driver. Leaving her, he sprang upon Victoire, whom he drenched with six copious outpourings in succession: she assured him she had got over her illness and besought him to distribute his blessings impartially amongst the three of them. He agreed.

"On the morrow, Madame Linars, who had overheard everything that had happened during the night, enquired of the three kinswomen how they had come to belong to Fysistère. 'We shall tell you our story,' replied Madame Guac. 'It will surely strike you as an odd and will also give you a clear idea of our common husband. He has a strange nature.' Madame Linars was nothing if not eager to hear the story, but she pointed out that it would also be relished by Fysistère's twelve other wives. Madame Guac fancied it would be indeed and so Madame Linars convoked Adelaïde, Sophie, Julie, Justine, Aglaé, Emilie, Lucie, Annette, Géoline,

Naturelle and Mariette; all took seats and prepared
to listen to the lovely Madame Guac. who spoke in
the presence also of her sister Doucette and of Victoire, the former Carmelite nun.' "

CHAPTER XXXV

The insatiable wench.

" 'Men have always desired me. When I was but
eight, a laborer doing carpentry in the house took
hold of my gem and as I uttered no protest, he niched
his member between my thighs, bade me squeeze
them together, and inundated my legs with his seminal
liquor. I reported all this to my mother. She
washed my buttocks and caused a row about that
carpenter and finally had him sacked. —This beginning indicates that my story will be rather free. But
one must be sincere.

" 'At ten, my father, untrousered, would have me
sit naked on his bare thighs, make his member go
to and fro between my legs like the clapper in a
bell and when well-warmed he used to go off to stuff
my mother, or a young and petulant creature who
was her sister, or my governess. At thirteen there
was a cottonlike fluff on my gem; 'twas so pretty my
father would come and lick it at night while I slept.
Then came the time when he felt my flanks heave
in sympathy with the movements of his tongue: he
knew I was enjoying the sport: his tongue probed
further and I discharged... Immediately my father
got upon me, sucked my burgeoning little titties,

posed his member at the entrance to my little cuntlet, and gummed my cottony hair with his sperm... After that, he washed me clean with rose-water. When I was fifteen, a young man, my seamstress' brother, grasped my cunt with his hand while I chanced to be looking out the window; he sought to tickle my clitoris with his finger, but hurt me and I gave him a slap.

" 'My father, obliged now to exercise prudence, had given up sitting me bare-assed on his knees and making me discharge by licking my cunt... He would cease his activities as soon as I gave the first sign of awaking; but as even then I had pretty feet and as Monsieur Dardevit, like every man of sensibility, had the most emphatic weakness for such charms, he ordered my shoes from a skilful shoemaker, the same one who was employed to make my mother's and the Marquise de Marigny's; my lecherous father would only present a new pair to me when I paid him a visit: he would have me put them on with cotton stockings, have me walk about for him, have me stand near the window or upon a stool so as to display my legs to better advantage, and then he would kiss them; next, he would have me sit down, would take off one of my slippers, plunge his prick into it, have me rub his balls with my other and shod foot, and would heave deep sighs. Then he would knock on the floor; upon hearing the signal, Madame Mezières, the neighbor downstairs, would come up, take off my remaining shoe or slipper, and lie down on her back. He would raise her petticoats and go into her, meanwhile having me lift my skirt to the knees and stand so that he could see my reflection in a mirror. "Your father's doing to me what he dare not do to you," Madame Mezières used to say, "because you are his daughter; but you're the one who stiffens his prick, you know... Ah, if you were to show him your

pretty little cunt, how he'd jump! what wonderful
blows of his prick he'd aim into my cunt!" Touched
by her pleas, I'd often hoist my skirts and exhibit a
downy, silky-haired cunt my father considered exquisite: I could tell that it pleased him, for the sight
would inspire him and he'd charge with redoubled
fury into the lady's trick. Leaving her, he'd himself
put my shoes back on, but Mezières prevented him
sometimes, and, raging with lust, she'd push me onto
the bed, lick my cunt, and into hers thrust the toe of
either my slipper or shoe, wielding it like a gode-
miche. While this was going on, my father would
gently fondle my buttocks or my breasts. "You'll fuck
her, you bugger," said Madame Mezières, "you'll
depucelate her, you'll get her pregnant, you'll have
to marry her..." These oft-repeated remarks led me
finally to ask my father's leave to marry.

"'I had an uncle, my aunt's husband; the stairway
leading to their apartment was poorly lit; one day as
I was climbing up, my uncle followed me; when
halfway up, he slid his hand beneath my skirts and
laid hold of what he called my cunterino; I started
in fright. "Keep still," said he, "do you want to
raise the roof?" I fell silent and he fingered my
cunterino, his one hand straying now and again to
my asshole, his other fastened securely on my breasts;
he put his member into my hand, had me squeeze it,
swore softly and while suckling my nipples, discharged between my fingers.

"'I was blushing furiously when we entered my
aunt's apartment, but I said nothing. My uncle
kept a stern eye fixed upon me and when I set out
for home, he said he would accompany me thither.
"You are going to marry soon," said he. "I have
someone suitable in mind for you. But only I can
persuade your father to agree to the match, and I'll
persuade him upon condition you let me stuff you

just three times before the wedding once the alliance has been made a certain thing." "Stuff me? With what?" I played the innocent, although I had witnessed my father cavorting with Mezières. We were in an obscure little alley. He brought his prick forth out of his breeches and grasped my cunt. "This, and into what I'm holding." I edged away, but said nothing. We were not far from my father's door; I broke away from my uncle and ran home; no one was at home. I waited for my father to arrive.

" 'Alone with my own thoughts, I resolved to sound my father out on the question of my marrying; he appeared and I was less restrained with him than usual: when kissing him, I placed my lips not upon his cheek but upon his mouth. He was delighted with that; I darted my tongue into his mouth, just as I had seen Mezières do it; he put his hand between my thighs, but not under my skirts— I abandoned myself, saying: "I want to marry... and you'll be well-caressed, you may be sure, if you give your consent..." "With all my heart, upon one condition: have you someone in view?" "My uncle has. I've never seen him, however." "Very well. 'Tis then no passing fancy on your part... I'd better give you a cunt-licking, it should seem to me..." "A what?" "I'll lick you there," he explained, putting a hand upon my gem. I pouted. "Now, now, be a clever girl. Take this soft sponge and wash yourself thoroughly. Scrub that pretty growth of fine hair down there, and the inside too. You'll find this enjoyable, believe me—you'll feel very silly for having been reluctant." He gently sucked my little nipples while my cuntlet, my buttocks and my rosebud were swimming in a rinse of luke-warm water.

" 'My impassioned father afforded me no time to pause and consider; as soon as I'd dried myself, he lay me down upon the bed, raised my clothing above my waist, and applied his mouth to my crack, into which he inserted his tongue, licking energetically until, after fifteen minutes of this, I gave out hints of an impending discharge. Observing I was on the verge of an ejaculation, my father got up and returned with a large lump of butter which he put into my cunterino, and then inserted his prick after it, causing me considerable pain; he squirmed and shoved, I discharged, such was my pleasure that I squirmed and shoved too despite my sufferings. Fortunately, my father's prick was not excessively stout, but it was long: he gave me the most complete pleasure, for he tickled the bottom of my womb and because I was very narrow there, he filled my cunt just as if I'd had a stallion's member between my cunt-lips: and that was how I lost my maidenhead.

" 'While he was at work washing my cunt, I besought my father not to delay giving his approval, which I did not want to owe to my uncle's intervention, and explained why. "Ah ha!" said my father, "so that's it! Don't let that bugger stick you, my dear. His prick's huge, he'll widen you noticeably, whereas I'll not harm things: your future husband, or any other of your fuckers, will swear you are a maid." I promised I'd not grant my uncle what he was after. "Oh, but you can amuse him all the same, you know. Frig him when he reaches for your cunt. You might even let him embugger you if he appears willing to be content to go no further." "How does one do that?" "Embuggery? I'll show you." And he embuggered me; it pleased me, for I discharged. "As for my consent," my father resumed, "send your suitor to see me: if he's the ugly rascal of a fellow I'm thinking of, you'll not be wild about him all... well, that's enough." Highly pleased, I returned to my uncle's; his wife and he introduced me to their protégé, a sort of mulatto they presented as a Monsieur Guac.

" 'That same day I had a very spirited interview with Monsieur Guac; during it, he did his level best to get at my cunt. His ugliness and stupidity did not repel me, since my uncle and aunt had forewarned me that he was no beauty but nevertheless most popular with women; this intrigued me. I informed him that my father was not opposed to me marrying; would he have the kindness to pay him a call? Indeed he would and he asked me to take him to my home: we agreed to confront my father the following day at noon.

" 'We arrived at a moment when my father was about to leave the house; Guac had fondled my ass upon the stairs and had engaged me to fist his prick, which put a glowing color in my cheeks; I was radiant; I presented Guac as my fiancé; his dreadful face, his mean appearance caused my father to smile and dispelled all his jealousy. "My children," he said, "I have some urgent business to attend to; it shan't take long. Please await my return." He left; when we were alone, Guac said to me: "From his tone it seems as though he'll keep his word to you and say yes." "I believe he will, for he never hides his reaction if something displeases him." "My beloved," Guac went on, his black eyes glinting with pleasure and lust, "allow me to put it in you here, right now, on your father's bed; do let me." I thought it a fine idea: after all, I had already been depucelated and, furthermore, my gem had been itching me furiously ever since my father had perforated it; however, I replied: "Oh my, no! What if Father were to come in? and he'll be back soon." "Why, when he sees you being screwed, he'll do nothing if not hasten your marriage."

" 'He lowered me upon the bed, I resisted feebly, clumsily; he thrust his prick between my cunt-lips, then pushed... but could not advance, even though he interrupted his struggles to wet the head of his device. He increased his efforts which resulted in his loosing a bucket of sperm all over my pubic hair, my belly and my thighs.

" 'I slipped away to wash myself. "Indeed, you are very thoroughly a virgin, 'tis clear," said he, putting his clothes back in order. While wiping and drying myself, from out of the corner of my eye I glimpsed my father in a hiding-place. I pretended not to have noticed. An instant after I returned to Guac, that cunning father of mine entered the room. Guac requested my hand in marriage; my father answered that he would allow me to make my own choice; he signed the documents. He then told Guac that he would like to have a talk with me and that he would conduct me to my aunt's—he wished also to speak to her. We would all meet there. Guac left.

" ' "Have you been fucked?" my father demanded directly Guac had gone. He seized my cunt and drew me towards him. "Have you, eh?" "You saw very plainly that I have not been." "Where did he discharge?" "Upon the hair..." "Some of it got between the lips?" "Yes." "Good enough. That will sometimes suffice to impregnate. You've nothing more to fear. Go visit him in his lodgings and give him a free rein. Between now and then I might just as well dig the ditch a little deeper." Aided by a large spoonful of butter, he penetrated me with some ease, and repeated the operation three times, excited by what he had just been watching and because I was extremely well shod in new silk slippers. I discharged three times within each encuntage: that totaled nine. My father affirmed I was a mettlesome, high-spirited girl and that I should turn into a good fuck-eress; I washed with care and he took me to my aunt's.

" 'We found Guac there upon our arrival; my appetite was rather whetted than satisfied by my father's triple stuffing. Said I to my fiancé: "Go to your place; I'll join you there, for I wish to have a conversation with you." He dashed off. My father spoke to my aunt, suggesting that the wedding-day be advanced; he feared, from the manner in which I had discharged, that I might become pregnant because of him and at the same time he desired that it happen; but at any rate I had to marry. My aunt went out with him.

" 'I too was about to leave, in order to let Guac essay a complete encuntage, when my uncle appeared, I was in such a sweat of lust that I was by no means sorry to see him, even though he did not please me personally. He turned the key in the lock and approached. "So you are going to marry? Well then, come along, let's have a look at the goods that are to be made over to him. You know, Guac has such a large prick he's likely to damage you lest we loosen things a little." This observation convinced me I ought to yield. He seized me. "Leave me, leave me..." I pronounced in a weak voice; my uncle paid no attention and seeing I was not going to cry out or scratch, he bore me to the bed, had up my clothes and directed his prick into my vagina. I feigned self-defense, but managed simultaneously to facilitate matters. He hurt me, I did indeed moan, and observing that my complaints were of some aid to him, I began to scream at the top of my lungs, which brought him trembling into the hilt, causing me such pleasure that my groans were those of ecstasy; I struggled fiercely, but my cunt hugged his thick member; my body thrashed, my ass heaved

with such fine effect that I discharged with terrible
convulsions and my cunt contracted so tightly that it
pinched my uncle's gland. He bellowed... and half
fainted from pleasure. "You fuck damned bloody
well for a virgin! What will you not be able to
accomplish in time! Let's begin again..." He had
at me three times in all, heedless of my tears—for
I thought it wise to weep. When he had his fill,
he decunted. "Oh celestial fuckery!" he exclaimed,
"were your cunt's merits more generally known, it
would make you your fortune." "Yes, you have
given me an excellent start," I answered between
sobs. He unlocked the door, emptied the bidet
containing a mixture of water, blood and fuck, then,
fearing his wife's return, he went out, saying: "You
owe me your thanks: without that preparation, Guac
would have disemboweled you. Come see me again
if I can be of further help."

" 'This kind of language neither surprised nor
upset me; as soon as he had gone, I dried my tears
and adopted an air of perfect gaiety. My aunt
returned; I notified her of her husband's attack, but
omitted to mention its success: my aim was to
encourage her to expedite my marriage. I begged
her to say nothing to my fiancé of what had transpired, pointing out that this might lead him to change
his mind. I promised always to protect my virtue
with the same dauntless courage which had just
animated me, and while I was speaking in this vein
the itch returned to my cunt; I asked to be excused,
left the apartment and raced to Guac's hoping that,
prepared as I was, he'd drive it home this time. He
was awaiting me. "I have a quantity of things to
tell you," I began; but he did not allow me to
continue further. He made for my cunt. "We'll
fuck first of all," quoth he, guiding me onto my
back. His impetuosity rather relieved me, for, in

truth, I had nothing new to say to him. I put up a calculatedly awkward resistance, as I had with my uncle and my father, but enlarged though I was, his attempts were in vain. I dared not tell him to resort to butter; that would have struck him as no virgin's advice. I waited for the idea to occur to him; it didn't. "You're devilishly mint in there," he muttered, rolling me over on my belly and spitting into my asshole. Wherewith, by dint of an unheard-of effort, he hammered his engine into that small orifice. I emitted ghastly shrieks, but he held me in such a grip while embuggering me that I was unable to budge; I endevored to reply to his buffets in order to minimize my suffering and hasten the denouement, and my bouncing ass did bring an end to the drama. That member in my ass seemed to have the proportions of a siege-gun's barrel; to feel it withdraw was a not unpleasant sensation. "You're worth your weight in gold, even bum wise; excellent." Then he asked my pardon. "Your lovely cunt, your lovely ass, your white breasts were driving me out of my mind; unable to encunt you, I embuggered you, in despair, as it were: forgive me, my dear creature. I have all sorts of plans for recompensing your stirling behaviour." My ass hurting, Guac dipped it in warm water, them he kissed it, licked it also, occasionally running his tongue as far around as my cunt. He had stiffened anew, but I wished to leave. He was obliged to bring me home in a carriage: to walk caused me pain, but the carriage afforded him an opportunity to frig me while he sniffed one of the shoes he had removed from my feet and into which he finally discharged a full pint of fuck. Delirious with pleasure, "My queen," said he, "my prick is over-large for you; pick out some handsome young lad by whom to be depucelated and I'll find a way to arrange everything without compromising you." The suggestion appealed to me; Guac got out and carried me into the house; I went to bed; the pangs in my asshole diminished and then vanished with sleep.

" 'The next day I went to my father and related everything Guac had done and said to me. "Good," he commented; "you are a fiery creature: you'll be fucked forwards and backwards and orally too and you'll adore it. You shall be married within a week's time. Between now and then I'll find you a more sturdily furnished fucker than I. For the time being, we'll do our best with a makeshift: ready yourself, I intend to put it in you. Impossible to give so pretty a cunt too many stretchings." My father encunted me thrice. "And still a maid, damn my eyes!" said he. "But that awful uncle of mine," I protested, "with his massive prick, has already raped me upon three occasions." "Three!" my father exclaimed. "What the devil kind of a cunt could God have given you! You could be sold a thousand times over as a virgin... Here, I'd better refuck you..." and he refucked me.

" 'While I was rinsing my cunt with warm water my father had gone to the window and was chatting with a young solicitor, his next-door neighbor, a strapping handsome buck of thirty. My cunt washed, I went to have a peep, raising the curtain, but having been observed by the young man, I withdrew. "Who is that heavenly creature?" he enquired. My father replied with a casual gesture which was probably meant to signify that I was his mistress. He was still gesturing when the solicitor took his leave. My father spoke to me at once. "How would you like that lad to put it in you? He'd pay." "Oh Father!" "Call me Sir in front of him." There was a knock, my father answered the door and I heard him ask in a low voice: "You brought it?" "Here you are. Fifty *louis*." "Mademoiselle," my father thereupon said to me, "you know that I love you for what you are. This young man, one of my very best friends, has come to make you a present; I am going out now; show him that you are capable of expressing your gratitude." My father concealed himself; the solicitor fancied he had left.

" ' "Have you been fucked today?" he enquired, coming up to me and grasping my breasts. I slapped his face. "Monsieur," I said, "we are in my father's house." "You are... Mademoiselle." "Quite, Sir, and am to be married next week." "A marriage, that would be, of interest or one born of affection?" "Having learned of my attachment, my father met my fiancé and discovered him monstrous; being a thoughtful father, he undertook to have me prepared for what lies in store for me; I thought you a friend of his: I consented after having seen you." The solicitor fell to his knees, he begged my forgiveness a thousand times over. "Therefore behave properly," I continued. Wherewith he caressed me, I at last returned one of his kisses. He drew me to the bed; his prick belonged to the same category as my uncle's but he was less adroit. I called out loudly for pommade. "My fiancé having once enticed me to his chambers, he shut and bolted the door and attempted to violate me," I explained. "Unable to make any headway, he pommaded me... and still had no luck. But pommade me nonetheless." While saying this to him, his fumbling efforts caused me to discharge; I sighed ecstatically, panting. My father mistook these sounds for those of pain; he emerged from hiding, pommaded me and guided my fucker's prick into my cunt. "Thrust," he said to me, "lift your ass, squeeze him in your arms, for every blow your depucelator gives you, reply with one of your flanks, lock your legs around his body and

tighten them as you move about; good, that's it...
excellent!... jump, my dear, throw caution to the
winds..." "Great God!... what pleasure," exclaimed
my fucker, "how narrow her cunt is... how deliciously
she moves under me..." I darted my tongue into his
mouth, murmuring: "My heart... my beloved...
I adore you..." "Ah, the dear little thing... what tenderness... I'm discharging... fucking her..." "Oh,
Father, he's fucking me!... do all men then fuck this
way!... ah, Father, what joy!... my soul is going to
flow out of the hole... he is in..." I discharged, my
whole body becoming rigid. "The little princess!"
expostulated the solicitor, "look at her come!... My
good man, give her to me to be my wife: I've depucelated her, I'll marry her!"

" 'My father, who had his own designs upon me,
refused; as a result the solicitor flew into a rage,
hurled himself back into my hole and fucked me
eighteen times: my father was obliged to pluck him
off my belly and convey him home, for he was unable
to walk. As for myself, I was hardly out of breath.
Once I'd washed my cunt and refreshed it, I felt as
good as new. Upon my father's return, seeing he
was deeply moved by the sight of my naked bubs,
I told him that, if he was stiff, he might as well satisfy
himself by fucking me two or three times. "What
a scene that was!" he gasped, "but you have a pitiless
cunt and a ferocious taste for the game. Your cunt
and taste will make our fortune. Let's see if you can
discharge again, my dearie... let's have it!..." And
while encunting me he praised me highly for having
avowed I was his daughter and given that slap to the
solicitor. "Fuckers," he observed, "have a certain
disdain for the fucked, but in your case it shall be
the contrary; I'd like to put you above those buggers—" "I'm discharging!" I cried. "And so am I,"
said he, shaking me with his thumpings. He

reëncunted twice over and I matched his discharges, indeed, I outdistanced him. "I believe I'd work ten men dry," I said as I washed. I asked him to advise my fiancé of what had to be done in order justly to encunt me; I shot my tongue into his mouth, smiled and left.

" 'I had been fucked twenty-five times in the course of the day, seven by my own father. I returned to my seller's house, but every man upon whom my glance stopped tempted me. How happy whores must be! I thought, they accost whomever they please. All of a sudden an idea popped into my head: I'll go to see Guac, I'll tell him to pommade me; let him cleave me in two, no matter so long as he fucks me! I quickened my pace.

" 'He was with an attractive young man whom he told to hide directly he heard my footsteps approach—but I saw the young man through the keyhole. Guac received me with a mysterious air and led me into the half-lit room where I'd seen him conceal his visitor. "My darling, my beloved wife-to-be," he began, "I believe I might stuff you today; you need but give evidence of some complaisance..." "To be sure... but don't overlook the pommade... my aunt..." "I understand..." I felt him turn me over to some gentler hands; someone seized my breasts, my cunt, a tongue insinuated itself into my mouth; I replied with caresses; a hand lifted my skirts, I advanced my cunt prettily. A body got upon me; I felt a lump of butter being inserted into the entrance of my cunt, another into my rosebud. There was a push, I responded; to my astonishment, I sensed virtually no pain at all. Finally, the invading prick reached the depths of my womb—still no pain—and now a discharge... The abundance and sweet warmth of the fuck brought word to my lips;

with an incredible pleasure, with wildest transports
I cried: "Dearest lover... divine lover... I am expiring
from happiness and voluptuousness... I adore you!..."
The young man decunted; he sucked my nipples, my
lips, had me stick forth my tongue; then, without a
moment's delay, he reencunted me furiously; I had
as much pleasure this second time as before; to be
brief, he did it again and again, incessantly, and it
was Guac who took him away at last—for my part,
already fucked twenty-five times that day, I believe
I could have stood at least another twenty-five with
these two men simultaneously, if both of them had
been able to stuff me. Guac, noticing that I was
having difficulty walking, sent for a cab while
I rinsed out my cunt. "Well, my charming queen,"
quoth he, "have you been satisfactorily fucked?"
I blushed. "Far from being tired," he pursued,
"I'm dying to fit my shaft in your asshole." "Oh
no, no, you mustn't!" I cried, alarmed. "As you
like, my dearie. But you will frig me a little, won't
you? Frig me with both hands, just as you are there
with your ass in the bidet." I frigged his heavy
member, so bulky I could barely get my hands around
it; when fuck was about to spurt forth, he fell to
shouting with pleasure. "Your mouth," he roared,
"your mouth, else I'll dip it in your ass!" I slipped
the foreskin clear of the gland, pressed the latter
between my lips; the fuck spurted forth. Fearing
lest it spill on my bubs, I opened my mouth and a
torrent of fuck shot down my gullet. I swallowed it
as one would a draught of good ale... A right copious
tankard of ale, and warm. "Fuck! fuck!" howled
Guac, "I'm getting dizzy... Ah, celestial slut—you're
worth more than all the rest of the women in the
world... Is it good, the drink? What causes so much
pleasure coming out must surely be good going in.
Ah, divine whore! I'll feed you a diet of that stuff!"

" 'The cab arrived at the door. Guac carried me out—I'd been fucked for the thirty-seventh time that day.

" 'My aunt's brother was alone in the house when I reached it. "Mademoiselle Convelouté," he complained, "you are cruel to me... I hear you are preparing to marry. It would seem to me you ought to favor a young man who adores you rather than this fiancé of yours who is ugly and a widower; you are a virgin and so extremely lovely! What is more, he's very thickly equipped—so at least your uncle has given me to understand—and he'll certainly hurt you. What if a more youthful prick were to ready you for your marital career? Look at it" —and he fetched out a truly charming prick— " 'tis a real maidenhead-tickler, and it'll never give you so much as a twinge of regret. I know my business, Mademoiselle. My sister's husband has a nervous device and is very quick on the tigger, and she has the good sense to call me in now and then to clean the cobwebs out of her trick."

" 'This language pleased me and the prick I was staring at looked inviting. "I, however," I replied, "have no cobwebs to be swept out." He saw from my manner that I was in a cheery mood, and laid hands on my breasts. "Have done, libertine," I said coaxingly, retreating in no great haste before his advances. His hand reached my cunt. "Oh, indeed! have done, this is too much." His breeches lay on the floor, his prick was nodding in the air... He deposited me upon his sister's bed, cleared away my clothes and got aboard me, whilst I said nonchalantly: "Ha, Sirrah! You are then capable of resorting to violence?" and I defended myself in a way intended to further his ends.

" ' "Ah heavenly girl girl, innocent thing, lamb, I'm stuffing my prick into your fleece." In it went.

I replied by twitching my ass in a feigned attempt to avoid what I desired, and managed to swallow two more inches of sausage. "No," he cried, opening the sluices, "no, nothing can be compared to encunted innocence!" However, fearing lest I get away, he thrice renewed his attacks without once decunting —that brought the day's total to forty—and did not leave me until he heard the approach of footsteps; I ran off to wash.

" 'It was my aunt; she said to her brother: "Fortunately you're with Miss Convelouté. Anyone else would have lost her nerve before the possibility of an interruption. Tell me, did you attack her?" "I did." "Well then I suppose you're about done in; come here, I'll comfort you." There was still some oil left in his lamp; the young man bolted the door, thus encloseting the three of us, and then sprang upon his sister, whom he penetrated in a trice. Great heavens, how her flanks heaved! "Stuff it deep!" she exhorted him, "I'm getting ready to discharge, fuck me, dig deeper yet, hug me, fuck me, gouge me, fuck me blue in the face!" I watched them... revived by the spectacle, my insatiable cunt was starting to yearn for a prick when a soft knock was heard at the door. I hoped it would be a cousin of my aunt who had for a long time been eager to put it in me, and I was determined to push him into an adjoining room and satisfy his ambition; but no, 'twas a handsome youth who looked very much like the young man Guac had had fuck me a little earlier in the day.

" ' "Mademoiselle," he began, "your name is Aglaé Convelouté?"

" ' "It is, Monsieur."

" ' "Mademoiselle is the fiancée of Monsieur Guac?"

" ' "That is correct."

" ' "Do you greatly love that gentleman?"

" ' "Sir, reason rather than passion makes for a wise marriage."

" ' "In that case, Mademoiselle, it shall cause you no distress if I reveal a secret to you."

" ' "And what secret would that be?"

" ' "This: a short while ago you supposed it was your fiancé who was possessing you—"

" ' "What tales are you bearing hither, Monsieur? Indeed—"

" ' "I was there, but hidden out of sight, Mademoiselle. His battleaxe being unable to cleave you, he sold me your maidenhead for one hundred *louis*: I deflowered you, no other. Might you prefer me to him?"

" ' "But can all this you tell me be possible?"

" ' " 'Tis the truth; his member is too thick: one has just been inserted into you. It was mine." (I knew all this perfectly well.) "There is but one thing to say," he pursued, "will you marry me?"

" ' " 'Ah, can you marry me?" I demanded in my turn.

" 'He hesitated. "Mademoiselle, I am already married—to an old crone of seventy-eight. She bestowed her fortune upon me. I am obliged to wait until she dies."

" ' "And were I to become pregnant, Monsieur? No; I shall wed Monsieur Guac."

" ' "Do you wish to be my mistress?"

" ' "That would not, I think, suit me."

" ' "But with his consent?"

" ' "Do you then have his consent? Why then," said I, "since you have had me once already, and since he agrees to the thing, I'll do as you like, provided he is not told that I know of his agreeing."

" ' "Splendid! this signifies your correctness and honesty. Are you presently alone?"

" ' "No, my aunt is here."

" ' "Could I have you tonight, after dinner?"

" ' "Gracious! I should never be able to creep out of the house—unless I were to give the excuse I was going out to look after my father, supposing that he was ill... But he isn't ill. No, it's out of the question."

" ' "With your permission I shall go and have a talk with your father; I am wealthy: better that I should give to you rather than to that poor wretch Guac the price of your favors."

" ' "Very well, speak to my father."

" ' "I'll come back to fetch you if he honors my request."

" ' "But don't come back alone; I want to hear his decision from the lips of one of his servants."

" ' "As you wish. Be easy."

" 'He repaired to my father's house; he related how Guac, unable to depucelate me himself, had sold my maidenhead to him for one hundred *louis*, which sum was in payment for four séances; a quarter of the total was already in Guac's hands. He told as well how he had encunted after pommading me; how he had found my gem delicious and so satin-like that he wanted no other; how he had asked to go to bed with me and how it had been by my advice he had addressed himself to my father. He then offered the balance of the fixed price: seventy-five *louis* for the three remaining nights. "Since Guac wanted to be a cuckold," my father answered him, "so be it. I agree, Monsieur, that you sleep with my daughter if you were the one who plucked her rose—and she will verify that. Go bring her here; I'll give you a note for her." He wrote a short message, then accompanied my beau as far as the door of my aunt's house, within which she was still being fucked by her brother.

" 'Meanwhile, I was enjoying myself watching the amorous strife progress on the bed; I was all afire when the young man reappeared, my father's note in hand; through the window I caught sight of the latter: he was waiting in my pretended depucelator's carriage. I left the house, saying I was going to keep my sick father company. When we arrived, the galant ordered a fine supper brought in and handed twenty-five *louis d'or* to the cashier. We ate, we drank, then I was tucked into bed; the young man demanded that my father undress me and wash my cunt; he himself in a flash removing every stitch he was wearing, he donned an out-sized nightshirt he had brought along: this garment permitted him greater freedom of movement. He summoned my father to insert his prick in the entrance of my cunt; that done, he pushed; and he had no less trouble now than previously at Guac's. This surprised me. He remarked to my father: "Her cunt is really tight: sh 'd grow a new hymen in a week if she were left alone." He fucked me six times. My father, lying next to us, each time inserted his blade into the scabbard. Soon after, my fucker fell asleep and I did also; the following morning he had chocolate brought in. I felt refreshed and refused the offer of his coach when he proposed to take me home to my aunt's in it.

" 'For it was not to my aunt's I wished to go. I had heard it said that fuck swallowed warm was excellent for the chest, fortifying it and whitening the tint of the skin; I wanted to quaff off a goodly dose of it, and my thoughts focused on sucking Guac's prick. As soon as I was free, I dashed to his lodgings and found him getting ready to go out. "I've come to give you some pleasure," I said, "but shall not take any, for yesterday you wearied me dreadfully." "Well, my dear, what's on your mind? An embuggery, a little thigh-fuckery? a frotch between the shoulder-blades or under the armpit? I can contrive to squirt into your ear, upon your neck, between your bubs if you'll squeeze 'em, over your navel, between your calves—if it's your calves, you'll have to squeeze them too—or would you like me to glove my prick in one of your slippers?... You have only to ask and I shall do anything for you, save encunt you... We seem rather a mismatch in that sense, but..." Instead of replying to this harangue, which was pure Greek to me, I unbuttoned his fly and set to frigging him with one hand while, by instinct, I tickled his nuggets with the other. He began to howl with delight: "Goddess... bleeding sacred bitch... divine whore... frig, frig, tickle... tickle my balls... oh! oh! what sensations!... buggeress, slut... tramp... whore... angelic creature... my fuck's coming!" Upon hearing this last exclamation I mouthed his large prick, rubbing the gland with my tongue. 'Twas then the good Guac, hurled into a delirium, through a wealth of allusions gave evidence of a learning which only increased his stature in my eyes: "Fuck!... heavenly mouth!... Aphrodite's cunt, cunt of Cleopatra, Egypt's queen, encunted by Anthony, Laïs' cunt, Aspasia's, Phyrne's, the cunt of Dame Agnes Sorel, of Marion Delorme, of Ninon, of Madame d'Aubigné, of Mesdames la Vallière and Pompadour and Duthé and la Lange, of the pretty Marc, of the adorable and provocative Mézerai, of the youthful and naive Henry, you are as nought compared to this mouth!... I'm fucking... fucking... fucking-ing-ing... discharging... oh swallow it, swallow it!... gorge yourself on fuck, my empress!" and he spewed forth half a keg of it... I kept on pumping at the source. " 'Tis too much," he cried, "one dies of that sort of pleasure." He had me take some coffee to rinse my mouth... Then I began to frig him anew. He sucked my nipples, my tongue and would have sucked my cunt; but I demurred, expecting to be fucked later that evening. He got stiff again, I shook and twiddled and stoked his machine, I tickled his spheres, more fuck appeared and I swallowed another brimming measure of it; and this happened a third time; mere lack of time forced us to separate.

" 'At nine that evening, a coach came to take me to my father's; there, we supped, fucked and slept as upon the previous night. On the morrow, after chocolate, I went to Guac's for my breakfast of fuck. Returning to my aunt's, her husband, probably having conferred with his wife's brother, was eager to put it in me; I gave him a firm refusal; he complained to his wife, who in turn reproached me, but once I had informed him that my fiancé had stuffed me ten times in succession with my father as witness, she begged my pardon and advised her husband to wait his turn in line.

" 'I was to be called for that evening. Before going, my aunt whispered in my ear: "Try to avoid a fucking so that your uncle can put it in you tomorrow; he's dying to." I found my lover at my father's house. We talked of Guac during supper. My lover said that, having been encunted in his presence, I ought not fear becoming pregnant. "That," he added, "is why I headed straight in and discharged in the cellar." " 'Tis a great pleasure for me to put your prick in my daughter's cunt," my father remarked, "I enjoy thinking of the horns growing on that confounded and most dishonest Guac who had the temerity to sell your pucelage." "That is just what brings me to a boil when I fuck his fiancée," my galant affirmed. "One more antler on that bugger Guac's head—the very idea refills my balls, no matter how often I've emptied them. It even occurred to me," he went on, "to give each of you fifty *louis* if you'd fuck together: the knave would thus be recornified and supercornute!" "Capital notion!" my father exclaimed, "very original indeed! After you've seen to your business, you can pop my prick into my daughter's cunt for me." "Oh no!" I cried; "gracious!" "You'll hold on to her if she appears recalcitrant—" "Those aren't my ideas," I told them. "If I wiggle my ass the way I do when my lover fucks me, it is because I love him. As for Monsieur Guac, I have much to be grateful to him for: he is like a nurse to me, you know. One might even say he suckles me." Neither precisely caught my meaning; they led me to bed.

" 'My lover fucked me six times; upon the sixth, he said to my father: "That's it, my friend. Get aboard and fuck her; I'll insert the engine." My father climbed onto me; the young man slid his prick into my cunt; Father pushed; as I was more fond of him than of any other living person, I put my flesh furiously into motion, doing as nobly as any princess fucking a page-boy; inspired by our frenetic activity, the young man waxed so violently hot upon beholding us discharge that he rolled us on our sides and embuggered me even while I was still encunted. I went to wash and then we three went to sleep.

" 'At breakfast the next morning, the young man seemed wild with joy. "Ah, by God! that one's been smartly cuckolded!" he cried. "Here, my good chap, here's the hundred *louis*. You'll really have to fuck her after she's married: I'll pay twenty-five *louis* per shot." He left and I hastened off to find Guac, whom I was growing to love as much as I loved my father.

" 'He greeted me with rapture, calling me his divine slut, his heavenly whore. I milked out his fuck six times over, and this hurled me into such an erotic panic that I dashed away to locate my father.

"Your solicitor," I panted, completely out of breath, "must surely have recuperated from his losses by now: I'm burning... Run fetch him, Father dear, if you love me!" He went calling me Cleopatra; he found the young man outside the door, his erect prick in his fist. "I was standing here when a moment ago I saw your daughter enter and I am frigging myself in her honor," he explained. "Don't you do it, my boy, you've not a drop to waste; come back in with me and stuff her, if you please." "Twenty-five *louis*—" "Nonsense. That's an outrageous price to charge a steady client; one louis per shot, that should be fair enough. But who knows? She may earn the twenty-five from you after all." They entered the room where I was awaiting them; as he came in, the solicitor tossed his purse upon the foot of the bed. "Come, show your calves, girl," my father said heartily. "That many fucks, that many *louis;* but you mustn't kill yourself, my little friend. He was frigging himself when I found him out on the sidewalk: he says he was thinking of you." Upon hearing this I cast my arms around his neck, thrust my tongue in his mouth, agitated, then withdrew it, and said: "Ah, dearest, most beloved friend! I adore you—" "And I you," he replied, fondling my breasts and cunt. I fell backwards, he fell on top of me, I plunged his prick into my cunt and in four heaves of my ass I felt him strike bottom; he discharged when he sensed that I was melting; he fucked me ten times. "I've credited you with fifteen *louis*," said my father as the solicitor cleaned himself and drew back on his breeches. "Come back whenever you like."

" 'It was but two days before my scheduled wedding; Guac had nursed me every morning, and the effects of this new beverage were to whiten my skin, brighten my coloring, make my cunt hair softer and fluffier, and to give me such violent penchants that I was not one minute at my ease unless I had a prick in my cunt. That morning, my solicitor said as we were taking breakfast: "Guac must be wondering what has become of me—we've not seen one another for a time. Perhaps he has conceived some erroneous ideas about my lovely fuckeress' cunt. Since the inflexible Agnes simply has got to marry, I'd like to buy her for the wedding night." I had repeated my intention to marry while we had been fucking, and my father had applauded me. But as he was accompanying me to Guac's, where I was to have my ration of milk, that good father made the following observations:

" '"You are not the common sort of bride; what would slake almost anyone else's thirst is but a drop of fuck to you. I have an idea: I think I can arrange to provide you a feast for the day after tomorrow: I'll recruit a team of fuckers who'll work over you till you've had enough. Let me see. I'll begin the thing, then your uncle, the solicitor will come next, then your aunt's brother and perhaps the neighborhood butcher; if I can find any stray buggers, they'll sodomize you—we'll say we are anxious to keep your maidenhead intact for the groom. 'Tis delightful to embugger a bride on her wedding-day; they'll all pay handsomely. I'll consult Guac and we'll make all the necessary preparations." We arrived before his door; transported with gratitude, I embraced my father and urged him to try to follow me into the house without being seen, for I wanted him to see me drinking my milk. I went in, he crept after me. Guac, his face wreathed in smiles, strode towards me, unbuttoning his fly; he kissed my feet, legs, ass, cunt and bubs; I prodded his gullet with my tongue, and after that he entrusted his prick to my hands. I was busily stroking it in a lively manner when he said; "Wench, I'm a reasonable man. I don't encunt you, but your father and uncle ought to fuck you on your wedding-day; I'll have three fresh pricks ready for our first night together... One of them will be that which depucelated you... Ah, the idea of you being encunted by your father is sure to make me release a pint of fuck—beware, here it comes, open your mouth wide! Come, wench, it's beginning to rise, get your lips around my prick... Ah! ah! ah!... The bugger fucks his daughter... Your father is fucking you, slut—fucking you, whore... Ah, that divine image makes me discharge... Houah!"

" 'He nearly collapsed. During the obligatory interruption I went to bring my father from his hiding place. "Fuck me," I said, "for 'tis essential to my fiancé's happiness." "Ah, goddess!" cried Guac, casting himself to his knees, "you commit incest for me, all for me?" He introduced the paternal device into me. "Jump, skip! Fling your ass hither and yon," he cried. "I'm dis-dis-discharging," I stammered, "come to me, my true love, let me frig you." Guac whinnied with pleasure as he sensed the fuck rising in him; he stoppered my mouth the while my father fucked me, and at the same instant I swallowed fuck I received a quantity of it in my cunt and ejaculated my own. My father had fucked me four times and Guac had four times given me pap when there came a knock at the door. Guac answered it at once, while I hastily rinsed my mouth and cunt. It was my uncle.

" ' "You arrive just at the right moment," said Guac, welcoming him. "We are trying out my fiancée and need your help." Further explanations were contributed by my father. Guac stretched me out on the fucking-couch and my uncle encunted me: he detonated six charges; Guac launched six more into my mouth; after that I was given a moment to catch my breath. Subsequently, it was decided that a dozen fuckers would entertain me, one after the other, on my wedding-day; I'd present my ass or my cunt as a target, whichever I chose; Guac would enjoy the exclusive privilege of my mouth, during the night he would have me fucked by three new pricks—these he would choose. Awestruck, my uncle exclaimed: "But she'll be a whore!" "Quite so, and such she must be if I am to adore her. However, neither of you need complain about it since you two will be the only ones who'll have free use of her..." As he finished pronouncing these words, he prostrated himself before me, acknowledging me as his goddess.

" 'I went back to my aunt's; her brother was there. Both of them argued with me, both tried to persuade me to open my cunt. "Just once, dearie, before you are a married woman," wheedled my aunt. They redoubled their importunings. I yielded. She guided her brother's prick into my cunt. I was fucked only once, this being a frail fellow and his sister being eager to get stuffed directly he was done with me. And now it was my hand which directed the sibling and irresolute prick into her blazing cunt. This operation concluded and indeed repeated, I bade them adieu and left the house; they wept to see me go. "One thing consoles me, since we must lose you: at least my husband and brother have fucked you. You have been an inspiration to them both... thanks to you, they now fuck me very frequently." As I was leaving, my uncle arrived; his wife told him what had happened. He said nothing, but took me aside, or rather to the bed, laid me upon it and fucked me in their presence, all this in complete silence. He wanted to begin anew; I refused, inviting him and his brother-in-law to come the day after the next, and stuff me on my wedding-day. They both thanked me."

CHAPTER XXXVI

Concerning the hirsute tailed man,
Convelouté, Linars, etc.

" 'Upon reaching my father's house, I brought him up to date, relating all these latest developments.
" ' "You know," he observed, "when one has so much paid work at hand, one should not accept to perform any for nothing. A chap with a rather agreeable appearance came today and offered an impressive sum for the privilege of sharing your company tonight. He looked vigorous to me, for he is dark-skinned and covered virtually everywhere with hair." "I hope you did not discourage him," I replied with a smile. "Little things of that order are no bother to me at all."

" 'Reassured, my father had me take a hot bath, then a cold one; he put me in bed clad in a generous nightgown and had me swallow some excellent broth: then he allowed me to sleep: it was five in the afternoon when I shut my eyes. I opened them at midnight, feeling someone licking my cunt; I requested my assailant to show himself: he lifted his head and I saw before me an exceedingly hand-some and exceedingly swarthy man. I smiled, he sucked my breasts, the while saying complimentary things: "You have a magnificent cunt, a superb mons Veneris, the belly of a maiden, an alabaster behind,

breasts white as snow, a prominent cunt, voluptuous
lips, fine teeth, the most lovely hair!... eyelashes,
eyebrows, hair that could belong to Aphrodite, a
perfectly turned leg, feet yet better formed!... After
I've fucked you, I'll have more to say." My father
bade me get up and come to supper. The swarthy
man lifted and carried me, naked as I was, to the
table, which was laid near the fireplace. There, to
my great surprise, I saw Guac; Fysistère (as the dark-
skinned man was called) laced up my corset, indicat-
ing that he appreciated an amply exposed breast; my
father put stocking and shoe on one of my legs and
feet, Guac attended to the other: my stockings and
slippers were of silk, and dazzlingly white. We sat
down at table; my fucker asked me to uncover my
breasts somewhat more; we supped, and I was hungry.
That dark fellow ate and drank like Hercules. Upon
quitting the table, he said to my father and to Guac:
"You have not deceived me: she even surpasses the
enthusiastic description you gave of her. If the
interior of her cunt is anything like the outside,
I shall have her at whatever the price." "Let's have
a look at your prick," said Guac. "Ah, yes, that
should make a very nice fit, a perfect one. A glance
at mine will explain why I've not been able to encunt
her, as Monsieur Convelouté, my father-in-law, has
doubtless informed you." "I shall soon see whether
she merits so splendid a name as Convelouté—but,
ye gods, Monsieur Guac! what's that you've got
between your legs! An appalling prick, I say!
Mademoiselle, fist that object, if you please, I'd like
to see how hard it is." I seized Guac's prick; he
straightaway began to roar with pleasure. "I'm
stiffening also," Fysistère remarked. "Make your
father rigid also, and we'll compare engineries." And
I grasped Father's member, which swelled as
I squeezed my hand; then the comparing took place.

Guac's was three times the hairy man's, whose was thrice my father's. "I'd like to have a word with her," said Guac, furious with lust; he steered me into a corner, drew a curtain to conceal us, and discharged into my mouth. Only my father guessed what Guac had just done. As for myself, that mouthful of custard braced me wonderfully; I too was afire.

"Fysistère's first words delighted me: "I must fuck her fully dressed, to begin with," said he. We retired to the bed: he removed his breeches and exhibited a body no less hirsute than an ape's; he had me take hold of his device, saying: "Introduce this thing into your cunt, and raise your ass in the approved style every time I give a thrust". I encunted myself at once; he pushed; I uttered a cry, for he was tearing me, having a prick larger than my uncle's and, indeed, than all the other pricks which had fucked me hitherto. "Don't be upset," he said, "I am deflowering you, depucelating you is the technical term. Move your ass, gyrate it." I moved and gyrated it as best I could, sighing with pleasure as I repaid his prick-strokes with heaves of my ass. He finally rammed his way to the bottom, my nippers closed upon his gland. "Adorable wench!" he exclaimed between shouts of lewd delight, "your satin-smooth cunt's biting the sausage! Your fortune is made, your future secure, as are your father's and your fiancé's who've sold you to me. Come now, let's fuck seriously!" I twisted and writhed, I leapt in the fashion my father and Guac too recommended. "Ah, this is sublime!" Fysistère rhapsodized. "She's discharging... Ah, she'll get me a little short-tailed bugger!" To my fiancé: "Come here, scoundrel, put your hand on my back, lower down, lower still —that's it. Now with one hand tickle what you find there, and with the other hand give my balls a massage." Guac obeyed.

174

" 'Later, I discovered that at the base of his spine the hirsute man had a stub of a tail, shaped just like a prick, but like the rest of his body covered with hair, and it was that tail my husband-to-be fondled. "This celestial cunt isn't something to be abandoned in a minute or two—no, I'll be at work for a good hour," said Fysistère, agitating himself happily. "Tickle away, bugger, tickle away, both my tail and my balls." He discharged six times before he came out for air... I asked leave to wash myself; my fiancé sponged my cunt and kissed me, calling me his cornucopia, his magival goose. Meanwhile, my father sucked my bubs.

" 'Said Guac to the dark-skinned man: "She's yours, but I'm as stiff as a goat. Permit me to embugger her." "Embugger her? No, 'tis good fuck wasted; nor shall you encunt her, for I want her to bear me a little one with a tail. But were she disposed to drink some fuck—and I've known a few high-spirited women who have a taste for it— I'd agree to let you enmouth her." Upon hearing this, I laid firm hold of my fiancé's prick and I'd have swallowed it had it been loose and not so bulky. He discharged while well within my gullet; he let go with guttural sounds, and the boiling seed splashed down into my stomach. "Ah, she likes fuck!" observed Fysistère. "She has every virtue, every quality and she'll be lovely so long as she is fecund. Well there, Papa, put yours into her mouth: of all fucks, paternal has the best flavor." I hurled myself upon my father, threw him down on the bed, seized his risen prick and made it move in and out of my mouth until he erupted. I savoured and swallowed his fuck delightedly. "Good!" exclaimed Fysistère, "she has had an exemplary upbringing, 'tis clear. The girl's priceless." He took off my nightdress and shoes and stockings; my father and Guac assisted him;

I was stripped to the skin, handled, caressed, kissed from top to bottom while I rinsed out my mouth. They passed me the nightdress; completely naked now, the tailed man raised it and got next to me, sucked my nipples and my tongue, then told my father to insert his prick in my cunt.

" 'Fysistère fucked me another six times without pausing to decunt. I felt tired; I wished to tidy myself; for an hour I sat astride the bidet, my cunt steeping in soothing tepid water. Fysistère amused himself by making Guac stiff and having him release packets of semen into my mouth. Then he summoned me, saying: "You have had ample rest, come to the couch so that I can give you the bouquet." He had my father introduce his member. "Courage, my child," Papa said, "this fucker is worth ten ordinary men; I'll try to provide you with some relief if this goes on for too long." Six more fuckings followed, fuckings of such extraordinary vehemence that I simply could not stand any more. I said I'd had quite enough: "But," Fysistère explained, "the bouquet is twice the usual attack." "What's this? How many shots do you propose to give her, then?" my father demanded to know. "Twenty-four in all. That's my accustomed dose." "That's too many, you'll drown the child if you've impregnated her, my good fellow. I have a suggestion: she has a younger sister, just as pretty as she is: I'll give her to you, for this poor girl won't be able to keep up with you." "I accept your offer," said Fysistère, "and I'll need a lot of others, for I stop fucking them as soon as they are full, or while they are nursing the little ones. Is the younger girl anywhere about?" he enquired, fucking me uninterruptedly. "No, you'll not able to have her until tomorrow night." "In that case, I'll finish giving this one all twenty-four. You may wash now," he said to me, decunting, "I've only five more to go. If your fiancé feels fit, let him give you a drink of fuck—'twill strengthen you for the rest." Guac immediately brought me his balls to fondle and his prick to frig. I acquitted myself so brilliantly that he was neighing before three minutes had gone by, and I had just enough time to get my mouth around his prick when he discharged, swearing like a trooper. "Yes, there's nothing missing in this girl, she has every talent a man could ask for," Fysistère declared as he reencunted. "If her younger sister is half as gifted, there are two matchless athletes." He ran off his last five fucks, one after the other. I can say in my own behalf that I discharged in reply to every shot he fired into the target, indeed, I sometimes answered with two or three to his one—whence the active Fysistère's admiring comments; he called me a fuckeress worthy of him. Wherewith my father said: "I doubt whether, even with the little one, you'll be well enough supplied. But I've got just what you're looking for: a niece. She's a nun and has the hysteric vapors, it seems: she'll be useful, however, in giving my daughters some respite." "A niece, eh? Excellent, I'll take all three and will give each an annual income of twelve thousand pounds," the dark-skinned man promised. "Bring them to see me every day, except for tomorrow. I'll be busy stuffing a tall blonde who has heard me spoken of and wishes to have a try." And he left.

" 'That scene altered all our plans. I slept till noon. We arrayed ourselves and were married at one o'clock. The wedding feast was gay. My sister was there, as was my hysterical Carmelite cousin, my father having found the means to have her there by alleging her need of the waters she had been for a considerable period requesting. I felt the most genuine pity for my sister Doucette's little cunt, and resolved to see her at some time during the day. My father cunt-sucked her while I looked on, explaining to her that such treatment was excellent for her health and prevented illness. Ah, how pretty she was! I'd have got my tongue in her cunt too, had it not been for my bridal dress and coiffure, for her dear little fuck tempted me sorely. Our father warned her that she would have probably to aid me in the course of my wedding night, and the amiable child naively and graciously agreed to do whatever would be of help. I also saw the cunt that belonged to my Carmelite cousin, the beautiful Victoire Loudo. It wasn't exactly sweet to see, nor cute, but was covered by a rich, superb black upholstery. One had but to touch it with the tip of one's finger to plunge her into an erotic frenzy, and my father was obliged to screw her in front of my sister and me; this quieted the poor thing for no more than a moment. We called my uncle; he fucked her three times. Then we put the young man to work; he was soon exhausted. Then we enlisted the solicitor's services. And finally we one by one applied to all those who were to stuff me on that glorious day. The embuggerers came afterwards: she was fucked, refucked and fucked again, nailed, hammered, cleated, planed, sealed and painted —and calmed at last. But we did not resort to Monsieur Guac—I was jealous of him; while all this multiple fuckery was proceeding, my father frigged my sister: the nun's embuggerage caused Papa such an erection that he thrust Doucette into a small chamber (I went with them) and there and then he depucelated her. I inserted the paternal sceptre into her dear little cuntlet—my function in this commerce was indispensable, for her gem, new and bright, was also very narrow.

" 'The nun was given a washing. Noticing that Guac coveted her, I expressed jealousy, which flattered him: he made me a promise to save all his fuck and his thick prick for my mouth while waiting for children to increase my cunt's diameter. "But you rented me out," I told him, "before having turned me over to the hairy man, in order to be fucked before and behind on my wedding night. How many cunt-fuckers and embuggerers am I to have?" "Six, at two thousand crowns a piece." "You see, then," I returned, "I shall need a little rest—but we should not let so pretty a sum go by. And have you insisted upon silence and no bright light?" "I have, yes, my beloved queen, I have contracted simply to produce you naked, without any night garment, and to be naked myself in the room. Silence and obscurity are essential—the six buggers have been discreet with me so far. After having seen you together in the salon, each of them will be placed in a separate room. You will move from one to the next: each will behold your entrance, survey and aspire after your charms, and suppose he is the unique possessor of all that tempts him. We will arrange everything by means of signals." "And, I take it, I shall be replaced by three persons? We'll allot my sister the smallest and most delicate prick. The Carmelite will get the most brutal and vigorous. I shall see you fuck my aunt—leave that to me: she'd like nothing better than to be fucked were the conditions such as would ensure her against compromise. See to it that each woman comes to grips with two men —you should have little trouble managing it, for only the men are to be deceived."

" 'Guac admired my grasp of the situation and my sense of economy. He promised he would submit completely to my orders and asked leave to call my sister or the nun, saying he wished to be frigged. I summoned them both. Uncovering her breasts, I bade the Carmelite take hold of my husband's prick and balls. Next, I placed my sister in the appropriate position, raised her skirts to above her waist, and adjusted her so that she would exhibit a view of her ass, which was exceedingly attractive to look upon. I stood beside her, likewise exposed, but showing Guac my forequarters. He, titillated by a soft and gentle hand and relishing the prospect of three eminently agreeable women, soon began to mutter and whinny with pleasure. From this amiable mood he went into a furious one, and he would without any doubt have encunted that nun had I not leapt to his prick and shoved it into my mouth. He discharged into my throat, howling with joy. We all four went out together to the dance and my sister, my cousin and I were greeted most warmly by the merry-makers come to the wedding.

" 'My six fuckers for that night had arrived. Guac, taking great care not to show me to any of those who were to have me, made much ado about me to those who were not. They were, taken all together, six monsters of ugliness. Guac found a way to get them to take off all their clothes: he led them into an isolated room, bade them strip, and rubbed their bodies with what he described as an invigorating balm: I observed this scene through the key-hole.

" 'The first was a fleshless skeleton having a prick resembling my father's. His nose was so long it touched his chin, he was hollow-chested, bright-eyed, and he had warts all over his body. I decided to bestow him upon my sister because of his prick's moderate proportions—and I imagined I'd find few moderately proportioned ones amongst these gentlemen—; his name was Widewit.

" 'The second was a stocky, stout little man with a considerable belly and having a prick the equal of my uncle's; his hide was the color of boiled lobster, by way of a nose he was furnished with a large beet;

he had bushy eyebrows, a funnel-shaped mouth and the slack lips of a great eater. He too was to be destined for Doucette if I failed to find anyone better; his name: Witencon de la Cowillardière.

" 'The third proved to be constructed like a heron or like a dromedary; he was hoisted up on long stilt-like legs or poles, lacking entirely in calves, upon his shoulders he carried a conical head; his visage was sharp and dark; his skinny thighs were mere continuations of his meagre legs, separated only by enormous knobby knees. Everything that was wanting in the rest of him was found in his prick, this article being sturdy, nay, massive, more so even than our betailed man's, and twice the diameter of Guac's. I selected Towtenwit for my aunt, who was hot-blooded, big-gapped and barren.

" 'The fourth was an important corn-factor as broad as he was tall, covered with black hair and with pimples, having balls weighing sixteen or twenty ounces each, a very long prick and as thick as my uncle's. I chose Witplongeardow for my cousin because of his balls.

" 'The face belonging to the fifth had the hue of a toad's belly, his head was monstrous and might also have been that reptile's, his belly was modeled after Desessarts', his prick after Guac's. (He was to embugger me—that had been decided in advance.) His glance was dreadful, his mouth disgusting and his nose yet more so. Witerwell was there to occupy himself with my aunt's ample cunt.

" 'Round-shouldered and stooped, bandy-legged, red-haired and rheumy about the eyes, the sixth and last was a tall man; he had a vaguely-shaped, lumpy prick, exceedingly long. He had however brought along an auxiliary and artificial member which, strapped into place, was to be used to embug-

181

ger me. Perceawant was to be my ardent cousin's second lover.

" 'Night fell. I was put to bed. Each of those six originals fancied he was going to have the pleasure of plying the carving knife upon my unsliced flesh. Guac conducted me into the nuptial chamber and made as if to tuck me in, but he distributed us, one to a room, and the lights were extinguished. As for myself, I remained up and walked about, providing each of my co-workers with a glowing portrait of the Prince Charming she was going to clasp in her arms. In all conscience I felt obliged to give them at least imaginary pleasures in the default of real ones. "My dearest," I said to my sister, "with what unlimited joy you'd sacrifice your night's quiet rest for me if only you could see the delicious young man who is to make gentle use of your sweet charms! He's a sylph, he's an Apollo, the very god of love, I assure you!" Next, I went to where the nun lay in great expectation. "You are going fully to sense the difference between the cot in your convent cell and a newlywed girl's bed," I told my mettlesome cousin. "A superb man, a majestic prick!" I betook myself to the room where my aunt was awaiting she knew not what. "Ah, you shall have your fill of what you love so, my dear Auntie: a matchless youth and perhaps two who desire me with all the passion of their young years: they're going to fuck me in your cunt, your burning cunt, and continue until their forces finally desert them. Think of it! Their pricks are solid; and so I advise you to grease yourself as though 'twere for the first time... pretend to be a maid and swallow those enormous joints of beef..." My aunt thanked me and besought me to bring these champions in with all possible despatch. I ran off to get her Towtenwit, the third.

CHAPTER XXXVII

Of the six fuckers and the three they fucked.

" 'Leapt upon by the horror she fancied an angel, my timid sister sighed happily; I heard her being cunt-tongued, I heard it when she discharged—"I'm dying..." she murmured... "How sweet your voice is, my beloved bride," Widewit whispered to her and he straightaway climbed aboard and encunted her. Although depucelated, the poor little thing uttered a cry; I spoke from the doorway close at hand, to disguise her trouble and distract her fucker; that old monster was literally eating her alive, caressing her, fingering her everywhere; she seconded his efforts with all her might and discharged afresh. Thanks to me, she had just as much pleasure as if she had been fucked by Don Juan; seeing that she was well enskewered, I went to find out how the nun was faring.

" 'Witplongeardow had decided not to employ his misshapen device, but rather his artificial one, and was nonetheless evoking groans from the poor martyr under his belly. I ran and informed Guac of what was happening, he came at once, plucked the villain from the breach and gave him a few cuffs: I heard him say in a very low voice: "Do you want to kill my wife, you scoundrel? Put in her cunt that damnable prick God gave you!" The fucker did as he was ordered and the fuckeress thenceforth knew pleasure only.

" 'Next, I repaired to my aunt's room; owing to his awkwardness, Towtenwit had been so far unable to encunt her; I lowered my head to the pillow and, between sighs, said: "Ask my father to introduce it for you." Guac, who had followed me on tip-toes, arrived to negotiate the insertion, and subsequently all went well.

" 'Each of the three girls was twice cunt-fucked; then, as though in concert, the three buggers wheeled as one and attacked the fort from the rear. Two of the three were therewith handselled asswise; my aunt naively supposed her cunt was about to be stuffed from behind, but the two others had not even an erroneous notion of what was about to befall them. Those three asses were pierced at the same instant and despite the instructions they had been given to avoid all outcry, they all screeched in chorus. Doucette: "Oh! the fundament!..." The nun: "Oh! the anus!..." My aunt: "Ah! the asshole!..." No one paid the least attention to these protests. Happily, my sister had a large ass: consequently, she suffered less than the others; as for the Carmelite, whom Witplongeardow was buggering with his infamous member, she had a veritable yardstick in her entrails and could feel it nudging her navel. She suffered much pain from this rude intrusion, for he withdrew and plunged back in again brutally; she had no pleasure until he discharged and she felt the agreeable warmth of his fuck flow into her large intestine.

" "My aunt was the worst treated by Towtenwit: her asshole was tight as her cunt was lack; his enormous prick was cleaving her in two, she gritted her teeth to stifle her curses. The discharge came at last, she imitated it with one of her own, his prick grew smaller, she felt much better.

" 'The three old lechers had had as much as they needed. Guac came to fetch them off their prey, and led them away without permitting the women a glimpse of the creatures with whom they had been struggling. The three cunts were wiped and dried and set to rights, the beds were made, the sheets changed, the three brides were tucked in again and Guac brought in the three new actors.

" 'He and I deposited Witencon in the arms and upon the belly of my sister, by now somewhat toughened by battle. She tenderly caressed the monster who encunted her, his prick guided by Guac to the mark (Guac took advantage of this opportunity to fondle and tickle my sister, which caused the poor little thing to tremble so, that her fucker exclaimed, imagining me to be his auditor : "Ah, but you are a bloody little whore, aren't you!").

" 'In that Guac seemed to have forgot everything but his immediate problem—namely, cunt-stuffing my sister. I left him to his affairs and went on alone to arrange the two other men. Perceawant I gave to the nun and saw to it his own prick was erect.

" 'Tis a gentle hand indeed that touches me," said he, wishing to seize mine, but I eluded him. "Get your ass to quivering, buggeress," he told his steed, "I'm entering your cunt, you can't get away from me now. I'm not your husband, I've paid hard cash to lie with you and depucelate you, and so you're my whore. Fuck, slut, and keep your ass in motion, that's what I've paid for." Guac heard him; he came in directly and seized him by the throat. "You've not fulfilled your end of the bargain, I need not fulfill mine. Get out of here, knave!" "Yes, but I was to have embuggered her!" And he charged into the Carmelite's ass despite the hail of blows Guac was showering upon him; the nun screamed like one of the damned.

" 'By this time, I was at my aunt's bedside; I matched her with the massively outfitted Witerwell.

He had contracted to embugger only, but the hot-blooded rascal he had beneath him herself directed his prick into her cunt. "Ah ha! so, wench, you're not a virgin after all," he declared (to me, he supposed). "How is it you know so much about prick management? Well then, whore, if you are experienced, fuck like someone who knows a little of the world, fuck, do you hear? for I've paid your pimp of a husband!" As she replied in earnest to all his thrusts, he went on, saying: "Ah, she's a whore, she is a whore, I say, she's what the others left me," and as he discharged he pinched and slapped her; she protested, defended herself. "Into your mouth it goes, bleeding whore that you are," he said, drawing out of her cunt, "and if you don't swallow my fuck to the last drop you'll wish you had!" Guac, having a moment ago driven out the nun's brutal fucker (after he'd been allowed to embugger her), now heard the hubbub in my aunt's room and hastened thither; he apostrophized that unclean wretch Witerwell, gave him a powerful blow in the face. "You might at least wash yourself before sticking it in her mouth, dog! I never give my prick to be sucked, never, do you hear? without first washing it in rose-water and soaking it in milk. Execrable bugger! you behave like that swine the Marquis de Sade; are you trying to nauseate us all? You've broken the agreement, and you don't deserve to spend another minute here." "There are a hundred *louis* in my coat pocket," said Witerwell, "take them in addition." "Wash yourself... Here's some rose-water... Some milk's over here... Well, my dearest, you'll have to put up with whatever comes along—he's got a hundred *louis* in his pocket, just as he says..." The old reprobate shouted like a lad of eighteen, enmouthed, embuggered, encunted, between-titted to his heart's delight. "Ah, by Jesus! what a whore they've given me!..."

Guac wished for nothing more than to prove to him he'd not got the partner he imagined; and when Witerwell was finished and dressed, Guac escorted him to the door, passing down a hallway and leading him straight past where I happened to be, fully clothed; it was as though he had seen a ghost, for I sprang out of sight. "Oh, I've been cheated!" the monster roared, "damn my eyes, he gave me a whore instead of his wife!" and he swore and cursed till he had stamped out of the house. While these scenes were in progress I was observing my young sister's fuckery: the poor little thing was encunted, embuggered and enmouthed like the others by her paramour Witencon de la Cowillardière, who did not pause before he had exhausted his last particle of strength. He adored me; what finally did for him was that when he felt himself drained dry, he had Doucette suck his prick (priorly very thoroughly washed in warm water) and kiss his balls. Again, he niched his prick and balls between her bubs and in the cleft between her buttocks, then he had his gland given a further sucking; wherewith he did get somewhat of an erection and promptly popped his device in Doucette's ass. He repeated this trick and, this last time, had a dry orgasm. He collapsed soon thereafter.

" 'I called for Guac, who pried him loose from Doucette's ass; he was unconscious and in that state was borne to his carriage; upon reaching home, liqueurs were given him in accordance with Guac's instructions to his footmen. Alcohol revived the aged libertine. "Ah," he cried, opening his eyes, "I am still alive, and I wanted to die in that asshole! I'm still hard, go fetch her here, bring her to me, I've got to stuff her again and... oh... oh... expire... oh—" and, indeed, he did expire.' "

"A heroic death!" Trait-d'Amour commented, and the whole company agreed it had been.

"Madame Guac went on with her story. 'And that was how I passed the first night of my marriage. Guac was, upon his return, furious with lust; he wanted to embugger everyone in sight, then enmouth us; we disposed ourselves. He enmouthed me, embuggered my sister and cousin, encunted my aunt, who ached for a month from his huge prick's effects and was furthermore impregnated thereby, and that probably was what prevented Fysistère from buying her too.

" 'As for Guac, I remain his mistress and his thick prick still fortifies me with its nourishing fuck. I'll be encunted by him soon after I've had my second child—he and Fysistère have agreed to that.' "

CHAPTER XXXVIII

The conclusion of the story of the three wenches.

" 'No one ever knew how the fiery man with the tail discovered that Guac had hired me out on my marriage night. He arrived in a towering rage; he demanded to know where I was; I was in bed—such was Guac's reply. "I dare say," Fysistère muttered, "and a man has died of exhaustion in her arms." "She spent the entire night attending to her duties." Guac explained, "but they were not lethal. Her cousin, the nun, having been somewhat wooed during the day, was attacked by her hysterics in the course of the night—she had a nightmare in which she fancied she was being fucked; I was summoned to her room; being unable to encunt her, I embuggered her instead. As for my wife, she's asleep and you'll be able to ascertain by the freshness of her cunt and asshole that she's not been touched." "We'll have a look at the Carmelite to begin with." "She too is sleeping." But they went in search of her.

" 'Guac drew back her bedclothes and pulled up her nightgown without awakening her. She lay on her side, unable to rest on her back because of her smarting ass—it was in dreadful shape. "She looks rather badly to me... And her cunt?" "It was less seriously maltreated. I strained it, but not gravely, by my vain efforts. After that she frigged herself."

" "Now let's see the bride." They came into my room. I believe I mentioned I knit up the raveled sleeve of care with a little repose preceded by a bath; my cunt and my asshole were found so appetizing and so pretty that Fysistère kissed them both, then he informed the good Guac that he had a secluded dwelling where he planned to sequester us, my sister, my cousin and I, during the whole of the time we produced children for him. When he looked in upon Doucette he found her dressed; she enchanted him.

" "The next day he took the three of us away, saying that, until the time our pregnancies were well under way, no one would approach us, we would speak to no one save through a grilled window.

" 'Fysistère is extremely wealthy; he fees Guac to the tune of twenty thousand pounds a year; my father receives forty thousand for my sister and my cousin. After a good supper, in the evening he has us all lie in a wide bed and he climbs into our midst. He fucks me first, then my sister, lastly the Carmelite; each of us gets two successive discharges between which he never decunts; then he returns to me, goes next to my sister, and so on; in a word, we are each given eight shots a night, meaning that Fysistère fires twenty-four times. While he is fucking one, the two others excite him, one attending to his sensitive tail, the other to his equally sensitive balls. That's how it was. We all three became pregnant simultaneously; he announced we were to have no more until we had given birth and finished nursing our offspring. He came here to Sens, he saw you, he fucked you, Madame, he married your eldest daughter, encunted your five other children, fucked your two nieces, got into your husband's bastard, raped your two servants, and made every last one of you pregnant. An unusual man. During the time he was operating here, we gave birth, nursed, found ourselves in a case to start in again, and he has fetched us here and he is going to fuck us some more. You too ought to try to be free—available, that is to say—when we are gravid once more; that way we will be fucked alternately.

" 'There you have our story. And now you know more about the man with the tail. I shall simply add that, when Monsieur Fysistère was not fucking us, we nevertheless did have desires to be fucked, and we satisfied them by resorting to my father, my uncle, and the stalwart Guac as well as to the solicitor and my first beau; they furbished us indiscriminately, Guac spilling his seed in our mouths, the others moistening our cunts. However, we all wanted Guac when the first pangs of labor began: his prick, as bulky as any infant, opened up the passage and his fuck greased it.

" 'After childbirth, we besought my father to hunt us up some pretty little boys not yet at the age of puberty, but capable of stout little erections, who would be able to keep our cunts from getting rusty. These youngsters were located; we used to oil their little members: they'd not discharge, but were able to keep us as clean as a whistle.'

"The twelve women were greatly aroused by this narration and some of them got up and went forthwith to have Fysistère give their cunts a polishing; he was greatly surprised by their eagerness and fell to with a right good will. He used his tail as well as his prick, thus handling two at at time, one on top of him, the other beneath. When this storm had blown over Fysistère returned to his three tried and true women. But it was not long before they were all pregnant. Whereupon he requested them, and Madame Linars too, to find him three or four new companions while his original three remained *hors de combat*. Madame Guac managed all by herself to procure three for him: one was Tétonnette, a childhood friend; the others were two sisters: Bienouverte, tall and blonde, and Dardenbouche, a pretty brunette, very affectionate and given to discharging like a fire hydrant. Tétonnette was one of those dark-haired but fair-skinned girls who are always found to have splendid breasts. Fysistère signed over twelve hundred pounds a year to each of Madame Guac's three discoveries, took upon himself the responsibility for their maintenance during the period of their fecundity, laid them side by side in the capacious bed and depucelated each eight times the first night. He began things with Dardenbouche, the youngest; she was so amorous, although a maid, that she replied to the initial prickthrust with a veteran heave of her flanks. It was with nothing less than heroical courage she sustained the eight successive assaults. Next, Fysistère turned to Bienouverte; her behaviour was more reserved; she wept and exclaimed, although not very narrowly cunted, because, not discharging from the outset, he only mildly wetted her cunt; nevertheless, she was a maid and acted like one : despite her languor, she was fucked the standard eight times—Fysistère would have been mortified had he failed even by one to live up to his lights. After Bienouverte came Tétonnette : she was less readily penetrated than the former, but so deliciously did she go into the dance, her bubs were so appetizing, her cuntlet fitted so snugly, that she gave him quite as much pleasure as had Dardenbouche.

"His two dozen attacks completed, Fysistère let his new wives sleep. Early the next morning, three menservants entered to receive his orders. He was awake but feigned still to be asleep, his mouth fastened upon one of Tétonnette's nipples and a hand on one of each of the other's breasts. 'Look ye at the bugger,' murmured one servant, 'he looks peaceful and contented, don't he?' 'Aye,' replied the other and they fell to frigging themselves. Whereupon Fysistère pretended suddenly to awake and said to the pair: 'I heard you two rascals. You'll not encunt them, no. by God, I want them to be pregnant thanks exclusively to me, but turn two of them over on their bellies and embugger them both, if you'd do me a favor.' He had scarcely concluded his sentence when the three sleeping beauties uttered simultaneous cries motivated by the three pricks burrowing into their assholes. Fysistère exhorted them to be patient and to think of all the encuntments they regularly had to every embuggerment; and, moreover, he assured them that the two servants and himself were going to eject their seed upon the floor. They were won over by these arguments and vied with one another in giving furious motion to their asses. A superior diplomat, that man with the tail!"

Everyone's reaction to this long story was the same : "What indeed are we but puny operators compared with those fuckers and fuckeresses! But we

192

do make the most of our limited abilities, don't we? A pity 'tis not tomorrow, wouldst that we could put our small wits to work!" "Now don't start frigging yourselves, my friends," I warned them, "save what little you have—" "Never fear; our fuck is not our own—it belongs to these lovely creatures." Who was surprised to hear us converse thus in my daughter's presence? Monsieur Brideconin and his good dame... but they were to have an even greater earful and see yet more.

CHAPTER XXXIX

Concerning the wonderful armchair.

It was Sunday. A fine dinner was prepared and served in my storeroom. Apart from the bed and the old sofa, I had a third comfortable piece of fucking furniture brought down there: I'd chanced across it in a locksmith's shop in the rue de la Parcheminerie, the locksmith had bought it merely for the steel and iron at an auction of a certain duke's belongings; I related the history of this object to the society.

"This armchair you see before you has unusual properties. It is more than at first glance it appears to be. The locksmith one evening shortly after acquiring it was about to sit down in it, for he had noticed it has an interior mechanism. The plump young wife of his old neighbor, the wig-maker Aupetit, arrived in his shop. All out of breath, the pretty woman sat down wearily in that devilish contraption; her arms were pinioned upon the spot, a spring mechanism drew up her skirts and another spread her thighs, a third forced her cunt forward, a fourth made it oscillate. "Eh, what the devil sort of a thingumabob is this?" she cried. "I've not the faintest idea," the honest lockmaker answered. "I was getting ready to try it out myself when you came in. Apparently it's what the Duc de Fronsac used to employ when dealing with reealcitrant girls sold to him by unwise parents. If you like, neighbor, I'll deal a little with you—" "Come, my good man! Is a woman ever to be raped against her wishes?... I'll bite, I warn you—" The lockmaker removes his breeches and gets aboard her; the lady attempts to bite him—and a gentle but irresistible device forces her mouth open and, exerting pressure, compels her to stick forth her tongue. Vulcan's minion takes full advantage of all that and nips into the wigmaker's wife, who's powerless to prevent it and even unable to scream. The operation completed, the spring and gear mechanism in the chair unwound and Madame Aupetit was released. 'Twas then she began to weep and sniffle, to complain about how she'd been used; 'twas as though she were in the depths of despair. "Why, you're a great silly," said the smith, "I managed so well you're certain to become pregnant—you'll have a baby the likes of which your old scoundrel of a husband would never have given you. But you've got to be clever. Tell him today that you've been doing penance or something of the sort, that you've got to go to the church tonight to receive some kind of a blessing... and when the curé gives it to you, stir your ass, say a few things to warm him up and when he discharges in you, make as though you're swooning and tell him he's shot to your gullet." Madame Aupetit left the shop

194

with her head full of these instructions and she followed them to the letter; the armchair was sold to me the next day.

"Having seen me passing in the street, the locksmith called me in, showed me his prize, praised it and explained its use to me; I bought it upon condition I obtained satisfaction from the apparatus; we'll use it on prudes, should we find any in the course of our orgies. We'll not have anyone sit in it until the proper time comes, otherwise the charm of its secret will be spoiled."

We were four at dinner: Madame Poilsoyeux, a pretty hatmaker from the rue Bordet or Bordel whom Trait-d'Amour had brought with him and whose name was Tendrelys, and myself. *In petto*, I decided to try the mechanical chair on the attractive Tendrelys, who was still a virgin, although Trait-d'Amour had made a steady practice of sodomizing her and had upon several occasions discharged between her thighs—or, if the hat-maker proved docile and compliant, I'd use it on Rose-Mauve or on her blonde sister Rosalie, or again on our landlady, for I was eager to initiate Madame Brideconin into our mysteries and her husband too, wishing to cuckold him in his own presence. We dined royally well, but avoided eating and drinking too much. Furthermore, we were served fowl and other readily digested things; the reader will soon see how I put my plans into execution.

CHAPTER XL

Of shaven cunts.

As we rose from table, Trait-d'Amour said to us:
"All week long I've had the idea in my head to
render the cunt of Madame Conquette Ingénue Poilsoyeux what it ought to be, that is to say, loose,
for I'm dead certain that after seven days of idleness it's tight as a drum. Brisemotte, Cordaboyau,
good fellows and mightily pricked, raise Minonne's
skirts and Connette's too, for it would not be meet
for them to bare their own bellies." They were
uncovered to above the navel; upon their cunts... not
a blade of hair! "I shaved them this morning,"
explained Trait-d'Amour, "to see the effect before
proposing the same thing be done to my goddess.
See how tidy they are, my friends; every bit of hair
removed from every part of the body. They have
bathed every day since learning that the beautiful
fuckeress daily dips her cunt in the limpid wave and
then plunges thereinto the rest of her incomparable
body. They tell me that when the fever is in them,
the cool water in which they soak their burning
cunts give them a nearly fuckative pleasure. But
behold those cunts: wouldn't you swear they belonged
to little girls of twelve or thirteen?" We all agreed
with Trait-d'Amour.

And I asked my daughter to consent to have her
cunt tonsured. She hid her face upon my chest.

Trait-d'Amour immediately laid her on the bed, her cunt sparkling in full and glorious view. "A pity though," he admitted, caressing, fingering, fondling, petting it, "the goatee is superb! I'll use scissors to start with; we'll mount this silken hair under glass and frame it in gold—it will make a precious relic." He snipped away and then from a rosewood box drew a perfumed shaving stick and for a long time soaped her cunt. As this operation excited Conquette, she besought me to lay my lips upon her mouth, and she darted her tongue into mine all the while her cunt was being razed, and when it was cleanshaven it was washed with rosewater, her thighs were dried with soft towels, and Tendrelys placed in a frame the wondrous hair that had been shorn away; after that, the beardless cunt was exposed to the company's admiring gaze. Everyone, especially the girls, and even the reticent Tendrelys, who, they said, had only come to see and blush at everything— everyone concurred in judging it superb, and found it so appetizing that it was subjected to a general kissing. The pretty hatmaker glued her lips to my daughter's pink cunt and her tongue roving in the crack succeeded in arousing her lust. Rose-Mauve, who could not stay away, leapt upon her like a tigress, plucked the hatmaker from the sacred object, and cunt-sucked Conquette with such zeal and energy that they both began to pant. The men had their turn: they sucked the discharging gem and made it discharge some more. As for myself, while staring at these stimulating goings-on, I rubbed and fondled Tendrelys' bubs, which she had in charming size and shape and dared not defend.

"Ah, what a party!" she said. "You've seen nothing yet," Minonne replied to her. Indeed, Trait-d'Amour, having liberated Conquette Ingénue's cunt of those ravening tongues which had been inceasingly active, spoke to his comrades: "Imitate me, dear friends!" Wherewith every prick, risen mast-high, was trundled from its hiding-place. "To cunts! To cunts!" was the next command shouted. Tendrelys lowered her lovely eyes; but Conquette, stretched out on the bed, her clitoris undergoing a gentle tickling at the hands of Rose-Mauve, raised her head to see the couched lances.

"Which one are you going to encunt?" my lusty former secretary asked me. "The voluptuous Conquette or Maid Tendrelys?" I hesitated before replying—that moment's pause was enough to bring a feeble cry from my daughter: "A prick... a prick..." Trait-d'Amour dashed to her side, took her in his arms and presented her palpitating trick. "Encunt her," he bade me, "the fuckeress' cunt's smiling at you." I plunged in; I was as stiff as a quarterstaff and as I penetrated her, my precipitation fetched a sigh from her lips. But a moment later she was fucking industriously back. "Ah, that's good!" she exclaimed, raising her ass to meet my attacks, "very good indeed... My but you're stiff today!... fuck, Papa, fuck... bury it, hammer it home, oh dear Papa, I'm going to discharge!" —Trait-d'Amour's finger playing about her clitoris was an additional inspiration. I discharged also, her delicious cuntlet gripping me like a pipe in a plumber's vice. That goddess made me positively drunk, Trait-d'Amour's ministrations made her fairly vibrate, as Petronius' Corax caused her master Eumolpe to tremble. Meanwhile, Brisemotte had flipped Rose-Mauve onto her back... Those two little witches, Minonne and Connette, as naked as your hand, had just peeled every stitch of clothing off the still hesitant Tendrelys and held her between them, frictionalizing and heating their cunts against her alabaster thighs, one tickling her clitoris, the other digitally investigating her asshole. They all three discharged at the precise instant the two encunted women erupted. "My stars!" cried the pretty hatmaker, "what a wonderful way to spend one's spare time!"

CHAPTER XLI

An unexpected prick arrives.

At this crucial juncture there came three swift knocks at the door—a signal I had given to the locksmith. I decunted and went to open; it was the good artisan indeed; he did not come in, but thrust at me a man wearing a blindfold and having his hands tied behind his back. He was covered by a great white woolen overcoat beneath which he was completely nude. I took him by the arm and pushed him towards the Fronsac mechanical chair upon which Trait-d'Amour seated his sister and set the thing in operation; directly the child had been seized by the apparatus, the individual who'd just entered was launched into the fray after his coat had been snatched off him. Now that he was naked, his massive prick provoked a general fright—remarks such as "Great God!" and "He's lugging a mainmast!" were heard all around. Conquette recognized who it was; she blenched. (The reader is to note that whereas everyone else could speak, Conquette and I had to keep silent.) Minonne, caught fast in the chair, was the only one this prick, which yielded to Fout-à-Mort's in no particular, failed to alarm. She grasped it courageously and popped its head between her cunt-lips, advising its owner to push with might and main. The bugger reared back, then lunged ahead, wielding that device like a battering-ram upon a besieged castle's gate; but it did not penetrate. "Raise your ass," the would-be fucker ordered in a brutal tone," I'm too tall." Minonne adjusted herself, the prick found the gap, and although it required a passage at least twice as broad, it forced its way in. Minonne underwent the ordeal like a true Christian martyr. Sweat and tears rolled down her cheeks. At last, that vast instrument touched bottom ans spewed forth its life-giving ichor, and by lubricating the damaged corridor lessened the pain the girl was suffering. Minonne's cries of distress were succeeded by others of bliss. "Ah!... ah!... he's inundating me... I'm fucked, I'm discharging, oh, I'm going out of my mind!" And the poor impaled little creature thrashed about like a whore being fucked by a monk in a brothel.

We were all at first dumbfounded with admiration, then, to a man, our pricks soared rigidly aloft like a quartet of demons. Brisemotte jammed Rose-Mauve from behind, Cordaboyau stuffed Connette from in front; Trait-d'Amour consulted my eyes, pointing first to Conquette, then to Tendrelys. I nodded to him to take the former, whispering to my lieutenant: "He's fucking your sister, do you fuck his wife—it's Vitnègre..." and Trait-d'Amour leapt with utmost avidity upon the scoundrel's lady, whom he encunted with such male fortrightness that she uttered a few expostulations... but discharged soon afterwards, her trouble metamorphosing into happiness. "Whatever wife discharges like that," her fucker stammered, "is a good one; only those who don't discharge behave badly."

While this was going on, Vitnègre was refucking Minonne and Minonne was redischarging. Rose-

Mauve shrilled with pleasure under Brisemotte,
Connette beneath Cordaboyau; Tendrelys, moved
by these proceedings, leaned languidly upon my
shoulder and gave me her pretty mouth to kiss;
Conquette, being reamed by Trait-d'Amour, was
weeping, bucking her ass, ejaculating, uttering little
cries of joy and envying Minonne her luxurious
agonies. "Hey, by God!" her fucker cried to me,
"are you standing by doing nothing? Grease this
little slut Tendrelys and depucelate her if you wish
to do some honest work." That dear child cast
a lingering glance in my direction, and put her hand
before her cunt as if to protect it. We had a supply
of butter in readiness; I annointed her cunt therewith, lay the virgin upon an unoccupied couch and
despite her earnest and touching prayers, my prick
entered her. "At least," said she, feeling herself
pierced, "you won't give me to that dreadful man
who's doing it to Minonne or to the others—you
won't, will you?"

"Wiggle your ass, my sweet!" the stern Trait-
d'Amour shouted from where he lay embottled. "Is
that the way one fucks? Look alive, d'ye hear!
Have a look at my beloved and at the other sluts in
the room... look, whore, look... we're dis... charging!"
Hearing this energetic exhortation, the poor little one
struggled beneath me as bravely as she could;
I penetrated slowly, cautiously, the while caressing
her, thrusting my tongue into her mouth, quenching
her thirst for tenderness.

"Oh, I say!" protested Trait-d'Amour, "you needn't
wear kid gloves with her; go heartily to it, like me
and like that blackpricked rascal who's stuffing his
victim on the chair. Notice how he bites her nipples
when he hasn't a spare hand to fondle them with.
Eh, bugger! don't hurt her, or not too much, she's
my sister and I'll cut your throat if we have any

nonsense from you... oh... oh, I'm discharging a-again!" Vitnègre pronounced an identical statement. "Ah, let him devour me," Minonne exclaimed, "so long as he fucks me!"

Ecstatic cries came from Conquette. As for Tendrelys, I was nearing the bottom of her cuntlet. "Oh, I'm a maid no longer... I'm discharging... whatever shall Mamma say?"

"She'll never know, my pretty fuckeress, my former master's prick does no harm to maidenheads," Traitd'Amour reassured her. At this point, Vitnègre backed out of Minonne, thoroughly done in; Rose-Mauve (whence Brisemotte had decunted) was lubricated for him: the steadfast and doughty Minonne's torments had appalled all the other girls. That mule's prick encunted Rose-Mauve with great speed owing to the pommade in her cunt, but she suffered nonetheless: she wept, bled and finally discharged... she was thrice sprayed, her fucker pausing not once to draw a breath; he'd let fly four times into Minonne's cunt. Connette's turn came. She was more scrupulously pommaded than Rose-Mauve had been, but uttered loud cries all the same; had she not been in the Fronsac machine, she'd have expelled her torturer.

She finally discharged, and waves of pleasure replaced those of pain. But no one expected the effect these butcheries produced; of a sudden, Madame Poilsoyeux announced a desire to be stuffed by her husband's gigantine prick; she made her request in a low voice and asked to be placed on the mechanical chair immediately Vitnègre decunted from Connette, whose trick was presently spattered with equal amounts of blood and fuck. But Traitd'Amour, then prowling on the loose, sprang upon and encunted her, saying in a whisper: "Wench, I am jealous of you, for the good Linguet as well as for myself, I'd rather strangle you than let you be fucked in my presence by that cuckold of a husband of yours."

"Forgive me, divine goad, the sufferings of the others tempted me. Run your blade deep and rid me of the desire, for I count now upon you only... there's Monsieur Linguet yielding up his precious f-f-fuck—oh I'm redis-discharging... ah!... ah! that blessed fuck-swallowing Tendrelys! ah, queen of whores, you're jealous; come, come, there're some prick-thrusts in your heavenly cunt... Ah, I'm discharging all over again... again..." she murmured.

And in the meantime, what was Vitnègre up to? He was resting himself and imbibing some potent liqueurs while he rubbed his prick against the bubs of his three victims who were frigging him by way of amusement.

Mademoiselle Linguet suddenly observed to her fucker: "But that bugger, you know, is another Guac, I'm going to get him to give me some refreshment; wash his prick in rose-water, I'd like to suckle it as Madame Guac used to drink the beverage supplied by her husband's ponderous device."

We had nothing to object to so reasonable a proposition. The monstrous engine was cleaned; two or three girls on either side of Vitnègre supported him and gave him their bubs to dandle. Rose Mauve tickled his balls and asshole. Trait-d'Amour lay down with his back upon the floor, my daughter knelt over him and packed his prick into her cunt. Mademoiselle Linguet was near enough to Vitnègre to be able to give his huge prick five or six preliminary kisses, all the while replying emphatically to the heaves and thrusts of her fucker who was on the verge of a discharge; she enmouthed that prodigy before her nose, moving her mouth so that the terrible engine slid to and fro twixt her coral lips and then advanced deep into her throat: when the monster belched forth fire and smoke, she bit it. Thus does the voluptuous mate of the giant serpent crush in her maw the head of the too amorous male. Bitten, Vitnègre screamed in ecstasy. He ejaculated a torrent, although this constituted his tenth emission, and Mademoiselle Linguet was all but drowned with fuck simultaneously pouring into her mouth and cunt. She wished three times to drain the mead from Vitnègre's drinking horn which his female aides tickled and stroked with such assiduity that, no sooner emptied, it rose up again, full, glistening and purple. While all this was happening, he kept repeating: "My wife lives yet, 'tis she I'm enmouthing; it must be so, for I feel the velvet softness of her mouth!" and this idea made him discharge whole floods. Mademoiselle Linguet was obliged to bring this game to an end before Vitnègre expired as a consequence of it. But she had sucked that double-sized prick with such fury that her mouth ached. Vitnègre was obliged to embugger the three damsels he had encunted, which brought the toll of his discharges, each copious, to sixteen, for the girls in question took turns manipulating his balls with unpitying persistence.

By now, no one was affrighted by the dolorous exercise involved in embuggerage by so elephantine a member; to the contrary, the patient's torments excited the onlookers' passions, and they pinched and scratched her to force her to agitate herself and thus to facilitate the huge prick's bumwise intromission. Vitnègre was at the end of his rope: it was precisely that which aroused Mademoiselle Linguet. She insisted we make him discharge a seventeenth time, and unload all he had left in her asshole; Trait-d'Amour saw that he had to consent to this sodomy. Vitnègre was manipulated once again, his balls were squeezed, kneaded, rubbed and licked, he was advised he was about to embugger Mademoiselle Linguet, his wife: upon hearing this, his weary prick rose proudly erect. He was given Rose-Mauve's nipples to suck, Connette's also. 'Twas stiff, rigid! The embuggeree was straightaway laid on her belly, her rosebud was buttered, then her rectum was tried and loosened with the large nozzle of a syringe. Tendrelys, with her sweet, soft hands, fastidiously guided the awful engine towards the expectant anus while Minonne and Connette each parted a buttock. Rose-Mauve, ready to manipulate the balls if need be, with a buttered finger rummaged in the patient's asshole to blaze the trail for the monster oozing already with impatience to plunge into the wilderness. It moves ahead, is stopped, it strains, then bursts through! From Madame Vitnègre's throat emerge guttural noises, her husband thinks he recognizes them, and his suspicions cause him to redouble the vigor of his assaults. Then came the moment when the embuggeree emitted a cry which completed lodging the monster in its lair. Vitnègre, his last doubts practically dispelled, rattled his weapon furiously about; he disembuggered only after he'd discharged... Rose-Mauve toiled over his testicles, his anus, and pressing her cunt to his ass, fucked in harmony with him, pushing each time he pushed. Vitnègre released three deluges of fuck into his wife's intestines, and that brought his total to nineteen for the session; having parted with his last shot, he fell limply backwards.

He was dragged from Mademoiselle Linguet's vent; she went at once to cool and close it in fresh water, for it was both red-hot and considerably agape. Vitnègre was pitched into a trough of wellwater standing in the courtyard, by this means to bring him back to his senses: the locksmith arrived; Vitnègre was transported into his carriage, and the vehicle rolled away with him inside.

"Do you know whom I fucked?" he asked the locksmith while they were en route. "It was in that bloody machine of yours and I can tell you the slut's learned a lot since the day she left me. I fucked her sixteen times, I believe, some in the mouth, others in the cunt, the rest in the ass..." Once he had deposited Vitnègre at his door, the locksmith left him.

Several months later, Vitnègre ran into the same tradesman. "Would you like to take me back there?" he asked. "Impossible," the other rejoined, "they've all vanished." "Vanished? Ha, the bitch! had I only kept my hands on her, I'd be able to spend the rest of my life in her asshole and cunt!"

And thus that adventure ended.

CHAPTER XVII

Two cunts are mutually jealous.

We were all seven still wonderstruck by Vitnègre's innumerable encuntries, enmoutheries and embuggeries when Trait-d'Amour, casting an eye upon the amiable hatmaker, naked like all the others, said to her: "Well, you've been depucelated, my pretty one, and 'twas my divine master who plucked your flower. 'Tis a very good thing—both you and I ought to be grateful and happy about it. I behold you now as pious believers gaze upon their Virgin Mary who, fucked by the Angel Gabriel, then by the Holy Ghost, whose whore she was, came away from these set-tos only the more virginal. You are now dedicated to Lord Linguet's prick; religiously guard your cuntlet from all stray tupperings, preserve it for him, you may not give yourself save with his permission. And now, my celestial creature, your pretty bush is going to be clipped—soaped and shaved clean."

Tendrelys objected, citing her mother's reaction to this haircut; that mother, she averred, inspected her cunt regularly every night to determine whether anyone had impaired her mint condition, for she had already been sold and was soon to be delivered to someone who fancied new goods only.

"What the devil do I care for your mother, buggeress?" Trait-d'Amour demanded, seeing me deploying the Fronsac and winding its spring. "We'll tell her the whole story." And he thrust her upon the Fronsac, which went instantly to work. He soaped her and prepared his razor.

At this point arrived Mademoiselle Conquette Ingénue, who had just finished rinsing her ass in well-water so as to shrink it back to its normal dimensions. "What's this? Mademoiselle's cunt is to be shaven also?"—there was a shade of irritation in her tone.

"Oh, my dear, don't let them do it, for Mamma won't understand what's happened to me," Tendrelys implored, kissing one of Conquette's hands which she had contrived to grasp.

"No, Mademoiselle, I'll not oppose their action; once shaved, your cunt will all the better announce to your mother the fact that you have been deflowered by my unfaithful father. We shall also see, after that charming toupée has been removed, whether your gem is superior to mine, weary and sore as it is at present."

" Ah, my adorable friend, there's no need for a trial, nothing exists to equal you."

"Very well, Sir, shave away; I believe that, when 'tis done, my fickle lover who depucelated this attractive gem, will have the kindness to allow you a moment's lodging therein."

Trait-d'Amour, all the while he was shearing off the golden fleece, explained to Conquette that all the pucelages were mine by agreement and that, in conscience, I was under an obligation to take them, for if I did not there was a risk neophytes would be injured by my colleagues' more sizable tools. Conquette did not know what to answer to that, but she maintained her air of arch disdain. I approached her and, as she was naked, kissed her breasts and deposited my prick in her hands. "You'd prefer to have Tendrelys hold it," she pouted.

"No," I protested, "I deny that; no one gives me an erection the way you do; but after you comes Tendrelys. Her bush's being clipped; it must be done if we are properly to compare your heavenly cunts—and yours is heavenly despite its severe usage this evening. First, both will be tongued: then I'll see to which my sultan-prick grants the apple; the better re-empucelated of the two will have it."

Mademoiselle Conquette smiled the little smile of a pretty woman beside herself with delight because certain to triumph; she said not a word. The cunt-shaving finished, Tendrelys' pretty trick was washed with rose-water; Mademoiselle Linguet proposed that they both rinse their assholes again; then the comparison was made. They were impartially scrutinized and judged the one as splendid as the other; which decision indeed awarded the prize to the lovely Conquette's so frequently fucked cunt. That was the general opinion.

Rose-Mauve and Minonne stepped forward to be compared, but their cunts were far from possessing that virginal aspect which characterized those of Tendrelys and of my daughter. "Your cunts are eminently agreeable to see," Trait-d'Amour declared to them, "and a hundred times better than whores' garbage pails, but I feel they do not belong to the same class as these two extraordinary articles we have just examined." Conquette preened herself; but she was generous by nature and soon found the tactful thing to say. "Since our cunts are of equal beauty," she observed, kissing Tendrelys' lips and petting her cunt in a friendly manner, "depucelate her and have your lieutenant refuck me, if he has strength enough left." She had not got the last syllable out of her mouth when she was encunted. "Fuck her for me!" she cried to me, "fuck the wench..." I ran my machine into the little nymph. But, ready now to discharge, Conquette Ingénue was plunging into an erotic fury, and after witnessing her I understood how it is that Sade's heroes, when about to ejaculate, become cruel. The encunted girl cried: "All of you, all, do you hear? fuck that damned Tendrelys, fuck that bloody little whore! Brisemotte, get into her at once, stuff her so that her anus and cunt are but one hole!" She discharged and, somewhat calmed, she asked Tendrelys' forgiveness. "Excuse it, my little sister, fuck rose to my head and made me cruel. No, leave her cunt as it is—trim, tidy, sweet, a maid's—let my fucking Papa have it thus to himself. 'Tis surely enough that mine be martyrized. Come, come Trait-d'Amour, push, my boy, fuck me, don't spare me, I beg no quarter," she said to her rider. She began to buck and rear and prance more energetically than ever, and this exhibition of enthusiasm and fire persuaded Rose-Mauve and Connette to lend themselves to some cunt-fuckery; Minonne still felt a little lame in her sensitive parts and so that obliging sister of Trait-d'Amour approached me and tickled my balls with such deftness that I ejaculated.

CHAPTER XLIII

How Minonne and Connette originally lost their maidenheads.

This business despatched, a period of rest ensued; we had dined lightly and now a collation: we ate strawberries steeped in Muscatel wine and buns, then we drank the excellent coffee Trait-d'Amour brewed for us, and we sipped Benedictine afterwards. Then we chatted together.

"You've dipped your tool in these two pretty lasses, Minonne and Connette, and in Rose-Mauve too, and you've just depucelated Tendrelys before our eyes; tell us the story of your first experience and tell us how you persuaded your first women." "Yes, tell us, tell us!" exclaimed Tendrelys, Rose-Mauve and everyone else. "I'll very willingly tell the story, but upon condition someone go and bring Madame Bride-conin down here so that she too can hear; we'll begin to initiate her in that way." My three blades, who envisioned her as one further morsel, were delighted with the suggestion. They took her away from her husband (who was at that moment holding her by the dugs) without even deigning to explain themselves and, two of them joining their hands under her naked ass and the third steadying her from behind, they bore her down the stairs, her skirts up around her waist, her bubs spilling gaily from her bodice. She was deposited upon Fronsac's wondrous machine and, had I not interfered and curbed their exuberance, they'd have told her a story rather than listened to mine. When peace was finally restored, I began.

"I entered as a pensionnaire in the home of Trait-d'Amour's stepmother, a laundress in the rue d'Abbon, while my wife ran about the provincial countryside with a gallant fellow, the same who used passionately to fuck her that he'd strip to his underwear the better to palpate and encunt her. Trait-d'Amour brought me my noonday meal every weekday, but on Sundays and holidays I went to dine at the house of the good Madame Wallon. One day when we were going there together, Trait-d'Amour asked me if I would not teach his little sister how to write. I agreed at once. The lessons started. While instructing her, my eyes often strayed to her budding white breasts, breasts white as a lily."

"One moment," Madame Brideconin interrupted, "get my husband to come down here. I'd like him to hear the story too."

Trait-d'Amour, receiving a nod from me, set off to fetch him immediately; I signaled to Brisemotte and Cordaboyau: the first laid hands on the landlady's bush, the second on her bubs. She was thus shining happily between those two males when her husband appeared. Brideconin was flabbergasted at first, then, waking from his stupor, he made a bee-line for Rose-Mauve's cunt and Connette's teats. Trait-d'Amour handled his sister's bubs; as for myself, I had Conquette sit on Tendrelys' lap between my legs, from time to time letting my hand fall upon my daughter's chest or her pretty rival's; thus situated, I resumed my narrative.

"I took Trait-d'Amour aside. 'Look here,' said I, 'I must stop teaching the little one; she gives me a fierce erection and I'll surely stuff her the first chance I get.' 'Oh, my good sir, 'twould be very fine

211

indeed for all concerned, were you to depucelate her...
The poor orphan has little enough pleasure as it is...'
(Their mother was dead; their father remarried to a
close friend of his deceased wife, whom he had chosen
in deference to his dying wife's urgent request, had
himself, as he died, left as a stepmother to the two
orphans this good friend of their tender and loving
mother.) I replied, saying the thing would involve
difficulties, for the child would doubtless talk. 'No,
I guarantee she won't. Minonne has already conceived desires for you. She's already told me she
likes it when you touch the thing under her skirts...'
This speech emboldened me. One Sunday, when
Minonne and I were alone together having a lesson,
I could not resist an impulse to kiss her pretty mouth,
then a bub, and from there my hand descended
rapidly to her hairless cuntlet; I sustained a terrible
erection; my prick was all but bursting from my
breeches, si I freed it, allowing it to protrude through
my fly, which I unbuttoned: it sprang nobly out.

" 'What have you there?' asked the child.

" 'A prick, my dear.'

" 'What's it for?'

" 'To put in cunts.'

" 'But I have a cunt, my brother says, and he says
my stepmother has a bucket-cunt. Since he's been
grown up and since he's got what he calls fuck, he puts
his thing in my stepmother's bucket-cunt, and that
makes her shout and wail and laugh and cry. He
wanted to put it in me, but my cunt's too little or his
thing's too big, he never managed to do it. My stepmother saw him trying to do it and scolded him. "Go
fuck yourself," that's what he said to her, and then he
changed his mind. "No," he said, "come here, I'll
encunt you, you old rascal, for I can't do without it,
I'm so hot." And he laid her on the bed and pulled

up her skirts and he fucked her, as he calls it. Oh, how she giggled, how she swore! and how pleased she was with what he did to her! And he said to me, "You see how much fun it is, Minonne, you see how crazy the old bitch is to suck the sugar-cane! Come on, show me your little cuntlet, so I can discharge for you." '

"Minonne's little speech put the finishing touches to my erection, which had reached outlandish proportions; I asked the child whether there were any butter available in the house. She fetched me some; I was on the point of greasing her when her stepmother, as good a woman as you could possibly find, returned, having gone out forgetting her fan. She spied my embarrassment, the tumult I was in, and saw the child's flushed cheeks. 'I wager you were about to torment her,' she said, 'you ought not: she's not yet ripe for that... come along with me...' The old girl dragged me off by the wrist; we got to her bed, up went her skirts and petticoats in a flash, she pulled me down upon her and engulfed me despite my resistance. To save her stepchild's maidenhead, she kept me busy for a solid hour; during it, however, I discharged only once to the old biddy's ten— I notice she found me to her taste. When this battle was over, she left the house without bothering to wash: 'I walk better with a little oil on the hinges.'

"As soon as she had gone, I went straight to Minonne, who'd witnessed everything through the partly opened door. I cleared her skirts away, buttered her cuntlet and my prick shot rigidly up immediately. As we started off, I told the little one to arch her back, so that her little hole would be within fair and easy reach of the prick that would soon pierce it. She took infinite pains to do her best, which was not at all bad, thanks to the way she wiggled her pretty ass, and I on my part managed well too because of the disgust I had experienced in futtering the old woman's grey-haired tunnel. I took Minonne from behind and worked my way to the bottom of her, for I felt her dear little matrix nipping and squeezing my inflamed gland. Following my orders, the child agitated her body, but did not discharge... Her brother's intrusion occurred just as I thought I was going to erupt. Trait-d'Amour surveyed us, transported with joy.

" 'Ha!' said he, 'so you're depucelating her, eh! Splendid! She's getting the best possible initiation. Does she discharge? Are you enjoying yourself, Minonne?'

" 'No,' I replied, 'no discharges thus far; the poor sweetheart's been suffering, though courageously... Do you see the way her ass writhes? That's rare and augurs well.' Touched, Trait-d'Amour slipped his hand down his little sister's belly and began to tickle the tiny clitoris lurking in her unfledged crack; the child's eyes became glassy, her body tensed, and turning her sweet mouth towards mine, she put her tongue between my lips, did indeed discharge, this being for the first time, and moaned with delight. I discharged too; never had I sensed such pleasure.

"Once I'd decunted, her brother asked me if I were a jealous lover. 'Yes,' said I, 'jealous of every rival but yourself.' 'Well then, your fuck will serve as pommade to help me ease into her pretty cuntlet.' However, Minonne was less willing to be stuffed by her brother and undertook to repel his assault: but Trait-d'Amour was soon master of the situation: he flung his sister upon the bed and was a moment later within the portal, making a difficult entry, for his prick, even in those days, was not by any means puny; his sister was all alarmed.

" 'Wiggle your ass and discharge,' he recommended, thrusting vigorously, 'tis lovingly you are being encunted, my sweet little orphan sister.' She discharged no less than three times over and then could do no more. Trait-d'Amour helped me clean my instrument and I went back into the fray. I had even more pleasure this time, because the youngster had by now got somewhat accustomed to the game, and because with his bulky prick her brother had cleared the way free.

"From that day onward, Trait-d'Amour and I fucked Minonne every Sunday and holiday. The stepmother was aware of what I was up to, but did not interfere. And then Trait-d'Amour one day asked me whether I would also mind giving some instruction in writing to Connette, presently his mistress and the girl he was later to marry, since Tendrelys' mother, always fearing lest she be depucelated, had ruined all his hopes of getting at her daughter. 'Certainly,' was my reply. I went therewith to pay court to Connette. Two months went by... Then, that young lady being one day standing at the window and leaning out of it, I caught a glimpse of some first-rate legs. Minonne, at the time practising her penmanship, looked up from her work and noticed me staring avidly at Connette's behind; I grasped Minonne's bublets and requested her to take hold of my balls. She rose from her chair, approached Connette and said to her in a subdued voice: 'Don't object to anything we do to you'; she raised her skirts, led me to her, buttered her cunt for me and oiled my prick too. 'Arch your back,' she said to Connette, 'be a good girl.' And to me: 'Run it square and true, you should find the way without any trouble.' Connette arched her back, obeyed her friend's every command, so that, although she was exceedingly tight, I penetrated admirably. In came Trait-d'Amour, always on time; he drew us to the bed, lay down, on his belly had his mistress lie with her back upon his, then bade me encunt her, asking his sister to guide my prick: with each thrust I made, he replied with a heave of his ass: these shocks imparted to his mistress' ass wedged me an inch further in every time. Connette's sufferings were perfectly dreadful. But when at last I struck rock-bottom thanks to a final heave of Trait-d'Amour's flanks, Connette winked, smiled blissfully and soon emitted with ineffable joy.

"I supposed Trait-d'Amour would hurl himself upon her and encunt her while she was hot. But no; 'We are engaged,' he explained. 'Were she to have a child by you, it would ennoble my family,' and he fucked his sister while I refucked his mistress. And thus it is that since then I have shared my most precious belongings with him."

CHAPTER XLIV

Final fuckeries.

"He merits your trust," all the company agreed. "Indeed he does," said Brideconin, who was at the moment employing both hands to do a homage to Rose-Mauve's cunt whilst Brisemotte and Cordaboyau were one of them handling his wife's cunt, the other her dugs. My story had made all those gay blades stiffen like honest Republicans, even though we were nearing the close of a trying day. The ladies, even those Vitnègre had encunted, were positively in rut. "How clever you were, and how delightful your instruction has made them turn out to be," said Conquette, darting her tongue into my mouth. "Oh indeed yes!" Tendrelys concurred, kissing me in like manner.

Meanwhile, Madame Brideconin was being pulled in opposite directions by her two young suitors, each of whom had absolutely to stuff her without an instant's delay. "I've only accommodations for one, dear boys," she explained in all modesty; "had I room for two, believe me, I'd keep neither one of you waiting outside in the cold. One first," said the landlady, "then the other." However, a happy expedient was discovered: Cordaboyau ploughed into her cunt, Brisemotte into her asshole. "They're doublefucking my wife!" cried Brideconin, "but what do I care? I've got a tidy little cunt around my prick." Trait-d'Amour, furiously ribald, laid hands on Conquette; I thought he was preparing to encunt her; I was mistaken. He lay upon his back and drew her down over his rigid prick; Minonne and Connette held her under the arms. She slowly lowered herself upon that veritable spear which Tendrelys' hand held steady in the exact position: thus Conquette managed her own embuggerment: the weight of her lovely body made it a profound introduction. When his massy device was buried to the hilt in her fundament, Trait-d'Amour called to me: "Ah, sire! the world's most beautiful cunt beckons to you." I headed directly for my daughter's gem, the helpful Tendrelys guiding my prick.

Madame Brideconin, a whore if ever there was one, since at this point she was having both her holes battered, made three signs of the cross; she was asked what the trouble was. "I'm being fucked in front of my husband, but I'm on some queer contraption which prevents me from protecting myself. My husband, seeing me cuckold him, cornutes me... all very well. But our master is fucking... is encunting his embuggered daughter!" "His daughter?" "Yes, his very own," Rose-Mauve stammered, discharging under Brideconin, "and what does that matter!" "Ha!" chorused the four fuckers and the four fuckeresses, "that gives us an appetite for the prick... and for the cunt," and they swore to fuck till they could fuck no more.

The encunters and the encuntees, the embuggerers and the embuggerees struggled and scrapped the one more vigorously than the other, underneath and above, in and out, to and fro, like so many devils and shedevils at a sabbath. Tendrelys tickled both my nuggets and Trait-d'Amour's, Minonne excited Brise-motte's and Cordaboyau's, Connette concentrated all her attention upon Brideconin's while poking her index finger in Rose-Mauve's anus. The fucker, to whom these refinements were novelties, exclaimed: "Ye gods, but you folks fuck wonderfully well; compared to this everything else I've seen is mere messing about," and he discharged like a siege-gun. "Oh, you're very right, my friend," said his wife as she discharged also; "I've never been given the working over I'm getting from these two dear boys, each of whose pricks is planting a horn, one in my asshole and the other in my cunt." Remarking that I managed more satisfactorily when Tendrelys fingered my privities, "Dear little companion," she said, "my hand will do the same for your encunter when you get your hole plugged... And you, Madame Brideconin, are you being suitably fucked?" This agreeable word *fucked* had so much grace when Conquette's pretty lips pronounced it, that I would undoubtedly have pitched into her cunt anew had not Trait-d'Amour, retiring from her ass and going off to wash, besought me in great earnestness to allow him to encunt her.

But my emotions were too great to permit me |to remain an idle bystander; I ordered Tendrelys to bring her cunt to the fore. Minonne and Connette toppled her upon her back and spread wide her thighs. Before being encunted by her indefatigable fucker, my daughter was fain to insert my prick in Tendrelys' tidy crack. "Move your ass, my beloved," she said to the dear girl, kissing her on the mouth, "and be sure to give Papa all the pleasure you can," and as she had noticed what a splendid impression the word *fucked* had produced upon me, the while seconding the extremely active Trait-d'Amour's efforts, she shouted a resounding: "FUCK! Fuck, by bleeding Jesus, oh blessed prick FUCK my bloody cunt... Oh Father, stab her, bury it in Tendrelys, tear her to pieces, dear Father, oh I'm discharging! dis-char-ging!..."

"How that modest lady does fuck!" murmured Brideconin.

That's how the séance concluded.

CHAPTER XLV

Farewell supper.
Madame Vitnègre recites a prayer.

We supped; bubs were no longer dangling, gleaming, swinging pendant in full view, the conversation was decent.

"They say, Monsieur," Minonne began, addressing me, "they say you've had at least eight pretty wives, and they mention their names."

"Ah," Conquette interrupted, "don't get him started telling more of those stories; the day's sport is over and we ought now to behave properly, like ordinary people do."

"You'll have to save it then," Trait-d'Amour put in, "for some interlude in our future games."

As we were all preparing to disband and as there was no further danger of a libidinous tolly-polly, I was asked to recommend to the company that our six cunts and twelve bubs be brought into sight and kissed indiscriminately in token of our separation for the week; I thought this a good proposal. Immediately, Conquette, Tendrelys, Rose-Mauve, Minonne, Connette and Madame Brideconin relieved themselves of their kerchiefs, bared their bottoms, betook themselves to the fucking furniture; their cunts were prodigiously licked; the five gentlemen present sucked their nipples; the ladies grasped, uncapped and kissed the five pricks; mine, however, was mouthed out of kindness: "Farewell for a week, adorable prick" was the valediction it received six times over.

We were about to leave when Vitnègre's lovely wife was seen to sink to her knees, her bubs flying. She raised her eyes heavenward and spoke:

"Holy and pretty Virgin Mary, whom the angel frigged, cunttongued and tit-fondled in the bed that was Joseph's, the cornute dupe of much blessed frolicking, from which fuckery resulted the gentle Jesus, that Good Fucker who stuffed the beauteous and public whore Magdalene, Marquess of Bethany, of whom the vagabond Jesus was, furthermore, the keeper and sometimes the pimp, who, to the infinite chagrin of the blessed Slut also embuggered His fairy companion, Saint John; blessed and pretty Mary, virgin as am I, we thank you for this happy day of fuckery; by the merits of your Son and in His name, grant us another like it next Sunday. And you, holy Magdalene, who was fucked by the grave prayer-speaking Jesus and by John the Embuggered as well, grant me my prayer, which is that I be enabled to fuck as often as you did, cuntwise or asswards, fifteen, yea, twenty times an hour, and all that without being wearied therefrom or sate. You fucked with the Pharisees, with Herod, and even with Pilate so as to have the wherewithal to feed that hungry rake Jesus, your lounge-lizard and the shiftless wastrels who collaborated with Him on His enterprises, O beseech your pimp Jesus—who, being God, has doubtless much power—to grant that I someday have between the hairs of my cunt that rich swaggerer whom I once saw get out of his carriage with an erection begot by the sight of me as I was returning home from the house of my friend, Madame Congrêlé; for, with the money I earn with my cunt, my ass, my bubs and my tongue and lips, I shall be able to relieve my worthy father in his old age; not only would I fuck with him and give him pleasure thereby, but I would sell myself as did the pious daughter of Eresichthon the fanatic, or the devout Ocyrhoë, daughter of the centaur Chiron, who both became mares, that is to say, the steeds of male riders, and whores. Model of a man, most excellent pimp, gentle Jesus, passionate fucker, complaisant street-companion of the burning, the oftfucking and exemplary whore Magdalene, who was so in love with Your divine prick and Your blessed balls, by Your omnipotence preserve my cunt's narrowness and satin quality, keep my bubs firm and round, allow not to desert me the fairness of my skin, my ass, my buttocks, my arms, my hands, my cunt, my shoulders; maintain forever the rigid stiffness of my lovers' pricks and above all my father's; maintain their balls full always of fuck, for You know the art and have the skill to do so, having inherited them from the blessed King David, beloved of the Lord and His favorite because that sovereign was the Number One Fucker of his age. O Jesus, grant that my high heels, which lend me such grace when I walk and cause so many men's pricks to harden, grant that they never give me blisters or put corns on my toes, but that these tempting and fuck-inspiring feet remain as now they are for many a long year."

"Amen!" murmured the entire assembly, pricks straining and cunts moist with emotion.

Everyone left edified by my daughter's extraordinary piety; as they filed thoughtfully out, they said: "That's indeed what one may justly call having religion... the true religion of Nature; and that's the proper way to address the divinity: one ought always ask Him for reasonable things... Oh, indeed, she's an unusual girl!", etc., etc.

CHAPTER XLVI

My daughter's cunt for sale; initial negotiations.

Two days later, when I went to see Conquette (I had stayed away from her on Monday), I found her, although fully dressed, blinking sleepily which, what for her large eyes and long lashes, made her appear especially charming; she was wearing a pair of new silk slippers she had put on for the first time.

I sank to my knees before her. "Conquette," I said to her, "no living mortal has prettier feet—they are a shade large, and these slippers' pointed toes and very high heels make them look half their actual size. How divine they are!... my prick is mightily hard, as you observe..."

"Dearest Papa, knowing how much you adore me, I wanted to consecrate these shoes before presenting them to you as ornaments to go on your mantelpiece. Here are the white ones I had on the other day, in which I was so often... so much and so well... you know what."

"What, my dear? Say it."

"Fucked, Papa, FUCKED!"

"Quite. Excellent. And those shoes?"

"Do you see the pretty shape my feet have given them? they are far more voluptuous now that they have been worn."

Avidly, I inhaled the scent that the interior of those slippers distilled. "Oh, but my prick is a veritable pillar!" I cried; "your blessed buggering shoes have an odor of paradise! I'm lost... I'm damned... I'll have the worst aches and pains in my balls if I don't shove it into your cunt one little time; are you going to let this paternal prick eject its seed upon the floor? No, I hope not—"

"Put your ass and your balls in this big flat bowl like a good loving papa. I had the water fetched up, it is nice and cool and will relax that poor darling prick of yours—that's what I do when my cunt is afire."

This all seemed like good common sense and I followed her recommendation. She hid her feet from my sight—that too was prudent of her. I felt much calmer.

"I had to cool myself a short while ago. Trait-d'Amour paid me a call; I was still in bed when he arrived: he laid hands on my cunt and my bubbies. Just to see his prick standing up on its hind legs made an impression upon me, but in my heart, do you know, I felt nothing. He said he wanted to cunt-tongue me and to have me frig him afterwards; I'm not a whore you know—"

"You are chilly, it seems to me—"

"That's because I have ceased to love... in a sense. You are my lover, dear Father, and your lieutenant Trait-d'Amour also has definite rights to my cunt: he's your prick's double, its *alter ego*, and when it buries itself in me it's you all the time who is fucking me. Anyhow, I felt a little sorry about my harshness with him; so I took his prick in my hand and he put it in my mouth, the foreskin pulled all the way back; I made him discharge and swallowed his fuck, which tasted marvelous, I must admit, after my morning chocolate. It was like a heavenly mouth-wash. But, as I was saying, if you would like to give your cherished daughter an unspeakable pleasure, kiss her, put your tongue in her mouth and she'll put hers in yours; she'll tickle your balls and squeeze your prick in her fist and she'll discharge like a goddess."

"Oh, you are too wonderful for words!—an end to them, let's fuck like intelligent human beings. Just a little bit."

"My cunt was cool a moment ago, but now you've gone and set it afire again—only fuck will extinguish the blaze, I'm afraid. Therefore, dearest Papa, let's fuck away! encunt your devoted daughter! but proceed softly so that I discharge several times; and I've something to tell you while we fuck—"

She leapt upon me, thrust my member into her cunt, advanced it gradually, by almost imperceptible little nudges of her ass. The water's coolness had checked my impetuousness and retarded my ejaculation now. Her movements grew more energetic and she began to moan, crying at last: "I'm coming, oh, sweet Jesus, I'm melting!" Then she lay still for a minute or two. "I forgot to give you the address of that man we saw in the street the other day. He handed me a slip of paper, on it was written a request that I come and see him for a—a—a fuck, oh FUCK! drive it in, drive it, Father, drive it all the way in, I'm discharging all over again... I'm coming... ah, heavenly Father!" and she leapt and danced and twittered and chirruped as never did fuckeress before her leap, dance, twitter and chirrup. After a copious discharge, she resumed what she had been saying: "Yes, that man in the street, his message. It's here, on the bedside table: tell him, or write to him, that I never go abroad, and enclose our address."

"Aye, it shall be done, O Fututrix!" I replied. Madame Brideconin brought us cups of chocolate and I left so as to attend to the business. I went straight to the lodgings of him who was so eager to be my daughter's lover and next fucker. I found him at home, transmitted a note Conquette Ingénue had written, in which she said that if he had any reply to make, he give it directly to her father. I was warmly received. The gentleman was well-to-do. He said he was searching for a mistress who knew how to please in bed.

"My good Sir," I made him prompt answer, "your quest is at an end. My daughter has been married. She may be yours upon condition she keep her present residence, which neighbors mine. You shall eat there with her if you like and sleep there too—I shan't be bothered in the slightest by whatever you choose to do. As for voluptuousness and ability to move the ass and flanks, a libertine husband saw to it she had the most arduous and thorough novitiate in this vocation. But in surrendering her to you I wish to be certain her fate will be a happy one and that her practical circumstances will improve a little each year; if you will guarantee her welfare, I shall take upon myself full responsibility for her fidelity. She is prudent, sensible, wellbehaved; the certitude of a future independent of her monstrous husband is the *sine qua non* of her consent to your proposals."

The gentleman found these conditions highly acceptable and the definitive decision was put off until after a business trip whence he expected to come back in a week or ten days. I returned to Conquette with this news.

"Papa," said she, "however much or little he fucks me, you will always be there, won't you, to take your daughter in your arms and perchance put your prick in her cunt? You and he shall be my two fathers; I'll even renounce your extraordinary former secretary if you promise to encunt no one but me. Where will you find a cunt better adapted to your requirements? Hold your fuck strictly in reserve for me, as you shall your heart, O most lecherous of fathers!" It was plain she was jealous; I encunted her straightaway. But I was too much of a libertine to confine myself to the exclusive fuckery of the woman I loved most.

Madame Brideconin brought us some cool lemonade. She was lame, had been born that way, but she limped in a seductive manner. She had arranged her hair in a new fashion. Though pockmarked, she was exceedingly provocative. I said so to my daughter.

"Even before our parties began," Conquette told me, "her husband was eager to stuff me, but I found him displeasing. Since last Sunday, his wife has approached me twice and asked to suck my cunt; they both adore me, but I haven't let them do anything serious... nothing but kiss my feet. He fucks her whenever I tell him to; I watch: it's a little pastime I indulge in while waiting for Sunday to come. All I need to do is sit down in front of

Brideconin with my skirts raised ever so little: that's enough to get him started: he grows so excited when he sees my ankle and then my lower leg that he hops aboard the whore; he keeps it up as long as I like: I give a tug at my skirt and he sets in anew. If he catches a glimpse of thigh, it's pandemonium: he begins to roar with lust—one day, when the weather was especially warm, I decided to give my cunt some air and raised my skirts all the way. That fucker saw the view and brayed like a mule and nearly split the landlady in two. He exploded fuck all over the room, continued to rummage in her cunt and was like to kill himself with overwork when his wife glanced at me. She finished her discharge and came over and pulled my skirt back down. Brideconin was terribly weary and didn't feel at all well, as a matter of fact."

Conquette's little story stiffened me, but I thrust my prick in cool water again; when my desires had subsided, I dried my engine, buttoned my breeches, and left.

We restrained ourselves throughout the remainder of the week.

CHHAPTER XLVII

The fucking club reconvenes.

Sunday arrived; with the exception of Rose-Mauve, who was indisposed, all the company assembled. Tendrelys came unescorted and of her own free will: Trait-d'Amour had called at her home and found her absent and that had annoyed him; but he was delighted, upon entering with his sister and mistress, to discover the young, lady already there and in Conquette's arms and having her nipples sucked by the latter. Trait-d'Amour thanked Ingénue for her tenderness toward the girl by kissing her asshole and cunt. Cordaboyau and Brisemotte were the last to arrive. We sat down round the table as soon as Cordaboyau, after having run to look for Rose-Mauve, returned to say that there had been some new developments since our last meeting; he handed me a note from the missing actress, and I passed it on to my daughter. Upon my suggestion, Trait-d'Amour read it aloud; here is what it contained:

"My divine friend,

"Accept the homage I pay your angelic cunt and matchless feet. Yesterday—I am writing to you on Friday—I put on the shoes you lent me in order to determine their effect upon the prick of a certain notary's clerk, my sister Rosalie's lover, who I have been eager to get away from her. I also wore her best hat which becomes me so well because of my dark brown eyes; I had your dress on—the white skirt with the pink background—; it seemed to me a good idea to borrow your pretty shape about the ass, and mine looked wonderfully well in your dress. Well, in the rue des Cinq-Diamants, I heard someone say behind me: 'Yes, 'tis she, 'tis she, my own goddess, no doubt of it!' The speaker approaches me. 'Ah, my beauty, we're just a short step from where I live; why not come along with me now, since your father has already talked matters over with me?' He took me by the arm; I let him lead me on, thinking that surely, when he recognized me, he'd release me and ask my pardon, especially after having fucked me. No, not at all; he noticed no error, or acknowledged none; he conducted me to an apartment on the first floor where, to be sure, there was not a great deal of light to see by. He fell to his knees before me, or rather before you. 'Most lovely one,' said he, 'your eyes are a little different today—they seemed to me to be of another color when earlier we met—but your brown hair is quite as lovely as ever; I confess that I always looked more closely at your feet than at your face—perhaps from shyness, perhaps not, for I am mad about your feet... charming though your face is. I recognized you perfectly from behind—who could mistake your walk, your figure? Do you love me?' I believe I replied affirmatively... 'Ah, my happiness knows no bounds!' he exclaimed, beginning to kiss me. He sucked my tongue, stroked my bubs, seized hold of my bush; we fell upon an ample sofa, my skirts were lifted, before I knew it I was being fucked... I pitched my ass furiously this way and that—I was anxious to please him, after all, and he did enjoy himself. 'Ah!' he said, 'you know what men like!' We concluded our frolicking, then he showed me where I could wash, had me pour water over his prick, wiped my ass and cunt and licked my cunt-hair and buttocks; next, he summoned his housemaid. 'Is dinner ready?' 'It shall be in fifteen minutes, Sir; will you take some wine first?' He ordered her to bring a bottle of Alicante. We chatted, we drank. 'Shall we go down now, my lovely one? We can settle it at once.' We applied to the notary next door: six thousand pounds a year—five hundred a month and a month in advance. What do you think of that? I signed on the spot. I went back up as well endowed as I'd gone down well fucked. We dined together, tête-à-tête. When the domestics had left us to ourselves, he bade me bare my bubs, then he got me drunk on champagne; he dipped his prick in some sparkling wine, I drank the glass down at once after having licked his prick dry. He found the gesture enchanting and decided to pop his prick into my mouth; he did, I sucked it. He found this better still. 'Ah,' he said between outbursts of pleasure, 'you are my goddess indeed, the whore Nature intended to be mine! I don't want to discharge into your mouth, for I simply haven't enough fuck properly to anoint your precious cunt. Show it to me, do, and let me kiss it!' He kissed it— 'Capital! Fare thee well till tomorrow,' and he called for his carriage. His serving maid sponged my ass and cunt. His carriage took me home.

"Tonight I am to install myself in his apartment; a suite of rooms has been set aside for me. I stayed in bed until late in the morning. And so, lovely Conquette, I owe my good fortune to you; I have your adorable cunt to thank for it, and above all your voluptuous footwear. While we were riding in his carriage, my generous fucker promised he would shortly have me bumfucked in his presence by a pretty jockey whom he has previously employed to embugger in two different circumstances. He admits to a violent predilection for the asshole from time to time. So he told me.

"Godspeed and godfuck thee well, O divine fuckeress!"

We were at a loss for what to say. Tendrelys embraced Conquette, saying: "Oh, if he only knew you better!" I was inclined to go and disabuse my self-deceived son-in-law; my daughter restrained me. "He loved no more than my shoes," she said, "and he was not unfaithful to them. He got what he wanted." Tendrelys applauded this observation. "It's not for me to say, but I agree with you entirely."

Madame Brideconin, wishing to be welcome at our parties, whence she extracted pleasures of which hitherto she had not even dreamt, had invited along one of her husband's sisters, a heavily pockmarked creature, but otherwise the most provocative and biggest-busted hussy of eighteen you could hope to see. The slut doubted whether we'd be much tempted by her ill-favored sister-in-law, for she knew we were accustomed to the best in good looks. But the landlady was mistaken. It was this big-busted wench who served us at table—she was solidly made, and had a splendid narrow waist. As soon as she'd got all the men's pricks aloft, they bade her stir herself no more and they themselves went to get and carry away the dishes. At dessert, I was asked to recite the story of the depucelated cunts Minonne had mentioned— the same story Madame Conquette Ingénue had stopped me from telling for fear lest it prove too stimulating. I agreed now to recount it, and Conquette was content to listen.

CHAPTER XLVIII

Certain conquests.

"I shall tell you," I said, wiping my lips on my napkin and kissing the bubs belonging to my active fuckeress, "how I depucelated Victoire Beaux-Talons, Virginie Motteblonde, Rosalie Conrose as well as Suzannette, her younger sister, then Manon Aurore, Souri Mignard, Léonore Robé, Jeanne de Margane, the perfume-seller, and Saccadine and Voix-Flûtée, two itinerant cunts.

"The first time I clapped eyes on the voluptuous Beaux-Talons, she was in a brown dressing-robe, wearing white cotton stockings, black patent leather shoes with heels higher than Conquette's. She gave me a promise of violent pleasures; unseen, I followed her; it was evening, she turned into the alley beside her mother's shop; the stairway was dark, I walked close behind her. She unlocked the door; the shutters were drawn in the room, 'twas pitch black in there; she shut the door. 'Ah, it's you, Monsieur Capahu,' she said, hearing my breathing, 'I thought I was alone.' I slipped a hand beneath her skirt. 'Oh,' said she, 'you're always up to the same thing. Shall we have some light?' 'No, leave the shutters as they are.' I hunted about for a bed... she retreated; I caught her, down we went ahead. 'Oh, but you're simply dreadful,' she declared, nevertheless readying herself for the attack. I delivered it; she replied thrust for thrust, saying: 'Ready, I must do my best, otherwise you accuse me of not loving you.' My pleasure-taking was delicious although straightforward and without accessory refinements... Victoire was so lovely, and I had had such a desire for her...

"I wanted to leave without being recognized—but a knock came at the door. I did my best to prevent my terrified fuckeress from going to open it, but she burst away from me. 'It's my mother or my sister,' she whispered; 'stay here or go, whichever you prefer...'

"I went ; she..."

MORE EROTIC CLASSICS FROM
CARROLL & GRAF

☐ Anonymous/ALTAR OF VENUS	$3.95
☐ Anonymous/ANGELICA	$3.95
☐ Anonymous/AUTOBIOGRAPHY OF A FLEA	$3.95
☐ Anonymous/THE CELEBRATED MISTRESS	$3.95
☐ Anonymous/CONFESSIONS OF AN ENGLISH MAID	$3.95
☐ Anonymous/CONFESSIONS OF EVELINE	$3.95
☐ Anonymous/COURT OF VENUS	$3.95
☐ Anonymous/THE COURTESAN	$3.95
☐ Anonymous/DANGEROUS AFFAIRS	$3.95
☐ Anonymous/THE DIARY OF A MATA HARI	$3.95
☐ Anonymous/DOLLY MORTON	$3.95
☐ Anonymous/THE EDUCATION OF A MAIDEN	$3.95
☐ Anonymous/THE EROTIC READER	$3.95
☐ Anonymous/THE EROTIC READER II	$3.95
☐ Anonymous/FANNY HILL'S DAUGHTER	$3.95
☐ Anonymous/FLORENTINE AND JULIA	$3.95
☐ Anonymous/A LADY OF QUALITY	$3.95
☐ Anonymous/LENA'S STORY	$3.95
☐ Anonymous/LOVE PAGODA	$3.95
☐ Anonymous/THE LUSTFUL TURK	$3.95
☐ Anonymous/MADELEINE	$3.95
☐ Anonymous/A MAID'S JOURNEY	$3.95
☐ Anonymous/MAID'S NIGHT IN	$3.95
☐ Anonymous/THE MEMOIRS OF JOSEPHINE	$3.95
☐ Anonymous/MICHELE	$3.95
☐ Anonymous/PLEASURE'S MISTRESS	$3.95
☐ Anonymous/PRIMA DONNA	$3.95
☐ Anonymous/ROSA FIELDING: VICTIM OF LUST	$3.95
☐ Anonymous/SECRET LIVES	$3.95
☐ Anonymous/THREE TIMES A WOMAN	$3.95
☐ Anonymous/VENUS DELIGHTS	$3.95
☐ Anonymous/VENUS DISPOSES	$3.95

☐ Anonymous/VENUS IN INDIA	$3.95
☐ Anonymous/VENUS IN PARIS	$3.95
☐ Anonymous/VENUS REMEMBERED	$3.95
☐ Anonymous/VENUS UNBOUND	$3.95
☐ Anonymous/VENUS UNMASKED	$3.95
☐ Anonymous/VICTORIAN FANCIES	$3.95
☐ Anonymous/THE WANTONS	$3.95
☐ Anonymous/A WOMAN OF PLEASURE	$3.95
☐ Anonymous/WHITE THIGHS	$4.50
☐ Perez, Faustino/LA LOLITA	$3.95
☐ van Heller, Marcus/ADAM & EVE	$3.95
☐ van Heller, Marcus/THE FRENCH WAY	$3.95
☐ van Heller, Marcus/THE HOUSE OF BORGIA	$3.95
☐ van Heller, Marcus/THE LIONS OF AMON	$3.95
☐ van Heller, Marcus/ROMAN ORGY	$3.95
☐ van Heller, Marcus/VENUS IN LACE	$3.95
☐ Villefranche, Anne-Marie/FOLIES D'AMOUR	$3.95
Cloth	$14.95
☐ Villefranche, Anne-Marie/JOIE D'AMOUR	$3.95
Cloth	$13.95
☐ Villefranche, Anne-Marie/PLAISIR D'AMOUR	$3.95
Cloth	$12.95
☐ Von Falkensee, Margarete/BLUE ANGEL NIGHTS	$3.95

Available from fine bookstores everywhere or use this coupon for ordering:

Caroll & Graf Publishers, Inc., 260 Fifth Avenue, N.Y., N.Y. 10001

Please send me the books I have checked above. I am enclosing
$_____ (please add $1.75 per title to cover postage and handling.) Send check or money order—no cash or C.O.D.'s please. N.Y. residents please add 8¼% sales tax.

Mr/Mrs/Miss _____

Address _____

City _____ State/Zip _____

Please allow four to six weeks for delivery.